Generation Karen

Erika Norrie

For Ken, Lorna, and Dorit

And with apologies to all the wonderful people named Karen out there.

Most of us have only two or three genuinely interesting moments in our lives; the rest is filler.

Douglas Copeland, *Generation X*

1984

When Vanessa was 8, she was overthrown.

It all started on a cool Tuesday night in late autumn, 1983. Vanessa, a wisp of a child with mousy blonde hair and cunning eyes, was engaged in a screaming match with her older and considerably larger brother Jason over what to watch during their allotted post-school hour of television. Tonight's showdown was between *The Muppet Show* (Vanessa) and *The Facts of Life* (Jason), and the bickering had deteriorated quickly into a full-out brawl.

"STOP!" shrieked Vanessa, on her back and kicking at the incoming sofa cushion with both feet.

"It's my turn!" shouted Jason, pile driving his entire body weight onto the cushion to buckle her legs.

The cushion – far too large and unwieldy for such a delicate manoeuvre – teetered and then tumbled to the ground beside her. Vanessa swivelled out of her brother's path and scrambled to her feet, making a dash toward the television. Just as her hand touched the dial, Jason's hands were around her lower legs and she was down on the carpet again.

"I'll tell mom!" she shouted, scraping her fingertips wildly against the door of the tv stand as Jason dragged her by her feet back towards the sofa like a plough.

"Do it," he sneered, gasping from the exertion, "and I'll tell mom you took her favourite seashell to school and lost it."

Vanessa twisted her body until she was on her side, propped herself up on her arms, and kicked her brother in the shin as hard as she could with her bare foot. This predictably hurt her far more than it did him and she started to howl.

Behind her, *The Facts of Life* theme music started up: *You take the good, you take the bad, you take 'em both and then you have...*

"I hate you!" she screamed as the sofa cushion came down upon her again, this time pinning her perfectly. Windmilling her arms on either side, she caught the sleeve of Jason's t-shirt with her left hand and gave it the hardest tug she could manage. Surprised, Jason lost his balance and let out a shout.

Vanessa was gathering herself for a follow up offensive of a swift crotch kick when a key clicked in the front door.

The siblings froze. Without a word, Jason was at the television switching it over to *The Muppet Show* and Vanessa was replacing the scattered cushions and herself back onto the couch. "Your braid," hissed Jason as he flung himself in beside her, pointing wildly at the bedraggled end where the bauble had slipped off. Vanessa flipped her hair over her shoulder and sat back hard to pin it down, as Jason kicked his feet out onto the coffee table and slumped. By the time their mother appeared at the door to the family room, shaking the rain from her hair, they were the very picture of cozy familial harmony.

"Awww," said their mother with doe eyes, "look at you two."

Jason wrested his gaze from the television screen, as if surprised to find her there. "Oh, hey mom," he said. "How was work?"

"Hi mommy!" added Vanessa brightly. "You look pretty!"

"Thanks peanut," replied their mother, shrugging off her navy blazer and slinging it over her arm. "Work was fine, and thank you for walking Vanessa home from school, Jason. You're a good brother." She unclipped the gold and pearl shells from her ears and juggled them thoughtfully in her hand. "Sloppy Joes for dinner?"

"Yum!" said Vanessa and Jason, their heads bobbing like the velvet dog that lived on the back shelf of the family Ford Pinto.

As their mother disappeared up the stairs to change out of her work clothes, Jason landed one final sharp punch to Vanessa's upper arm. "OW!" whispered Vanessa, rubbing her sore shoulder but unwilling to risk a grounding by retaliating. Then, grudgingly pacified, the siblings settled in to watch Gonzo fall in love with Madeline Kahn.

Momentous life change came for Vanessa in the second commercial break. At first it was merely another advertisement, thirty more technicolour seconds nestled innocuously between peeing babies and plastic soldiers, but tiny Vanessa, cross-legged in front of the tv with her jaw open, was defenceless.

Cabbage Patch Kids.

Stuffed animals are all well and good, insisted the commercial, but Cabbage Patch Kids are a whole other level. They are an extension of you, a reflection of your very soul, each one as special and unique as the child who loves it. Do you have glasses? So does your Cabbage Patch Kid! Do you have curly hair? So does your Cabbage Patch Kid! Do you like to bake cookies with grandma? So does your Cabbage Patch Kid, and imagine how much more wonderful it will be with *three* generations baking together! Forget that pile of generic infants and faded teddy bears, the children sang in jubilant harmony, there is no love that could ever compare to this.

You need one, the children said. Trust us.

And, oh, how Vanessa needed one.

Over the next weeks, all else in her life took on a drab, grey sheen. "What's wrong?" asked her mother, when she found her youngest sitting glumly in a semi-circle of toys. Vanessa's little mouth twisted down. How could she ever explain the melancholy of a Cabbage Patchless world? Strawberry Shortcake had gone sour. Tenderheart Bear was trite. Barbie had lost all the sheen in her matted golden hair, along with one pink shoe. Vanessa's yearning for Cabbage-y motherhood was all-consuming: her baby – literally made for her, destined to be hers – was out there waiting for her.

When it came time for letters to Santa, Vanessa selected the most perfect piece of cream construction paper and her favourite red marker that smelled like cherries, and positioned herself at the kitchen table with the intensity of a NASA launch. Holding a tassel of hair under her nose like a moustache, she and her father wrote in her very best handwriting:

Dear Santa,

How are you? I am good. I have been good this year mostly.

I would really like it if you could bring me a Cabbage Patch Kid for Christmas. She should have long blonde hair and blue eyes and a dimple like me. But not glasses because I don't have glasses. I promise I won't fight with my brother if you bring me this.

Please give the reindeer some carrots from me. Is it true you go around the whole world in one night? That is a lot of work. I wish I could fly.

I love you.

Vanessa

"We're up," Vanessa's father notified her mother while getting ready for bed that night. He felt slightly sick. The stampedes, fist fights, and baseball bats at toy stores were the primary topic of conversation between the parents on the school run, who traded rumours on which tiny shop the next town over might be getting a shipment like rare and valuable baseball cards.

Vanessa's mother grimly closed the drawer of the bedside table drawer harder than was entirely necessary.

At 8am on Christmas morning, Vanessa clattered downstairs and into the arms of Nicole Geneviève, an amiable baby-powder-scented bean bag with bright blue eyes and two fat braids of lemon-yellow yarn. Vanessa' parents, bedraggled from sleep and barely into their first coffees, bowed their heads towards each other. They hadn't even needed the baseball bat.

The bond was instantaneous and profound, and everything the advertising had promised: Vanessa and Nicole Geneviève went everywhere together, did everything together, were everything to each other. Nicole Geneviève joined the family for meals, though much to Vanessa's wailing disapproval was never given her own plate. Whenever Vanessa went for a bike ride, Nicole Geneviève would be tucked carefully in the front basket. When her brother drew a small line in marker on Nicole Geneviève's chubby pink cheek in retribution for Vanessa poking through his room when he was out and disturbing his geode collection, Vanessa moped and raged for two solid days. (Forgiven but never entirely forgotten, this grievous betrayal would be brought up in the speech she gave at his wedding.)

Most thrilling, however, was the small but notable ripple in the echelons of power at Clifford Scott Elementary School.

"NO!" screamed Norah when Vanessa first appeared holding Nicole Geneviève triumphantly aloft.

The other kids came scattering over, scrabbling over each other like a pack of overexcited puppies. The doll was passed around and every inch appreciatively examined.

"Her dimple is so cute!" shrieked Amy.

"Look at her dress!" bellowed Ruth.

"There's a name written on her bum!" squealed Timothy.

"BUMMM!" howled the children with delight.

As the proud mother Vanessa felt visible and powerful, and it was a provocative sensation. In one fell swoop she had gone from miscellaneous classmate to person of interest, person of value, person of renown. Ruth shared her green grapes at lunch in exchange for being able to hold Nicole Geneviève for the hour; Timothy targeted her twice in their game of Tag.

In the volatile politics of elementary school, however, one Cabbage Patch was a mere entry step – a taste of the high life without being a part of the establishment. The real power remained with Natalie, who had two

4

Cabbage Patch Kids and steadfastly maintained her position by bringing them into class in a double stroller and rationing out time with them. When Timothy's attentions wandered predictably back to Natalie over the next weeks, Vanessa knew she needed to go bigger.

So, a few months later with her birthday looming, Vanessa made a bid for more power.

"It's my birthday soon," she said to her father with calm reason and calculation, "and I would like a sister for Nicole Geneviève please."

'Prove it,' she seemed to be saying to her father. 'Prove that you are the best daddy.'

But he paused, slightly longer than Vanessa had anticipated, so she went all in: "Natalie has two and I only have Nicole Geneviève, and everyone wants to play with Natalie at recess and they don't want to play with me." It was a calculated exaggeration and a bold play.

"Natalie has two?" asked her father. He wondered how that was possible, who they must know, what they must have had to do. He faced his wife with his mouth open.

"Well," said her mother through thin, determined lips.

Predictably, when Vanessa arrived at school the day after her seventh birthday with curly-haired brunette Emilie Beth in one arm and blonde-tufted Montgomery Nathan in the other, Nicole Geneviève sticking merrily out of her backpack, her classmates went wild.

"Nooooooooooooooooo!!!!" shrieked Norah in pure ecstasy and wonder. "YOU HAVE THREE?!"

Vanessa had become a Cabbage Patch Vanderbilt. Not only did she now have one more Cabbage Patch than Natalie, Montgomery Nathan was a "Preemie" – smaller, cuter, balder, and completely oblivious to any medical challenges associated with his difficult start to life. In elementary school accountancy, this was the equivalent of a vault full of gold bullion.

Vanessa instantly became ruler of the playground, exalted by a grovelling crowd of children desperate to hold her plastic offspring and share in their wonder. She was in her element, confident that she had achieved her destiny. She was a benevolent if firm leader, carefully deciding each day who was It and who got to go on the swings first and who would have the esteemed honour of sharing lunches with her. She married twice, both times for love but neither time lasting past the home time bell. It lasted four entire months, and it was a golden era for all involved.

Whether Natalie had intended a coup when she showed up after the summer holidays with caramel-skinned Cora Delilah – a startling and wondrous change from the previous five peach ones – a coup is what happened. The class defected from Vanessa's court without a backwards glance, and Natalie was once again surrounded by adoring minions and suitors while Vanessa could only watch jealously from afar. Even Montgomery Nathan's jaunty new purple dinosaur romper failed to turn any heads.

"Don't worry," said Norah reassuringly, carefully dividing her ham and cheese crackers into two sharable piles. "We're still friends forever."

And just like that dinnertime was back to the human four, no benign plastic faces staring blankly ahead as the others ate.

"But won't they be hungry?" asked her father.

"They're going to a restaurant later," said Vanessa, aggressively stirring her buttered noodles with her fork.

When her mom found the three dolls in an unceremonious pile in the corner of the room a few days later, she asked, "What happened? Did you guys get into a fight?" while tenderly tucking them back into Vanessa's bed.

Vanessa made an angry huffing noise. "Cabbage Patch dolls are for babies," she jeered. "I don't want them in my bed."

"Oh well," said her dad from the doorway, sad as much for her as for his own wasted superhuman efforts.

The rift was permanent, and Vanessa and her abandoned Cabbage Patch Kids would never again share a bed. All three dolls eventually found a new home via a garage sale, sold for $1 apiece which Vanessa promptly spent on a bottle of Coke, some candy cigarettes, and two chocolate bars.

Vanessa would make another bid for power a few years later with a veritable stable-full of My Little Ponies, but lost points for several of them being garage sale hand-me-downs, and never climbed higher than courtier again.

2022

She had promised not to say anything but, by nature impatient and prone to a good bit of gossip, Vanessa couldn't stop herself. Besides, she reassured herself confidently, it really was in the group's best interest to be forewarned of something so significant.

Becca was the obvious first call, but she was at some work event that evening and wouldn't be answering her phone. Robert, Vanessa's husband, was home but was toodling away at his book in the dining room with the door closed – his signal for 'please give me space' – and, anyway, Vanessa wasn't sure how he would respond to the news given who it was about. That only left Nick.

Nick picked up almost before it rang.

"Nick, it's Vanessa."

"Hey V."

"Am I interrupting anything?"

"Just scrolling Facebook."

"Got a minute? I have news and I have to tell someone."

In the diminutive "third bedroom" of his cramped and damp apartment, Nick ran his fingers hard through his thinning hair and watched the fine dusting of dandruff that wafted down to the surface of his desk. He drew a faint smiley face before sweeping it onto the floor with the palm of his hand.

"Always," he said, but with nominal warmth.

Vanessa felt a tingle of anticipatory gratification. Good old reliable Nick, she thought, always there when you need something. She should really call him more often.

"One sec," she said, suddenly aware of the acoustics between the kitchen and the dining room. As much as she loved the house – "charismatic" the realtor had called the tidy two-story, repeatedly pointing out the dark wood focal staircase, attractive location to schools, "and it has both a sitting AND a dining room!" – the paper-thin walls were regularly an issue when her husband wanted to, say, watch a hockey game while she was trying to sleep. She refilled her glass of white wine and headed upstairs to the guest bedroom, making distracted shushing noises into the phone.

As she closed the door quietly behind her, she asked, "Did Conrad call you?" When she coughed at the end of the sentence, she realised she had been holding her breath.

"He did not," replied Nick.

Vanessa kicked off her moccasins and tucked herself into the emerald velvet armchair in the reading nook by the window, where she could be comfortable while keeping an eye on the happenings of the street outside. This was her spot, of the entire house. She had meticulously cobbled the room together with her mother in mind (her father had inspired the sitting room, with its dark tones and leather), taking care that the limited-edition lithograph of Georgia O'Keefe's vaginal irises brought out the red tones in the raw silk bedspread. It was this room that had called out to her when she and Robert had their first viewing: the house had been wildly out of their price range, even despite Robert's healthy inheritance from his father, and far beyond their requirements as a child-free, pet-free couple, but they made an offer as soon as they got home and added the extra to the mortgage total. Something about the way the light streamed through the second story bay window made Vanessa feel like she could breathe.

"Then you haven't heard…" she said, with a lingering dramatic pause.

"Heard what?"

"About Conrad."

"I've not heard anything from or about Conrad, no."

Nick gave his Facebook newsfeed a vigorous scroll of the mouse wheel and landed on an article about the Western Canadian independence movement. It was one he had read before – it was a good one. He shared it on his profile with two quick clicks.

"Guess where he is!"

"India?" said Nick. "Or was that where he was last? He sent me one of his weird artsy woo woo postcards. I'd have to check the fridge."

"He was in India before the whole pandemic thing kicked off, in the Before Times – ha ha! – but he got out just in time. He spent last year in California. Thank goodness. Can you imagine being trapped in India through all that?"

Nick was distracted by a photo of an ex-girlfriend and her new husband on holiday somewhere. "Yeah," he said, pleased that his biceps were bigger.

"Though I wouldn't have minded getting trapped in, like, Bali, you know? All that free beach holiday time…"

"Totally," he said. "Yeah."

Annoyance flashed under Vanessa's sternum: this was not how this conversation was meant to go. She waited for him to prompt for details but he was busy leaving a laughing emoji on a post denigrating the Canadian prime minister.

"Anyway, guess where he is now!" she said brightly.

Nick pulled at a loose thread on his bleach-spotted navy bathrobe and noticed a faint stain on his favourite South Park T-shirt. He licked his thumb and rubbed at it, then fished around in the drawer for his nail clippers and snipped off a looming hangnail. "Can you just tell me?" he said, too tired to play one of her endless guessing games.

The irritation in her sternum began to smoulder. Vanessa breathed in for four counts, held it for four counts, breathed out for four counts, and put on a smile you could hear in her voice.

"Utah!"

Nick was only half listening as the "Like" reacts started trickling in on the article.

"Conrad's in Utah!" pressed Vanessa.

When he finally heard her, it caught him off guard. He had expected something far more exotic and therefore, for Conrad, less exotic. "Utah?" he said. "As in the state?"

"That's the one."

Nick shook his head. "What the hell is Conrad doing in Utah?"

"Absolutely no idea," replied Vanessa, reasonably satisfied with the strength of Nick's eventual response. "He just called and told me. *Utah.* Can you believe it?"

"I actually can't."

Nick flicked over to Conrad's Facebook page. The last post was a photo of feet silhouetted by a sunset over rippling water. *#blessed*, read the caption.

"I'm picking him up from the airport on Monday."

Nick leaned back in his chair and hooked his hands behind his head. "How long's he home for this time?"

"That's the big news, the reason I'm calling – he says it's for good this time."

Nick's jaw dropped. Conrad discovered in a random location was at most banal trivia, a frequent occurrence over the years, but a final return to Canada was actual news.

"For good, for good?"

"Apparently so."

"What's brought that on?"

Like a maestro conducting an exquisite symphony, Vanessa calibrated her response for the appropriate blend of mystery and revelation. "He's had an epiphany…" she said enigmatically, stroking the skin over her collarbones with the tips of her fingers.

Nick brayed with laughter, which Vanessa found disappointingly aggressive. "Classic. About what this time?"

"He didn't say."

"Too bad."

"I did try."

"I bet you did."

"This sounds different somehow."

"It'll be another one of his *passions du jour*, no doubt."

"He said he's seeing his life in a whole new way now and it's time for some changes."

Nick wiped a tear from his eye and snorted in some snot. Vanessa silently gagged on the other end of the phone.

"I sure hope it isn't just another *passion du jour*, anyway," said Vanessa. "He's nearly 50 after all! At some point you have to put away the games and grow up."

"Maybe he likes the games."

"Psh. I bet his life looks far more glamorous and appealing from the outside than it actually is, anyway. Like, fun, yeah, but what does he have to show for it all? It must get a bit same-y after a while."

"Conrad's in Utah," wheezed Nick, largely for his own benefit. "Maybe the epiphany is that he's become a Mormon."

"I asked that! He said it's –"

"And he's about to marry his fourth wife."

"He's only been gone for eight months, Nick."

"That's enough time."

Vanessa was grinding her teeth. She wondered what time Becca would be getting home.

"Could be sisters even," Nick continued, starting to enjoy himself. "Don't they do that, Mormons? Sister wives? Or maybe that's not what that means, I'm not sure."

"Nick…" managed Vanessa plaintively.

"Did you know they have special underwear that they have to wear?"

He could tell by the silence on the other end of the phone that Vanessa was getting irritated. "Sorry," he said.

"That's fine," replied Vanessa.

"So he's coming home Monday. Where's he staying?"

Vanessa felt as though someone had punched her in the sternum. She patted her forehead with the palm of her hand for being so ridiculous.

"He's going to crash in our guest room for a few days until he gets his feet under him," she said with what she hoped was a breezy manner, shifting to her feet and starting to pace the length of the guest room.

Nick partially closed his laptop. It was unlikely there was anything between Conrad and Vanessa anymore, and certainly it had been literal decades since their failed attempt at a relationship, but Vanessa's benign, genial husband Robert was never able to entirely conceal his deep dislike for Conrad, and Nick enjoyed how deliciously defensive Vanessa got when this topic came up. He couldn't resist.

"How does Robert feel about everything?" asked Nick. "About Conrad staying with you, I mean."

Vanessa pulled the duvet on the bed taut and smooth. "Robert will be fine with it," she replied tightly, rotating the decorative throw cushion by three degrees. That creak in the hallway: was that Robert? Vanessa crept to the door to listen just as her husband atonally belted out a few stanzas of "Hit the Road Jack" from the kitchen downstairs.

"You haven't told him yet?"

"I mean, I only just talked to Conrad, like, immediately before calling you."

"So why did you ask if I'd spoken to Conrad?"

"I wasn't sure if I was the first person he had called."

"You're always the first person he calls, Vanessa."

"There is nothing between us, Nick, and you know that."

"And does Robert know that?"

"Yes, Robert knows that."

"And does Robert believe that?"

Vanessa reached the end of her good humour. "Oh, grow up, Nick," she snapped.

The silence buzzed on the line. Nick opened his laptop back up.

"Anyway," said Vanessa, smoothing her hair, "I'm calling because I thought we should do something, the four of us. Make a big deal out of this for him."

"Sounds good," said Nick, casually 'liking' a link to an article about the fallacy of white privilege without reading it. "Let me know what the plan is."

Deflated, Vanessa sank onto the edge of the bed. "And partners, of course," she added quickly. "Becca could bring Max and maybe you could bring Eleanor?"

Over on the other end of the phone, Nick audibly shifted. The silence was suddenly electric.

"Oh no, Nick," she murmured. Vanessa had been hopeful about Eleanor – a no-nonsense PA who swore like a frat boy and seemed to roll easily with Nick's mood swings.

Nick made an unfriendly expression in the darkness, entirely unwilling to get into it.

"Oh Nick." She clicked her tongue at him in sympathy. "When?"

Nick thought about just hanging up, pretending he was out of battery, but couldn't bear the thought of the fallout. He could hear Vanessa puffing excitedly into the phone.

"A couple weeks back," he shrugged. "It's no big deal."

"Oh but it *is* a big deal," replied Vanessa, having to sip her wine to subdue an eager smile. This was her happy place: being the concerned friend, the compassionate confidante, talk to me and tell me everything. "Are you okay? Do you need to talk?"

"I'm fine," said Nick. He opened a link to an article about the declining economy under the Liberal Party and scanned it for bombshells, but the article was a dud. Woke socialist propaganda denying them their due responsibility.

"Are you sure?"

Nick let out an irritated puff, which even Vanessa in her enthusiasm could hear and understand.

"Okay, well, I'm here if you need to talk," she said with a pout. She watched through her gauzy curtains as a neighbour took out the garbage considerably before the allowed hour, and chewed on the side of her cheek in annoyance.

"A get together sounds good though," he said, while typing a comment to the effect of "Blue Lives Matter" in response to one of his leftie friends spouting about cultural appropriation. Vanessa, hearing the clicking, gave up.

"Right, well, I will let you know the plans once I figure them all out," she sighed. "Enjoy Facebook."

"You bet," replied Nick.

"Say hi to the girls from me."

"Will do."

"Be nice to people."

"Always am."

And they hung up, both knowing he would be into a full social media flame war within the hour.

1995

When Vanessa, Becca, Conrad, and Nick were all somewhere between the ages of 19 and 23, they stopped believing in Santa Claus.

It was a Friday evening and the group was gathered in Vanessa's living room to console Nick, who had received yet another rejection letter from a potential employer. It had been a year since Nick had graduated with a solid grade point average and a Bachelors of English, and the subsequent twelve months of futile job hunting had ravaged both his confidence and his general mood.

The foursome had met over the course of about two years, starting with Conrad and Vanessa bonding in high school over a mutual dislike of Chemistry. When Conrad, a year ahead of Vanessa, went off to University, Vanessa sought out and conscripted the charismatic and moderately famous Becca into the group, while Conrad appeared one evening a few months later with the affable and awkward Nick as a souvenir from their brief stint with the university's meagre Croquet Club. The motley four had settled immediately into an easy rhythm of friendship, like cats from the same litter, disregarding any age gaps and varying levels of life experience.

At the apartment that evening, commiseration Spaghetti Bolognese simmering on the stove and filling the air with the sickly smell of off-brand tomato sauce and discount ground beef, the friends formed a circle around him in an attempt to soften his despair by sharing it.

"That really sucks, Nick" said Becca from her usual place on the futon, pouring the last of the cheap red wine into her glass. Her teeth were stained faintly blue from the first few glasses.

"I guess I thought it was going to be easier with a degree," Nick said to the tipsy group and to himself. "Wasn't it supposed to be easier? I mean, isn't that the entire point?"

"It'll happen, Nick," soothed Vanessa. She was perched in a ball in a bean bag chair in the corner by the window, legs curled underneath her, listening and occasionally bringing the acidic wine to her lips. The damp air of summer clung to her skin despite a faint breeze dusting through open windows. "It's only been a year," she reminded him.

"It's the system, man," was Conrad's response from where he was lying on the floor, blonde curls spread out around his head like a halo. "They don't value general Arts degrees because they don't want us thinking too much. An ignorant population is a compliant population."

Nick, positioned upside down on the battered wing chair with his lanky legs hooked over the top, his soft brown hair obscuring his eyes, groaned. "Is it my fault? Maybe I'm shooting too high. What would a publishing house want with a Bachelors in English?"

"Hey," said Vanessa, "better than Art History! What am I going to do with an Art History degree?"

"What about doing a PhD, Nick?" suggested Becca.

"And do what then?" said Nick.

"Become the foremost expert on Dickens? Share your passions with the next generation? I could see you being a really great university professor."

Nick's unhappy face was like a Greek mask of suffering.

"Or something else maybe?" offered Becca, with a faint tinge of impatience. "I'm sure you have plenty of transferable skills."

"I guess maybe I could teach," he mustered unconvincingly.

Vanessa scoffed. "Do you really want four-plus more years of school, Nick?" She shook her head. "Nah. You'll find something, trust me. You're very smart. You've got this."

Conrad was languidly waving his arms and hands in the air above him. Halfway through an Economics degree himself, none of his friends actually believed he would go on to be an Economist as, the more he learned about free market capitalism, the more ragingly anti-capitalist he became.

"Why do you even need a job, man?" he asked Nick.

"To pay rent?" replied Nick. "To buy a house someday?"

"Ha!" said Vanessa, her cheeks pink from the wine. "Buy a house! Have you seen house prices these days?"

"It's all part of a capitalist lie that seeks to churn out people as commodities to be traded and sold," asserted Conrad. "Rebel, Nick. Walk away. The gold watch when you retire isn't worth an entire life in soulless servitude."

Becca looked horrified. "Don't give up, Nick," she said with a furious glare at Conrad. "It'll happen."

"Becca, you're spilling your wine on the futon!" cried Vanessa, deeply protective of one of the few items of any value she owned.

Conrad passed Becca a napkin with which to daub the droplets on the sofa; Vanessa watched Becca try and fail, and felt relieved she had chosen the dark blue washable cover over the more decorative embroidered one she had briefly considered.

"The problem," continued Conrad, deeply engrossed in his left thumb, "is that it won't happen because it doesn't exist. We're all obediently chasing the dream that capitalism sold us: career, wife, kids, white picket fence. All we need to do is work hard and sacrifice everything and it's all ours."

"Meh," said Vanessa.

Conrad propped himself up on one elbow and waggled his hand at Vanessa. "Why are we paying into Canada Pension? Do you really think you're going to see that money in fifty years? Bullshit we are. That'll be long gone paying out the Boomers, the coffers empty by the time it's our turn. We're on our own. It's time we face it."

Nick placed his arm across his eyes.

"I don't blame our parents' generation," said Becca thoughtfully. "It's not their fault they had so many opportunities. It was after the war – all their competition was dead."

"Nah nah," said Vanessa, "I blame them because they took all the opportunities and didn't leave anything for us."

"Basic labour market supply and demand, man," huffed Conrad. "The Boomers get all the good jobs because they got there first, and now we come along and there are more of us than there are jobs."

"There *are* jobs out there, though," retorted Becca. "Lots of them."

"Not good ones," said Vanessa with a scowl.

Conrad was impressed. "And capitalism requires us to remain poor in order to fill the crap ones."

Vanessa noted his approval and blushed.

Becca, the only one of the group not currently at or through university, had many unspoken opinions about what she saw was her friends constantly making excuses and wasting time. Becca's attitude was to get on and make the best of things, no moaning allowed, and in that vein was carving out her desired future career in theatre with taciturn determination. She was at that time in rehearsals for her latest dinner musical, which would feature her laying on a piano in a yellow bikini belting out Dusty Springfield songs to bored bus tours benignly contemplating their over-salted chicken, but it paid reasonably well and would hopefully be good exposure for further work.

She was also the only one among them to own her own apartment – albeit vicariously through her parents, who had recently expanded their multi-home property portfolio to acquire a charming apartment in a historical building with their daughter's name on the paperwork. It was an impressive place for a 19-year-old budding actor, and she assumed the fact the group spent so little time there was due to jealousy.

"If the world was ever our oyster," rhapsodised Conrad, "that oyster has gone bad, and why even bother because we're all going to fry like hamburgers under the expanding hole in the ozone layer anyway."

"Oh god," said Becca, "I am so tired of that green shit."

"It's not 'shit', Becca," scolded Vanessa, "it's important."

"So what do we do?" asked Nick for the hundredth time. "What can we do?"

"What do you *want* to do, V?" asked Conrad, rolling over and putting his chin in his hands.

Vanessa looked blank, then concerned, and then she shrugged.

"No," said Conrad, "you're still thinking like your parents. Money. Career. Think big. Go against the grain. Nick, what do you want to do?"

Nick buried his face in his wine glass to buy time. He felt pressured to come up with the correct answer to the question but had no clue where to begin. "Maybe something in an office?" he ventured.

"Do you really want to be a three-piece suit, Nick?" asked Conrad earnestly, "inhaling a hot dog in the square at lunch time because you only have twenty minutes between meetings during which you discuss nothing? Do you want that? Is that what you want?"

"At this point I just want a job," said Nick, righting himself on the chair with a desolate thump.

"V, do you want to cross off the days of your life sitting in an airless office just so you can afford the more expensive dish soap that doesn't dry out your hands when you soak in it? Who cares if your kids are kind, moral contributors to society – you have a brand-new car!"

Vanessa shook her head but felt ass though she were adrift in boundless space.

"Think bigger, people!" said Conrad in a near-shout, "We were promised the world, and we got IKEA. You're never going to get your dollhouse so stop waiting for it!"

Becca threw back her head in a wave of nostalgia. "Oh I had a dollhouse when I was a kid!" she said, closing her eyes. "I *loved* my dollhouse. My total dream home. Nothing fancy: a modest two story, two bed, one bath.

Nice sized kitchen. Man doll in a felted suit and painted eyes that stared off in different directions. I think the lights even worked at one point."

"Was there a Mrs Dollhouse?" wondered Nick.

"Oh there was. Little brunette with a bun. Grey dress, white apron, sturdy practical shoes. Disappeared one day – not sure what happened to her."

Vanessa stood up and stretched her fingertips to the ceiling. "Were the police ever called?"

"Not to my knowledge," mused Becca. "Perhaps she ran off with my brother's GI Joe."

"Poor Mr. Dollhouse," said Vanessa.

"He did alright: he married Barbie in the end."

Vanessa grabbed at Becca's hand and pulled her to her feet. "Come on, help me dish up the spag," and the two women wandered off to get dinner ready.

"See, Nick," said Conrad, shuffling on his hip to get within conspiratorial distance of Nick, "there's the problem right there – did you see it? Dollhouse. Marriage. We've had this message of superficial consumption defining success baked into us since we were fetuses."

He thumped his fist emphatically against the dusty carpet and coughed on the resulting cloud. "V, you really need to vacuum!" he called out.

"I know!" she called back from the kitchen. "I've been busy!"

Nick closed his eyes and let his head fall back against the chair, then said quietly to Conrad, "I have had one job offer."

Conrad sat up quickly. "What? Where?"

"Nothing special," said Nick, opening his eyes but avoiding eye contact. "Just stocking shelves at a warehouse, but it'll cover rent while I figure out what to do with my life."

"Oh my god that's great, Nick!" exclaimed Becca, re-entering the room balancing three bowls of spaghetti and a towering plate of garlic bread. She set down the food to high five him but only managed to connect her pinkie with two of his fingers, generating an underwhelming 'thwick' noise. "Congratulations!" she said, grinning like a proud mother. "See, there *are* jobs out there if you look for them."

"In a warehouse, Becca?" said Vanessa, pouring everyone more cheap red wine. "Kill me."

Nick cracked his neck slowly and deliberately: first one side, then the other. "It's okay. Buys me some time to think at least."

Conrad was unimpressed. "You really want to spend your days making The Man richer?" he said incredulously. "I'm disappointed, man."

"I want to eat," said Nick. "This is really great, speaking of, Vanessa. Thanks for making dinner."

"My pleasure," she said. "I love having everyone together here."

"So what's your dream, Conrad?" asked Becca, sucking up a few strands of saucy noodles suspended between her fork and her mouth. "All this anti-establishment talk: what's left?"

"What's left," replied Conrad, now folded cross-legged onto the futon beside Becca, pasta bowl to Vanessa's dismay perched precariously in his lap, "is living." He looked forceful and serene, punctuating each word with closed eyes and a shake of his head. "Connecting. Experiencing. Feeling, properly feeling things for once. Letting go. Carpe diem."

"Mmmm," chorused Nick and Becca noncommittally.

Vanessa stuffed pasta in her mouth to avoid having to say anything. She had always somehow trusted that her dream would come to her eventually, with patience. As a child she had fluctuated between wanting to be a nurse discovering the cure for pneumonia in time to save her ailing grandfather to wanting to be a popstar and screen sensation beloved by millions. She had once won an award for a poem she had written about autumn and her teachers had regularly told her and her parents that she should consider becoming a writer. She was drawn to history and archaeology and had in her teens made the local paper with an amateur production of *Iphigenia in Aulis* on warehouse scaffolding, but was content to leave the acting to Becca in pursuit of something that might actually pay off her student loans one day. She was good at spreadsheets and bored easily by repetition. All of her dreams felt tepid and uninspired.

Honestly, she hated this conversation every time it came up. It made her profoundly uncomfortable – a pantomime of anarchic bohemia that spoke of rebellion without any view of a viable alternate path. What did it even mean, 'to feel, to experience'? How could you pursue something so consistently ill-defined?

"I am already living the dream," she said instead. "Today the hotel fed us the leftover baked ziti from the restaurant, and they gave me an additional navy uniform to switch it up from the bottle green. What more could a girl want from life?"

"A husband? Babies?" Nick's eyes shone over the rim of his cup. "Say the word, V, and you know I'm there for you."

"She's way too much woman for you, Nick," teased Becca.

"I'll take that challenge!" said Conrad.

"I'd leave you behind," said Vanessa. "Today I broke my personal best of eleven simultaneous incoming calls on the switchboard. 'Thank you for calling the Holiday Inn, how may I direct your call? Thank you for calling the Holiday Inn, how may I direct your call?' I am a switchboard ninja, Wonder Woman with her magic cuffs against the onslaught of punters. Pow! Pow! Pow!"

The group fell silent, only the sound of sullen chewing.

"Huh," said Nick softly. "None of us has dreams."

"Not our Becs, isn't that right?" asked Conrad, leaning his whole body towards her on the couch in attentive sympathy. "You're living your dream."

Becca couldn't tell if Conrad was being serious or insulting. "Working towards it at least," she replied with defensive humility.

"Small town dinner theatre musical revues…," said Vanessa.

"That pay the bills," added Becca quickly.

Nick pursed his lips. "That's adulthood, though, isn't it?"

The group fell into individual contemplation, mouths on glasses.

"When I was a kid," said Conrad, "I wanted to be a police officer."

"Imagine," said Vanessa.

2022

Vanessa got the idea of throwing a dinner party for Conrad's return from Virginia Woolf's *Mrs Dalloway*. Not the book itself, per se, which she had yet to read, but rather the film inspired by the book in which Nicole Kidman wore a fake nose and looked dowdy and won an Oscar.

She tested out the idea on Becca as they pushed into the spa's gilded changing facilities following their recently launched Sunday "Girls' Morning" Pilates class.

"I've been thinking," she pitched with her best Cool Girl confidence as she fumbled to retrieve the locker key from where it had slid to the back of the strap of her tank top, "of throwing a dinner party for the group."

"Are you!" exclaimed Becca, dropping her towel and water bottle on the bench and cracking her upper back with satisfaction.

"A proper formal one, with name cards in calligraphy and everything," Vanessa added, feeling her cheeks grow warm. "There's something refreshingly old school about it, don't you think?"

"Oh absolutely," replied Becca, flicking her long honey blonde ponytail over her shoulder as she rummaged in her locker for her toiletry bag. "Since when do you do calligraphy?"

"How hard can it be to do name cards? And if I run out of time I can pay someone to do them."

"Be good to use your dining room for something other than Robert's research papers," agreed Becca, assessing her figure in the mirror as she brushed out her glossy hair.

As the strokes grew increasingly vigorous, Vanessa, well-trained through going on 30 years of friendship, waited patiently. Becca took a step back, her lips pursed. She twisted one way, then the other, then turned fully sideways. She pinched a centimetre of skin on her taut stomach and chewed on her bottom lip. She leaned in close to the mirror and scrubbed at some invisible pores.

"You look great, Becs," Vanessa swooned on cue. "I don't know how you do it. You haven't changed a bit since high school."

"Psssh! You!" replied Becca, massaging out an invisible blemish somewhere near her right kidney.

A dark-haired woman in a pink puffer jacket stuck her head through the door and glanced around. "Liz?" she called out, her voice muffled and dull through a facemask patterned with multi-coloured sloths. Becca and Vanessa paused to allow a response. An awkward number of seconds passed.

"Liz?" called the woman again, looking at the two women with what Vanessa took to be a hint of judgement. Vanessa started to fish in her bag for her mask, but the woman gave up before she could put it on. Becca, however, spotted the mask hanging from Vanessa's finger and cocked a disapproving eyebrow.

"Anyway," said Vanessa, plonking herself onto the padded bench with a synchronised puff of air from both her and the cushion and starting to put on her street shoes, "I want it to be big and special. Full Martha Stewart: ludicrously large centrepiece, charger plates, our wedding china, a seating plan – the whole shebang."

"Are you going to change?" asked Becca lightly, surveying her sweaty friend.

Vanessa passed her hands over her T-shirt and leggings, suddenly embarrassed. "I didn't bring a change of clothes. Is this not okay for brunch? I didn't think we were going anywhere fancy."

"We don't have to, don't worry," replied Becca, quickly checking her rear end in the mirror. "Besides, check you in your fancy new workout outfit."

In truth, Vanessa was feeling very fancy indeed: it had been an exorbitant amount of money indeed for mass-produced lycra, but the pneumatic salesgirl had been shocked and delighted by what the uplift technology had done for Vanessa's middle-aged derriere, and the credit card had come out easily.

"Thanks Becs! It's infused with crystals to align your chakras or something. Total nonsense of course but I saw it in the window and loved the colour, and I had to have it! You know, treat myself."

"You deserve it," said Becca warmly, "and it looks great on you."

There was a moment between them. Vanessa felt validated.

"I stink. Do you mind if I have a quick shower before we go? Just want to freshen up a little."

Without waiting for agreement, Becca took hold of the bottom of her yoga top and pulled it up off over her head. Vanessa had seen Becca's bare breasts arguably more often than she had seen her own, yet as always couldn't stop herself from ogling. Becca had the breasts of a 22-year-old porn star: they were impossibly pert for being comparatively large on her petite frame, to the extent that Vanessa theorised based on absolutely no information other than good, clean jealousy that Becca may have had surgical help at some point. Becca of course always denied having had any help but took every opportunity she could to get them out.

"No problem," said Vanessa, tapping on her phone. "I'll take this chance to get caught up on my socials." She started to absentmindedly scroll through a Facebook feed composed almost entirely of friends' babies and fitspiration memes.

Becca grabbed a fluffy white towel from a stack in the corner and opened the door to a nearby shower stall, giving it a quick glance over to ensure it was stringently clean before stepping daintily inside. "Won't be long!" Becca hollered over the noise of the water.

"Really not a problem!" hollered Vanessa back.

"How's Robert doing anyway?"

"Good. Still working on his book!"

"The same one?" There was the sound of a nearly empty bottle being squeezed repeatedly, banged against a hand.

"The same one!"

Massaging organic vanilla and shea butter shampoo into her hair with the tips of her fingers, Becca pursed her lips. Robert's placid perseverance – his ability to focus on something unceasingly, for months on end, without wavering or doubt – was the thing Vanessa liked most about him, but he was now three years into this book and there had been as yet no draft to show for it. Becca respected him for pursuing his passions, but the lack of quantitative progress was very… well, it was very Vanessa is what it was. The two of them were positively made for each other.

"Gosh, he's thorough," hollered Becca.

"I think he's nearly there."

"That's good!"

Out on her pouffe, Vanessa briefly lingered over a photo of an acquaintance's handsome husband: tanned, bare-chested, and smiling gleaming white teeth over an idyllic campfire cookout of freshly caught fish, Greek salad, and two enormous glasses of white wine. She tried to remember if the acquaintance and her husband had kids, and when was the last time she and Robert had gone camping. She couldn't remember if she even liked camping, or if Robert did, though their history of quaint Bed and

Breakfasts suggested a definite shared preference for comfort and warm showers.

"What's it about again?" hollered Becca.

"Something to do with Renaissance poets?"

"That's right, poetry."

Vanessa closed Facebook and did a quick check to see if she had any Instagram notifications. She did not.

"Nearly done!" hollered Becca. Something clattered to the floor and the silhouette in the glass door front stooped to pick it up.

"No rush!"

Vanessa jiggled in her seat, tugged down her lycra bra top that suddenly felt scant, then caught sight of the top of her head in the mirror and absent-mindedly wandered over to study herself the way Becca had. Robert had generously described her one damp night early in their relationship as "made for sex," but she thought herself frustratingly more rectangle than hourglass. Her hair – fine and silken, the colour of plain potato chips – was prone to breakage if she allowed it to grow much past her shoulders, and defiantly resisted all attempts at a style more complicated than "sleek." A solid 6.5 out of 10, she reckoned.

Vanessa had always reassured herself that average looks forced an above-average personality. Plus the alchemy of night creams seemed to be keeping all but the most determined wrinkles at bay, and she had fewer white hairs than Becca even if Becca's were less noticeable under the dye. She could totally still pass for 35, she thought confidently, examining her skin up close and scratching at the rough edges of a healing pimple.

She looked at herself in profile and instantly regretted the change of angle. She puffed out her stomach and her cheeks despondently, then sucked both in, crooked a leg and her head and took a selfie that she immediately deleted. She was about to start rummaging curiously through Becca's bag when she heard the water switch off, which sent her scuttling back to the bench to pretend she had been on her phone the entire time. She had No new notifications.

A young woman with large curly red hair peered shyly from the doorway.

"Liz?" asked Vanessa brightly.

The woman looked confused.

"Someone was looking for you."

The woman nodded and disappeared.

Becca stepped out of the shower with her hair in a towel turban, naked and dewy from the eyebrows down. "Ah," she exclaimed, "that feels much better."

Vanessa made a point of staring in the other direction, ostensibly to give Becca her modesty but mostly to deprive her of the satisfaction of being admired again. She felt the cushion of the bench she was sitting on depress and then the air was filled with the scent of Becca's heavily perfumed body moisturiser.

"So is there an occasion?" asked Becca. "For the dinner party, I mean."

Vanessa turned to reply and found her face in very close proximity to Becca's naked crotch. She let out a surprised yelp.

"Oops," said Becca. "Sorry. Let me put on some clothes. I'm so used to being naked in public from my acting days, I forget that not everyone has the same body freedom."

As desperately as Vanessa wanted to prove her cool cred and dispute this, Becca was entirely correct: if Vanessa had to change so much as a sock in public, she would find a hidden nook or discrete corner in which to do so. It was the respectful thing to do, after all. No one needed to see all of that.

"Thanks," said Vanessa. "You've stopped..." and she waggled her fingers in the general direction of Becca's bikini area.

"Yeah," blushed Becca, "Max likes it better this way. I feel a bit, I don't know, *uncultivated*, but I'm saving tons of money not having to buy my aesthetician dinner every few weeks!"

Vanessa laughed loudly as though she related entirely, realising that she had no idea if Robert had any preference and did it actually matter as would she ever do it anyway even if he did because she was pretty sure she wouldn't. Becca pulled a trendy yoga top over her head – no bra, noted Vanessa with envy – and stepped into some skinny jeans.

"Anyway," said Vanessa in a serious, topic-changing tone, "the dinner."

"Yes!" said Becca, examining the immaculate paint on her perfectly pedicured feet.

"I want to get everyone together," started Vanessa, dragging out the words for maximum dramatic effect, "because... Conrad... is coming home...tomorrow... *for good*."

"Is he!" exclaimed Becca delightedly, shaking her fingers through her hair before pulling it up into a perfect messy wet bun using only gravity, luck, and a couple of bobby pins.

"I'm picking him up from the airport next week. He's had a major life revelation that he wants to tell us in person."

"It'll be a woman, I bet you anything," mused Becca. "It's always a woman."

"I will let you know," replied Vanessa, "or he will, you know, at the dinner."

Becca stuffed her workout clothes and toiletries kit haphazardly into her matching gym bag and slung it over her shoulder. "Well that all sounds very exciting," she said, "and I can't wait to hear more." She checked her watch and squinted her eyes at Vanessa. "I could murder a green smoothie before brunch."

"I have a spare mask if you need one?"

Becca waved her hand dismissively. "You and your masks, V. If anyone is so sick that they need a mask, they won't be at a gym."

Vanessa pointedly wore hers to walk to the juice bar in the lobby of the Pilates studio, and felt superior when she spotted others noticing.

"So, the dinner," Vanessa persisted after they had settled in, determined to have the conversation. "I thought Conrad telling us about his big epiphany would be a great excuse to get everyone together for a fun formal dinner at my house."

"Oh!" exclaimed Becca, clapping her hands, "I know a great recipe for grilled eggplant and herbed quinoa that would be perfect!"

"I haven't started planning the menu yet."

"This would be genuinely perfect. It's healthy and full of flavour and you can easily make it organic. I'll email it over as soon as I get home."

The bronzed god tending the counter gave Becca a flirtatious wink – "What can I get you, beautiful?" – and she absent-mindedly twirled a tendril of hair that had come loose from her bun and now lay attractively against her cheek as she ordered a medium high-protein kale and ginger smoothie. He was twenty at most, with shoulder muscles straining against his t-shirt and smelling faintly of cinnamon and patchouli.

Vanessa blushed. "I'll have a large blueberry and banana," she said softly.

"So much unnecessary sugar, V," tsked Becca, "but go on, you've earned it. You worked hard in class today."

The barista winked at Vanessa as he left to make up the order, his back muscles flexing attractively. "Such a flirt," she remarked to nobody, to ensure Becca was aware.

Becca, however, was head down, rummaging around in her bag at her feet. "When are you thinking for dinner?" she asked, pulling out a smart red leather diary and flipping through it. "This week and next are not too bad, then Max and I are off to Seattle for some quality Us Time. What about this Friday?"

Vanessa lifted both hands as if to say something, then dropped them into her lap. "I'll have to check with Robert," she replied evenly, "but that's what I was thinking, yeah, Friday."

Becca marked the date in her book with the matching red pen. "Fantastic," she said, closing her diary with a smart snap. "I doubt Nick will have plans – he never does these days – but I can confirm that with him tonight. Plus ones I assume?"

"I suppose?" replied Vanessa weakly. "I mean, yes, of course."

Becca chewed thoughtfully on the end of her pen. "I think maybe he and Eleanor might have broken up anyway?"

"They have!" said Vanessa, thrilled to have known something that Becca did not. "Nick told me yesterday."

"I knew they would," mused Becca. "It's been coming for a while. That's fine: there are still six of us with Max and Robert, so that's a good number. Do you have a theme yet?"

Vanessa put her hand firmly on her friend's arm and gave it a hard squeeze. "Becca," she said firmly.

"I'm just trying to help," Becca shrugged.

The barista arrived with their smoothies and winked at both. Vanessa wondered if he just had a convenient facial tick.

"Here's to your dinner party," said Becca calmly, raising her smoothie for a toast. "Can't wait to see what you come up with."

"Cheers," chimed Vanessa, rallying a smile.

1997

When Conrad was 22, he broke his own heart.

He had been dating Caroline for four months and things were going well. She was an exuberant, bubbly girl with a shiny brown bob and a booming belly laugh, and conversation flowed easily between them. They had met in a Women's Studies course in which he was the only male, and he fell for her instantly when an angry classmate called her a tool of the patriarchy for wearing skirts and makeup and she replied with an eloquent and impassioned rant about second versus third wave feminism. Conrad didn't understand the rant, if he were honest, but something about her fire inspired him to chase her down the hallway after class and invite her for coffee.

And then there was Vanessa.

To the deep chagrin of Becca and Nick, who were reasonably worried about future group dynamics should it all go awry, Conrad and Vanessa had attempted coupling up briefly the year prior. For the greater part of a year they managed a sweet if not entirely convincing relationship, which ended amicably with what both parties fervently insisted was a mutual understanding that they were different people on different paths. In the moment, however, it had been heady, needy stuff. Years later when Nick's eleven-year-old stepdaughter wailed "This is LOVE. You don't understand!", Conrad patted her head and assured him that, oh honey, he sure did.

On the night they all went for margaritas, Conrad and Vanessa had been apart for nearly as long as they had been together and the water around them seemed smooth. Vanessa was happily dating Kevin, a long-nosed Ethnomusicology student who wrote her esoteric erotic poetry and sent her

27

on treasure hunts to find love letters, and Conrad was happy and fulfilled with Caroline, so they decided it sufficiently safe to congregate over drinks in the name of restoring their healthy, adult friendship for the good of the larger group. That the tension still hung between them like Philippe Petit on the Twin Towers, pointless and spectacular, remained an unspoken truth.

Vanessa came prepared, downing half a bottle of Tia Maria prior to leaving the house and wasting no time before starting on the cocktails once she got to the restaurant. Before Conrad and Caroline had even arrived, she was sufficiently sozzled to have completely obliterated any nerves. There is no better excuse than drunkenness to behave abominably, was her motto: it's like a Get Out of Asshole Free card.

"Hiiiiiiiiiiiiiiiiiiiiiiiiii!" she cried as the other couple appeared beside the table, tumbling out of the booth to embrace them both. Kevin caught her by the arm at the last second to keep her from ending up on the floor.

Caroline, who had been warned by Conrad about Vanessa's proclivities for the dramatic, held up her hands in self-defence but smiled. "You must be Vanessa," she said warmly. "I've heard so much about you."

"All good stuff, I'm sure!" bleated Vanessa, wrapping her arms around herself in a hug and rubbing her upper arms for self-comfort. She gestured towards Kevin, who was trying to make himself as small as possible. "Please, please, sit," she said. "This is Kevin. Kevin, this is Caroline, and of course you know all about Conrad."

Behind Caroline stood Conrad, dressed like a 65-year-old philosophy professor in a battered grey cardigan and brown corduroy slacks he had found during a particularly productive poke through a thrift store, his perfect curls shivering in the air conditioning. He watched Vanessa swoon and fawn and make introductions around the table, accepted Kevin's limp and slightly sticky handshake, and wondered feverishly and not for the first time what they were doing by bringing them together.

"Oh my god, you're like a shampoo commercial. You're very pretty!" slurred Vanessa to Caroline as the group settled into their booth. "Seriously, what shampoo do you use?" Without warning, she reached over and stroked Caroline's hair.

As Caroline recoiled, Conrad clapped both hands on the table to draw attention away. "Can I get everyone a drink?" he asked.

Kevin pointed to the mostly empty margarita pitcher. "We've already started."

"I'll get us another one then. Lime again or…"

"Frozen strawwwwwberry!" sang Vanessa, waving both arms in the air in anticipatory celebration.

Conrad headed to the bar to order. Why this restaurant?, he thought peevishly. If there were such a thing as his and Vanessa's place, this would be it. Surely she knew that when she picked it. Surely that was why she had picked it.

Or had he picked it? He couldn't remember who had first had the idea for a double date.

Back at the table, Caroline was hospitably attempting to keep the conversation flowing. "So how did you two meet?" she asked Vanessa and Kevin with genuine curiosity.

Vanessa grinned wetly at Kevin.

"At the library," replied Kevin, patting Vanessa's lap. "I helped her with the microfiche machine when it got jammed."

"That's right!" crowed Vanessa. "I was researching beauty standards in early 20th century art."

"Such a fascinating topic," said Kevin with baby cow eyes of complete adoration. "One of her best papers too."

"And I had spent all day scrolling, scrolling, scrolling, so much scrolling, god, you know how looking through microfiches are. A surprising number of murders back then, actually!"

"Right? I thought that too. I don't know why!"

"So I'm scrolling, when all of a sudden…"

"It jammed!"

"It jammed! I couldn't scroll in any direction. I tried everything."

"She looked so sad."

"I was so upset, Caroline, you have no idea. And then he appeared, like a vision, an angel. A microfiche angel!"

"'Excuse me, do you need some help?' That's what I said to her, all slick like that."

"And just like that he fixed it for him, just like that, presto."

Kevin couldn't take his eyes off her. "And the rest as they say is history."

"Love at first fiche," said Vanessa with her lips against his neck.

"That's cute," said Caroline obligingly, trying her best, wishing she were about anywhere else at that moment.

Conrad got back to the table in time to hear Vanessa ask Caroline: "So how did you end up with this loser?"

Caroline glanced at Conrad apologetically.

"But you're not a loser, are you, Conrad!" shouted Vanessa, using her full body weight to shove Kevin to the edge of the bench to make room for Conrad to sit beside her. "You're not a bad guy at all, are you?"

"I like him," said Caroline, patting the bench beside her. Conrad sat down and squeezed her hand under the table. Kevin looked faintly relieved.

"This is nice," said Kevin warmly, filling everyone's glasses. "To new friends, may they become old friends. To old friends, may they become family."

"CHEERS!" cried Vanessa, clinking Kevin's glass so hard he worried for a moment that she had cracked it.

"So Kevin," asked Conrad, "what are you studying?"

With the tolerant grimace of someone accustomed to having to explain his field to people who would not try to understand it, he replied, "Music, in its cultural context." Seeing Conrad squint and inhale to speak, he quickly added, "I don't play an instrument."

"Wicked," said Conrad. "Cultural music."

Vanessa beamed with pride. "He's doing his master's already, my Kevin. He's very smart." She nuzzled his arm, then fake chewed on his shoulder.

"Very impressive," said Conrad, absolutely not interested. "I'm finishing my degree in Economics – real mind-melting stuff when you get deep down into it. I'm a free market socialist, myself. Market and individualist anarchy and all that. Capitalism is a prison, man."

Kevin twitched, then turned conspicuously to Caroline. "And what about you? Are you at university too?"

Caroline choked on a mouthful of margarita and fluttered one hand to eye level. "Oof," she said, "brain freeze. Yes, sorry, yes, a Bachelors in Women's Studies with a focus on gender and sexuality. Religious Studies minor."

"Oh!" said Vanessa, eyebrows high with surprise. "Are you... religious...?"

"No no," tittered Caroline, "comparative. Lots of them, ideas across them. I like to understand what makes people tick."

Vanessa threw back her head and cawed like a raven. "I was wondering!" she howled. "Conrad with a religious girl, do you know what I mean! Can you imagine it!?"

The other three at the table just stared, not entirely sure what she meant.

"I mean..." started Caroline, wanting to defend her partner, but he hushed her by shaking his head imperceptibly.

When "MMMBop" came over the restaurant's sound system, Vanessa started to grind sloppily in her seat. "I love this song!" she cried, clutching at Kevin's shirt. "Come on, baby, let's dance!"

Kevin captured her hands in his and, holding them pinned, looked significantly at the other couple. "This is a restaurant, babe. There's no dance floor. Shall we order food?"

"Good idea," said Conrad. "Quickly."

"Conrad will have the fish tacos," Vanessa declared to Caroline. "He always gets the fish tacos here. I really love your dress."

Kevin selected the steak fajitas; Caroline went for the boneless buffalo chicken salad; Vanessa settled after much internal conflict on the loaded nachos – extra cheese, extra tomatoes, jalapeños on the side. After studying the menu at length, Conrad shyly ordered the fish tacos.

"Told you so," said Vanessa.

"So do you guys come here often?" asked Caroline, sweetly but with the slightest undertone of menace.

"So many times," said Vanessa, "when Conrad and I were…"

"Let's not talk about that tonight, V," said Conrad quickly.

"I don't mind," said Vanessa, lolling happily on the table. "I'm not embarrassed about the fact we used to be a couple, Conrad, are you? What do you want to know, Caroline? I'll tell you anything. Like, literally anything. Like, did you know that Conrad used to have the biggest crush on Posh Spice?"

Conrad excused himself to go for a cigarette outside.

Vanessa watched him walk away and then staggered to her feet. "Actually, Caroline, would you mind taking care of Kevin for a minute? It's just I gotta' pee." She teetered on her heels before heading off in the opposite direction to the washrooms.

Conrad was standing immediately outside the front door of the restaurant, his back to the glass, one hand holding a lit cigarette, the other balled in his coat pocket. The wind was toying idly with his hair. He looked strained.

"Oh hey…" said Vanessa, masquerading surprise at having encountered him there of all possible places.

"Hey V," deadpanned Conrad, facing her out of politeness only to be zapped with a familiar twinge when their eyes met. He realised he had been subconsciously avoiding looking at her all evening.

Vanessa gazed up at him through her eyelashes, clear-eyed and staggering no more. Ah, thought Conrad. She had planned for something to happen after all.

"Can I bum a cig?" she asked, placing a hand casually on his arm. He felt his muscle unconsciously flex. Electricity there still, always. He fished one out and lit it for her from the end of his.

Had her eyes always been that blue? Those golden flecks that made her eyes appear as though they contained the entire universe in their depths. They got bluer when she cried, he remembered. Why are all girls pretty when they cry?

"Thanks," she said, inhaling appreciatively and taking in the deserted city street. "Nice night."

Conrad watched her lips around the cigarette, blowing out the smoke. He had always loved her lips: the way she pursed them when she was reading, the way she would wet them with her tongue when she was feeling sexy, the way they would bruise and swell after…

"Yeah," he said. "Beautiful night."

Vanessa shifted her weight onto one leg and braced a foot on the glass behind her. "It's supposed to rain tomorrow."

He thought about the little freckle on her left shoulder, right below her clavicle, and how she used to giggle and squirm when he kissed it. Did Kevin kiss that freckle? He felt a flash of jealousy.

"Is it?"

"Yeah."

She tilted her head down and peered sideways at him in that way he found devastating. Who was better, would she say, him or Kevin? That part of their relationship had always been excellent.

"You look great tonight," said Conrad huskily. "I like your dress."

"I liked Caroline's too," replied Vanessa. "Very pretty. Green."

"I like this one," he rasped.

"Thanks," she replied, holding onto the 's' longer than necessary.

"Is it new?"

"No."

"I've not seen it before."

"You wouldn't have. I don't see you much anymore."

"No."

"You're very busy nowadays."

"So are you."

"I am. But happy."

"That's good. I'm happy too."

"I'm glad."

Conrad dropped the spent butt of his cigarette to the sidewalk and snuffed it out with his heel. Vanessa likewise dropped her half-smoked cigarette and crossed her arms behind her back. There was a foot and a half, at most two, between them. They had ceased to make eye contact but she noted that his feet were pointed directly towards her, splayed on either side of hers.

"I remember those shoes," she said thoughtfully. "You had those when we were together. I remember them in my front entrance, so… big… compared with mine."

"They're very comfortable."

"They seem comfortable."

"I'll need to replace them soon though. They're wearing out."

"That's a shame. It's hard to find really good shoes."

"I'm going to miss them a lot."

Heavy, thick silence. At the nearby intersection, a car honked twice. The lights on two floors of the skyscraper across the street flickered and went out. Conrad thought he could hear his own heartbeat in the stillness, or perhaps it was hers he was hearing. The blood was whooshing in his ears.

"Kevin seems nice," said Conrad finally.

"Yeah, he is. Really nice."

"You guys look great together."

"Thanks," she said with an unconscious wave of dismissal. "I like Caroline. She has a good energy."

A young man reeking of stale alcohol and body odour approached the pair with his hands open in supplication. "Sorry buddy," said Conrad defensively, "I don't have any cash on me." The man flicked his gaze over to Vanessa, who shook her head and stared at the pavement. "Sorry," Conrad repeated as the man shuffled away.

"Good luck," said Vanessa to his back.

Conrad wanted to kiss her more than anything in the world.

"Caroline's a lucky lady," Vanessa said with her lips. Her eyes were saying infinitely more: invitation, temptation, surrender.

Conrad glanced away, suddenly uncomfortable. Vanessa grabbed his hand and swung it around playfully, her palm hot against his. "Hey, we're friends, right? This is what friends talk about. She's important to you, so she's important to me. Tell me how you two met. Was it through a friend? I don't think I know the story."

This was, of course, a lie. Vanessa knew all the details of their relationship, as he did hers, spread by whispering friends trying to pave the way to resolution and calm between them.

"How long have you been together?"

"A few months, I guess."

"Only a few months! The way you two act towards each other it's like you've been married for years."

"Yeah, we get along well I guess."

"I'm happy for you, really. So great. So what makes her so special? Excellent conversationalist? Fantastic cook? Loves football and beer?"

Vanessa was trying to tease but there was a distinctly hard edge to her words.

"Does your mom like her? I bet she does. She reminds me of your mom a bit, in a good way."

Conrad licked his lips.

"Did she sleep with you on your first date or did she make you wait?"

"Vanessa…"

"I just know how you feel about women who sleep with you on the first date. I mean, I know *now*. Too late for me but maybe this one's a keeper, hey?"

She punched him playfully in the arm, harder than would be considered playful, and immediately rippled with regret. She could tell by the shadow on Conrad's face that she had gone too far.

"I'm kidding, you goon," she quickly corrected. "This one won't last either. You're going to die alone."

Conrad looked over her shoulder back into the bar to where their partners sat, visibly engaged in light-hearted conversation.

"Hey, I'm sorry," blurted out Vanessa, desperate to restore the electricity. "I'm sorry, Conrad. That was uncalled for."

He looked back at her and softened. "No problem, V."

A taxi went speeding past, with a young man spilling drunkenly out of the rear passenger window. "WhoooOOOOOOOOOooooooo!" the man shouted.

"I'm a bit drunk too," she admitted. "I was really nervous about tonight."

Conrad was staring straight into her eyes.

"I didn't know what it was going to be like, meeting her and seeing you and… And I thought it was going to maybe be really difficult, you know? And it was in a way, but also not, because it's you, but you're with her and…"

The two stood still, eyes locked, breathing shallow and fast.

She didn't mean to say it, didn't want to say it, but the words were in her mouth before her brain could sense check.

"Do you love her?" – a pitiful, spurted plea as she squared off her body and braced herself for impact.

Every nerve in Conrad's body exploded at once in a melee of love and lust and regret and confusion. He could feel Caroline's presence not more than 20 feet away, remembered the way she laughed, imagined running his fingers across the soft skin of her cheek, the way her eyes grew dark when she was passionate about something. And all of this while Vanessa, furious, ferocious Vanessa, stood there in front of him, frozen, unblinking, tears making her eyes glint in the streetlights, the scent of her soap familiar and comforting,

"I don't know," admitted Conrad. He shifted his gaze down. "I think so. Yes."

"That's great," said Vanessa, one fat tear rolling down a cheek as she gazed up at the sky. "Really, that's great."

"Except…" said Conrad, soft and yearning. "It's just… the way I feel when I look at you is the way I should feel when I look at her…"

Vanessa raised her face up to his invitingly. He studied the soft curve of her bottom lip.

"And?" she whispered.

The city stood still around them, on its tiptoes, holding its breath. Time stopped, waiting.

"I should get back to Caroline," he said. "Sorry."

And he went inside.

2022

Exactly one week and three hours after the phone call from Conrad, Vanessa was at Vancouver International Airport waiting to collect him.

The Arrivals area was humming with the animated anticipation of a thousand reunions. Rain pattered on the glass panelling of the roof, and someone nearby smelled thickly of sweet cologne. Beside Vanessa a mother in a beautiful green and yellow sari and two small children under seven in pristine special occasion outfits waited with a handmade cardboard sign that read, "Welcome home daddy!"

Cute, thought Vanessa, although "Welcome" was missing an 'e' and the painted hearts were sloppy.

The mother caught her staring. "Cute kids," Vanessa said, so as not to appear creepy.

"Thank you!" said the woman, affectionately tousling the head of the little girl. "Little troublemakers but they are my life. Do you have kids?"

"Oh," said Vanessa abruptly. She fiddled with her mask, tugging it up and pinching in the nose bar. Something about the woman was disarming, nurturing: her eyes were impossibly kind. Vanessa felt a simultaneous need to run away and to ask for a hug. "No," she said finally, almost apologetically, "it didn't work out for us."

The woman's expression flashed with regret and pity.

"My daddy's coming home today!" said the little boy to Vanessa. "I made him a sign!"

Vanessa looked down at the beaming child, his eyes wide and dark. His wide grin was missing both front teeth. He had the same disarming energy of his mother.

"It's a wonderful sign," said Vanessa.

"Are you waiting for your daddy?" asked the even-littler girl.

"No," replied Vanessa, "I'm meeting a friend."

"What's your name?" asked the boy.

"Vanessa."

"What's your friend's name?" asked the girl.

Vanessa checked her watch: Conrad's flight was still half an hour from even landing, much less getting through Customs and Covid testing.

"Conrad," she replied.

"I'm so sorry about this," said the mother, cupping both kids by the back of their heads. "They're very excited. Their father's been on a business trip for a few weeks now, and I think they're a bit sick of me."

"They're adorable," replied Vanessa, imperceptibly starting to move away from the family as she pointedly studied the Arrivals board.

"Aarav!" called the woman to her son, who was slaloming through the barrier poles, "come back here please." She sighed deeply. "Honestly," she said to Vanessa, reaching down into her lap to cup the little girl's ears, "they're the greatest thing I've ever done in my life, but if I could go back – Aarav, I said NOW! – if I could go back, I'm not sure I'd make the same decision."

Vanessa could feel the sweat starting to form under her arms. She tried to smile but her lips wobbled and distorted. "Ah," she forced out.

The women gazed up at her. "I actually really envy women who don't have children. You have so much *freedom*."

PING, said the announcement board: Conrad's flight was delayed.

Vanessa saw her escape. "Ah shoot," she said. "That's my friends flight."

"Oh no. Well, you're welcome to hang out with us if you want company," said the woman. "Farhan's flight has landed but..."

"That's so kind," said Vanessa, her feet already moving, "but I think I might go grab a coffee and sit down. Nice to meet you though. Enjoy your reunion."

The mother looked faintly abandoned. "Say goodbye to the nice lady, kids," she said.

"BYE!" they chimed in unison.

"Do you like my sign?" the little boy asked of the man standing behind Vanessa.

Vanessa walked hurriedly in the opposite direction, feeling petty and mean. The sweat was beading on her forehead and running in rivulets down her back. She started gasping like a fish pulled from the water, her face hot and damp, clawing at her mask until it was in her hand and she could get fresh air into her lungs again. It took several moments before her the flight response began to subside.

"A medium latte with oat milk, please."

The Starbucks barista squared her shoulders. "I'm sorry, ma'am, I have to ask you to put your mask back on until you're at your table."

"Please," Vanessa begged, "not right now. I need some air for a minute. You know how it is."

The barista lifted her chin. "I appreciate that, ma'am, but it's store policy and I am not allowed to serve you if you're not wearing a mask. You can take it off when you're seated."

The barista couldn't have been more than 18, with a broad forehead and a swirl of shining black and pink braids neatly pinned up on top of her head. Her dark eyes flickered and flashed behind her Starbucks-branded mask. "Harriet" said her name tag in looping cursive, alongside a hand painted cartoon of a mermaid. There was a jerky awkwardness in her movement that implied an innate discomfort occupying space in the world, which Vanessa instantly recognised.

"Harriet…" tried Vanessa, going for sisterly empathy, but the barista didn't react. Vanessa glanced around for support, but the tables were all empty. She opened her mouth to speak again, then grudgingly looped the damp cloth back around her ears.

"Thank you," said Harriet. "I know, I hate them too."

"I don't…" said Vanessa, but was suddenly too tired to explain herself. "A medium latte with oat milk please."

"Ahh," said Harriet, "I can do the latte for you, ma'am, but we're all out of oat milk."

Vanessa's cheeks grew hot. She fixated on a tuft of baby hair peeking up from the woman's braids and fought the urge to wet her finger and paste it back down. "You are a major coffee chain located in a major international airport and you are out of oat milk – how is that even possible?"

"We've had quite the run on it today, I'm not sure why. Guess it's been an oat kind of day! We have all the other options though: regular, skim, soy, even coconut which is delicious in a latte."

Vanessa counted her breaths. "Could you check the back maybe?" she asked.

"No oat, I'm sorry, ma'am. Have you tried coconut and vanilla together in a latte? It'll change your life."

Vanessa shifted her weight onto one leg and checked her watch. Momentarily drowned by the feeling of being overwhelmed and hard done by, she concentrated on inhaling through her nose to avoid hyperventilating. "Could you check please? In the back I mean? Check to make sure?"

"I promise you we have no oat milk at all, ma'am," insisted Harriet, her head still high but starting to pull at her fingers. "I checked for another customer earlier and we are definitely all out. We do have several other delicious, non-dairy options though – soy, coconut…"

"Is there somebody else I can speak to?" asked Vanessa, exasperated. "Your manager, perhaps?"

Harriet's eyes darkened behind her mask. "I'm afraid my manager is on her dinner break right now. If you want to have a seat…"

Vanessa pinched the bridge of her nose with her left hand and scuffed away an angry tear. "Just… check…" she said in a low, near-growl.

"Of course, ma'am," said Harriet, heading for the back, "in case."

Vanessa rolled her eyes toward an imaginary table of supporters. "And stop calling me ma'am!" she snapped, leaning over the counter.

Harriet paused briefly with her hand on the door to the back room before quietly pushing through. Vanessa thought she heard the girl say something as the door banged shut but might have imagined it. Her stomach churned with rage and regret.

"It makes me feel old," blurted Vanessa the instant Harriet re-emerged from the back empty-handed. "Ma'am," she clarified. "You keep calling me ma'am. It makes me feel old."

"I'm sorry," repeated Harriet, those customer service crinkles firmly fixed but her eyes now dull. Vanessa wondered if she could make the girl cry, or perhaps even snap and start yelling. She found the idea of testing out the theory oddly compelling.

"So no oat milk then."

"No ma'am," said Harriet in her practised customer service manner. "No oat milk. Would you still like the latte? We also have cold drinks, baked goods, muffins?"

Resistance clearly futile, Vanessa knuckled. "Fine. But only the latte, nothing else."

"One medium latte, with…?"

Vanessa pursed her lips. "Coconut milk, I guess, if those are my only options."

"Any flavourings?"

"No," said Vanessa firmly.

Vanessa filled out the comment card as Harriet twiddled the knobs and dials on the coffee machine: *It is unacceptable for a major chain in a major airport to run out of basic ingredients, especially given your prices for a cup of coffee. I won't be back.* She declined to include her name and contact information.

"The lids are over there," said Harriet, placing the latte on the counter between them. "Have a great day!"

"Mmm," replied Vanessa, her mask already off and in her hand before she reached the table. The seething resentment outlasted the coffee.

An hour and a half later, Conrad came bursting through the doors from Customs like a hurricane. It took Vanessa a few seconds to connect the neatly coiffed, beautifully suited man who threw himself in her arms for a bear hug to the handsomely scruffy man she had been expecting. Tall and willowy, with the nose of Adrian Brody and the wide, gap-toothed smile of Condoleezza Rice, Conrad always made Vanessa feel dizzy and a bit stupid when she first saw him after a long absence. His halo of golden curls, as usual appearing as though he was not long past a swim in the ocean, gave him at 47 years old both a youthful vibrancy and the classic beauty of a Botticelli painting.

"Oh my god, Conrad, look at YOU!" she exclaimed, holding him at arm's length and taking it all in.

Conrad gave a girlish titter and twirl. "You like?"

"I like! I almost didn't recognise you without the puka shell necklace! Does this have something to do with your revelation?"

"It does," replied Conrad with a mysterious twinkle.

"Wow, well, you look really great. And I'm so curious about what's going on."

Conrad grabbed the handle of his suitcase. "And I can't wait to tell you," he twinkled, "but not yet. Where are you parked?"

As they trundled off to the carpark together, Vanessa caught a spicy waft of cologne that made her head spin. "So how long were you away this time around?" she asked, to distract herself.

"Eight months! But time is an illusion, V. It's been eight months, an entire lifetime, and just one single day."

She peered up at him. "So this is real, hey?"

"I'm a whole new person, V. Just wait. Life will never be the same." He whooped and clicked his heels.

They walked to the car in what fundamentally amounted to silence: Conrad monologuing about the smell of Vancouver air and the ghosts in the shadows in the concrete parking garage, and how the call of a starling made him think of European kings; Vanessa hearing almost none of it, lost in the white noise of her own head.

As they reached the car, Vanessa stepped briefly to the side to toss her coffee cup into the garbage.

"Have you ever had coconut milk in a latte?" she asked Conrad. "It's actually really good."

"Shotgun!" he called.

1998

When Nick was 27, he became a senior manager.

Management wasn't a step he particularly wanted, more an opportunity that he felt compelled to seize. There was nothing ostensibly wrong with Franklin & Co., purveyor of intricate parts for large machines to the mining industry: it was a solid, dependable income stream in the tenuous years after university, when most of his classmates slung plates of overpriced food or broke themselves to hit sales targets for disposable clothing. In the space of only two years he had risen through the ranks, from shelf stocker to shift supervisor to team lead and most recently to assistant manager. They paid him well, treated him well, he got on with his (predominantly male) colleagues, and he didn't dread going to work most mornings. It wasn't his dream job by any stretch, but it sufficed.

To offset the lingering sense of personal failure and to hold onto the disappearing tendrils of his passions, Nick threw himself into the online community circle of wordsmiths and poets publishing pseudonymously on Blogspot. He started *The Chaucer Chronicles*, writing as "Argus" after Ovid's failed perceiver, initially writing simple book reviews and progressing with growing confidence to opinion pieces on modern socio politics and economics. He discovered that his more pointed or opinionated pieces garnered the most attention, with commenters crowding his inbox to applaud, contribute, disagree, or dialogue. He followed everyone who followed him, and rapidly built up an online community of interesting and engaged friends. Clicking "Publish" at the end of a post became the highlight of his week.

"What a great way of keeping your writing muscles strong until you find the right job," approved Vanessa after visiting the blog for her first and, as it would turn out, only visit.

"Super cool, Nick," agreed Becca, who went so far as to create a username – "NoSpoon" – in order to be able to comment but then never actually did.

(If Conrad ever read it, he never said so. Nick was if anything relieved, content to express his thoughts in a world that welcomed good, honest debate without constant judgement.)

His most inadvertently life-changing post was innocuous as these things go: an off-the-cuff rant inspired by an article sycophantically extolling the many wondrous virtues and nobilities of the glorious and proud nation of Canada. Hunched in front of his computer on a chilly spring evening, bundled in his favourite flannel pyjama bottoms and his Roots hoodie, Nick succumbed to the joy of an unedited tirade:

This country is the little sister desperate to join her brother's gang - "I can fight! Oh, I can!" We are a growling Shih Tzu pretending it's a Doberman. We don't have the legacy of Britain or the might of the United States, the struggles of Russia or the population of China. We trot along mindlessly, clinging to our legal code and a deep-seated fear of/worship of the United States in order to define ourselves, and actively re-electing a government that admits to embezzling millions of dollars of taxpayers' money.

The world likes us for the same reason we are drawn to baby animals: we are cute, quiet, and altogether harmless. Play with the US and they might bite your throat, but you can roll around on the floor with us for hours and the worst you'll get is a bit dusty.

Our greatest strength – our rabid determination to let everyone hold tightly onto their cultural history and individuality – is also our greatest weakness, resulting in a collection of people who feel little connection with each other. If we're good to tourists, it's because we're all essentially tourists ourselves: fifth, sixth, seventh generation tourists who pin up pictures of the Motherland and wonder out loud whether our Native people might actually have the right to be peeved with us for outstaying our welcome.

And so on, relishing the ways the words rolled through his mind and into his fingers, the physical release of finding the best turn of phrase to capture an idea, the admission and on-the-fly development of his truth and worldview, until, finally, petering out, he rubbed the back of his head, cracked his knuckles, and hammered out his grand and unapologetic finale:

We are passive and apologetic hypocrites who bask insolently in the worldview that we are lovely and sweet and polite. Life is easy here for the most part and we take it for granted, planting jovial flowerbeds in front of the graffiti, and doing a very good job at distracting others and ourselves from the serious issues.

And with that he hit Publish and waited, one ear on the hockey game, for his online community to respond.

They did not disappoint. Zarathustra – a sharp-tongued Torontonian with a passion for graphic design trends – was right on it:

We as a nation are far too self-congratulatory.

Nick was pleased: he had expected her to come at him for a fight and he felt validated.

Thinker #9 – a baleful Scot with a profound emotional investment in the ins and outs of the UK Premier Football League in the UK – commented:

I think of Canada as a place where spoilt kids go in their gap years, to do white water rafting and kayaking and bungee jumping and all the stuff they could've done in Yorkshire for a fraction of the cost but it's worth the quadruple figure plane fares, I'm told, to see racoons in the wild.

ST – a tenacious Englishman with an almost-encyclopedic knowledge of pop music, chipped in with:

I once drank a bottle of Molson and so I feel qualified to claim that I know what all Canadians are like. Also I quite like watching Due South.

Nick felt pleased and rewarded. It didn't matter that he couldn't have picked any of these people out on the street: it was all the love and satisfaction of attending a house party full of friends without all the hassle of leaving the house and making small talk. The human connections felt real and rich.

And then, a comment appeared from someone new: Ladyfox.

Your words are opium.

Nick paused, intrigued by the intimacy of the comment. He clicked through to check out her blog, *The Manchurian Manifesto*, which ended up being a mixed bag of thoughts and arguments, beautifully and passionately written. She attacked the patriarchy, railed against inequality, dissected politics, and challenged cultural norms. She wrote of her complicated relationship with her parents and her penchant for odd, quirky, simple things of joy. She shared micro stories about aliens impregnating cows and ancient travellers taking the wrong turn in time travel.

Scrolling through the first twenty or so of her posts, Nick found himself chuckling, speaking back to the screen, stopping to re-read sentences multiple times to savour their eloquence. He felt light-headed and realised he was hyperventilating slightly.

He peeped at her profile picture: an artistic portrait cut on the bias, showing only a wisp of dark brown hair being tossed by the wind, one lens from a pair of cat's-eye sunglasses, the very edge of an open pink mouth. The skin of her forehead was smooth and calm, visibly glowing in the reflective sunshine. There was something evocative about the sunglasses: he thought he could make out the outline of one inscrutable eye through the darkness of the lens, or perhaps it was merely a reflection of the person taking the photo. She seemed young, possibly around his age, but her "About" section frustratingly only said "Regret nothing." Her hair looked soft.

"Who are you?" he wondered out loud, smoking a cigarette by the back door of his house. He watched the smoke trail off into the starry sky and attempted to complete the entirety of her based on the profile photo. For the first time since he had started blogging he felt annoyed by the anonymity of the internet.

Thanks! he replied to her comment on his post. *Welcome to my blog!*

He followed her back, and then he waited.

Previously rewarding, the blogosphere took on a new energy now that she was in it. Every time she published a new post, Nick would consume it like a starving man presented with an unimaginable feast. He scoured her posts for clues about who she was: one about a hilariously bad date with a cocaine-addled PhD student confirmed that she was single, one about the emotional fallout of seeing off a centipede with oven cleaner confirmed that she lived alone, one about an adventure at work suggested she was a teacher. Her words carried hidden undertones of someone with uncommon curiosity and humour, intelligence, and depth. He imagined them having feisty debates in quirky coffee shops. She would probably punch him playfully on the upper arm when he said something too conservative: she seemed very liberal but he liked the way her perspectives made him think about his own.

He did his best to play it cool – a feat made easier by the medium – but she was now commenting on everything he posted, regardless of content and it was growing increasingly difficult.

"Listen to you! Nick, you're adorable," gushed Conrad when Nick eventually told someone about her. "Talk to her already."

Not yet up to that, however, Nick made up an excuse to post a particularly flattering photo of himself in his blog and was rewarded when, within a couple hours, under the auspices of an examination of feminism at the start of the millennia, she shared one of herself making a face at a meercat at a zoo. His desperate imaginings had not done her justice: she was radiant. She was petite with a sharp pointed chin and dark pink lips and dark eyes – possibly Italian or Spanish. Nick contemplated taking a language course to impress her, if he could figure out which. He studied the pointed pink tongue, the comforting creases at the corners of her eyes, the down where her hair was being pulled back from the sides of her neck by the sunglasses – the same sunglasses! – on top of her head, the smattering of freckles across her forehead. He imagined himself in place of the meerkat, with her sticking out her tongue at him. His eyes traced the ambiguous curve of her breasts under the sage green linen shirt she was wearing.

He printed it out and stuck it up on the corkboard above his desk, and brought it with him later to be propped up against his bedside lamp so it would be the first thing he would see in the morning.

Nice picture, he emailed her. *You're very beautiful.*

It had taken him an hour to come up with that.

She emailed back: *You're not too bad looking yourself.*

He believed her for some reason. While never a handsome man – the most he would have given himself was that he had "character" – he had struggled in recent years with how the thinning of his previously-thick, ash-brown hair made the clumsy largeness of his other features loom unattractively forward. Under her gaze, however, his heavy brow ridge became strong and intelligent, the pockmarks dotting his cheeks scars of a turbulent and interesting youth, his thin pale lips and prominent ears adorable quirks that set him apart from the conventional crowd. Big boned with a propensity to put on weight around his middle? Solidly built with the physique to lead a family through a hard Nordic winter! And hadn't he read once that the thinning of his hair was a sign of excess testosterone? Surely nothing of which to be remotely ashamed or embarrassed.

Flushed with potential, Nick managed to type out and hit send before he had time to second-guess himself: *I can't stop thinking about you. Is that weird?*

If it's weird, it's mutually weird at least.

Nick's eyes filled with happy tears. "Oh fuck," he whispered to himself, alone in his office at the warehouse. He rubbed his mouth and nose hard with both hands and exhaled slowly. He briefly contemplated vomiting.

And so began a new literary love affair for the ages, told in Arial 10 point. They emailed each other multiple times a day, sharing the trials and joys of their daily minutiae and asking all the questions they had both been trying to answer via close reads of blog posts. She lived in Mississauga, she was indeed a teacher and she loved it, her favourite colour was a rusty orange, and her dream was to scuba dive in Egypt for which she would first need to learn to scuba dive. She had one brother and one sister with whom she got along well, a controlling father with whom she did not get along, and a beloved mother who called her "Button." Her blog pseudonym referenced Disney's *Robin Hood* – her favourite movie and, as was common to many girls of her generation, her sexual awakening.

"You seem different!" said Becca, after Nick surprised her and Vanessa by treating them to lunch out of the blue. "Is Nick in love?"

He was, such that anyone could be in love with someone he had never actually spoken to, much less met in person. He barely recognised himself: he had never felt so full of light and energy.

The emails ramped up, increasingly personal and vulnerable. Before long they were brainstorming the details of their future together: she would move to Vancouver (she had always been planning to so why not now?) and they would find a place together (rents being expensive and all, it made the most sense, and how else can you really get to know someone?). They flirted with the idea of phone calls but stayed with the written word, both too consumed by the joy of the other's writing to be able to move onto more modern mediums. Nick, who was not a phone person at the best of times, argued that there was something romantic about waiting to speak in person.

I need to be with you, she wrote one evening, and Nick replied, *Tonight, tomorrow, next week, soon, now. Say when and I will be the one with the red rose in his lapel.*

When she came through the arrivals gate, he not only had a red rose in his lapel but two dozen of them in his arms.

"How cliché," she said, as they fell into each other's arms.

The plan had been for her to stay in a hotel, but she never made it to check in. They periodically emerged dazed and delirious from his bedroom to scavenge for food before succumbing and tumbling back into bed, transforming words into touch like the world only existed for them. Nancy, her name turned out to be.

"Nancy, Nancy, Nancy," he said, kissing her all over her face and on the tip of her nose, "my life starts now."

Little of note changed when the weekend ended and she was back home: the distance created distance and their phone calls lacked the poetry of their emails, but they doggedly proceeded with the logistics of their life together.

And then one night, while chatting about a student in Nancy's class, Nick heard a distinctive cry in the background.

"Do you have visitors over?" he asked.

Nancy grew quiet. "No," she said finally.

"Oh," said Nick, puzzled. "I thought I heard a baby."

"You did."

Nick's stomach lurched, not for the first time with Nancy but never like this.

"Her name is Hayley," she said in a strange, strangled tone.

"Someone's on the other line," said Nick, and he hung up on her. Twenty minutes passed before he was able to work up the courage to call her back.

"Sorry," he said, "accidentally cut you off there."

"It's okay," she replied. He could hear *Sesame Street* in the background: Big Bird was waxing poetic about the letter L. "I'm sorry I didn't tell you."

Nick started tugging at the stubble on his chin. "And why didn't you tell me?"

"I meant to," she replied, her voice cracking, "but then it got serious and I couldn't bear the thought of losing you. I'm a single mom with a toddler – what guy's going to want that?"

"And her dad?"

"He's out of the picture. He was out of the picture before she was born."

Nick busied his hand coiling and coiling the phone cord to remove a kink. He suddenly needed to pee desperately. Everything in his body was telling him to hang up, run away, change his name, start a new life. The Yukon maybe. Become a bartender in Whitehorse. It was appealing.

"Is it over then?" she asked.

Nick desperately wanted it to be over, needed this to not be happening. This was not what he had signed up for.

He heard Nancy start to cry quietly on the other side of the phone. The sound lashed at his conscience.

"It'll be okay, Nance," he hushed her. "You've caught me off guard is all."

"ARE YOU OUT OF YOUR MIND?" asked Vanessa, over drinks the next evening.

"She needs me," said Nick, "and I love her. Nancy, I mean. I love her." He looked small and lost. "I need to meet her... the girl... But she needs a dad."

"Fair, but does it have to be you?" asked Vanessa, staring at him as though he had started speaking in tongues. "What do you know about raising children?"

Nick shrugged.

"It's your life, Nick," said Vanessa, shaking her head.

Oh my god, congrats! wrote Conrad from an internet café in Berlin, on one of his first stops on his European tour. *That was fast! Well done, bro!*

Nancy and Hayley made the move to Vancouver two months later, as soon as Nick had signed the rental agreement on a tidy two-bedroom apartment in Coquitlam. At the same time, the position of manager came up at work, accompanied by a fat pay raise, and Nick accepted it.

"I guess this is it," he mused aloud as he waited at the airport to meet his new instant family.

They married two years later in a beautiful non-religious ceremony in the Stanley Park Pavilion, surrounded by 200 friends and family. Their bulldog, Chippers, was the ring bearer.

2022

"Conrad!" exclaimed Robert, meeting them at the door with his hand politely outstretched.

"Rob, you old mucker!" boomed Conrad, dropping his backpack with a thud and wrapping his arms around the other man. "Bring it in, man. Handshakes are for in-laws, and I am triple vaxxed and ready for fun." Robert patted Conrad's back awkwardly a few times before limply succumbing to an extended and enthusiastic embrace.

"Vanessa tells me you've had some life revelation," Robert mumbled into Conrad's shoulder.

Without releasing him, Conrad replied, "Not yet, not yet. Soon! But not yet. Patience! Your guest room's upstairs, right? Second door on the left?" and then he was off into the house with Robert left standing dazed on the stoop.

Vanessa gave him a supportive rub on the shoulder. "You're okay, honey," she said, pushing him back inside the house.

Upstairs, Conrad was making a lot of noise unpacking in the guest bedroom. Already he had music blaring – a deep pulsing tonal sound that resembled dissonant whale song – and at times it sounded like he was singing along wordlessly in full throat.

"Shall I lay out dinner?" said Robert hopefully, glancing up the stairs.

"I can do that," said Vanessa, "if you want to pop up and see if Conrad needs anything."

Robert widened his eyes in feeble protest but Vanessa was gone.

Conrad lit up when Robert knocked softly on the doorframe, "Rob!"

"Robert, please…"

"Come in, come in! Sorry to have been in such a rush there, but I'm desperate to get out of this suit and into something more comfortable." He

49

casually indicated the pile of clothes that had exploded from his backpack into the corner of the room, across the armchair, and half-covering the side table.

"No problem," said Robert. "Vanessa wanted to me ask if you needed anything. I mean, do you need anything?"

Conrad gazed at Robert beatifically. "You're so good to me, Robert. You and Vanessa, always there for me, helping me. I won't forget that."

"Okay," said Robert, his eyebrows starting to tick.

"I think I'm fine for the time being though, thank you very much. Or maybe a glass of water? Dehydration from the flight and all that."

"There should a clean glass in the bathroom," said Robert, indicating the door in the far corner of the room.

"Perfect," said Conrad, unbuttoning his shirt. "Good old Canadian tap water. You really take things like that for granted until you get out into the world and see how others have it."

"Sorry, I should let you get changed. You said you wanted to change your clothes and I didn't think..."

"You're all good, Rob," said Conrad, pulling off his shirt. "Nothing you've not seen before."

Robert looked at the ceiling. "You know, let me get you a glass of water from the kitchen!" he said, pivoting on his heel and speed-walking back downstairs to where Vanessa was carefully placing cutlery alongside the plates on the kitchen table.

"All good with Conrad?" she asked as Robert came breezing into the room.

"Yes, fine," said Robert, grabbing a glass from the dishrack and filling it from the fridge dispenser. "Do you think he would like ice? Or maybe lemon?"

Vanessa walked over to her husband and planted a wet kiss on his cheek. "Thank you for doing this for him."

At dinner, Conrad was in fine form, regaling them as always with stories that always seemed to linger somewhere on the line between irresponsible and implausible. Vanessa had a far greater tolerance for these tales than her husband, who found them insufferably pretentious and attention-seeking.

"So there I was on this narrow path halfway up this mountain in Tibet, the rain sheeting down around me, guide nowhere in sight, one missed step and it's 200 feet straight down..."

Robert contemplated the boiled peas on his plate with inordinate interest, shaping and reshaping them into little green mandalas.

"What did you do?!" asked a rapt Vanessa.

"I said a prayer to the mountain, asking it to rise to meet my feet, and the next thing I know I'm safely around the next corner and there's this charming little cave and my guide's there with a fire lit, singing with his pipe going."

"That's incredible. Robert, isn't that incredible?"

"Incredible," agreed Robert in a low voice that failed to cover how not incredible he found it.

Blissfully inobservant, Conrad bathed in the light of their attention.

"So how did you get from Tibet to Utah?" asked Robert in a conscious effort to please his wife.

"The long way," said Conrad, "but first: do you have any more potato salad?"

"I do," said Vanessa, "hang on," and she pulled out a Tupperware container from the fridge and placed a large splotch on Conrad's plate. "More?"

"Yes please," said Conrad, smacking his lips and spearing a potato with his fork. 'More' ended up being over half his plate and piled unsteadily high before he finally gave the thumbs up.

"This potato salad is amazing," he said, gesticulating with his fork and spattering the table with a light spray of mayonnaise.

"It's Robert's specialty, isn't that right, dear?" said Vanessa, nudging her husband.

"So good," said Conrad. "What's your secret?"

Robert blanched. "Um," he said, "maybe the white vinegar?"

"Mmmmm, no, I don't think that's it," said Conrad, smacking his lips. "It's something more... unexpected. Something.... joyous... Something that dares you to stop eating because you can't and you know it."

"Celery?" Robert offered, looking bemused. "Or... sweet pickle maybe?"

Conrad waggled his finger triumphantly. "That's it," he said. "The sweet pickle. POW. Yes. Joyous!"

Vanessa and Robert made furtive eye contact. 'Joyous?' Vanessa mouthed with a twinkle.

As the potato salad mountain disappeared, Conrad's entire demeanour changed: he became shifty, animated in a fluttery way that Vanessa had not seen in him before. "Can I tell you?" he said, fluttering his hands over his chest. "My news, I mean? Why I'm home? I know you've planned the dinner on Friday and everything, and that means so much to me, but I'm not sure I can wait that long. We can use the dinner to tell the others and really thrash it out, you know?"

Vanessa made no attempt to hide her excitement. Even Robert leaned forward with curiosity.

"Ah, I'm actually nervous!" said Conrad. "This is incredibly important to me. I've never felt this way about anything before."

He fiddled with the edge of the tablecloth; Vanessa watched with concern that he might tear it – it was her favourite: the one with the little strawberry vines that reminded her of her mother.

"Please don't judge."

"I don't judge, Conrad," said Vanessa; Robert raised an eyebrow. "Fine," she corrected, "I won't judge."

"And listen to the end. Don't jump to any conclusions."

"Absolutely no jumping, I promise."

"You might not get it. And that's okay," and he slowly and very dramatically exhaled.

He had met her in the restaurant beside his hotel in Lhasa, at the bar as they both waited to order drinks.

"Ha, I knew it was a woman!" exclaimed Vanessa to Robert, before settling back in her chair and graciously indicating to Conrad that he could continue.

She was American, with black glossy hair that brushed her shoulders, and eyes that looked at him and through him at once. As they waited for service, Conrad looked her up and down appreciatively, squinting at the top shelf bottles when she caught him looking. When the bartender finally came over, they both gestured for the other to go ahead once, then again, and then a third time, and then attempted to order at the same time. The bartender was unimpressed; they, in contrast, thought it uncommonly hilarious.

"What are you drinking?" she asked Conrad.

"Gin and tonic," he replied.

And she ordered his along with hers, blocking the path to the bartender with her body and paying for the lot with a fan of cash.

"Thanks," said Conrad, in awe of both the casualness and the abundance of the money, both of which were rarities in his backpacker circles. "How can I pay you back?"

"Remember this moment," she said, disappearing into the crowd with one hand in the air.

"And did you see her again?" asked Vanessa, pausing with a cube of steak halfway to her open mouth.

He did: two days later, on the night train from Barhni to Delhi. In an example of fortuitous coincidence, she was in the same sleeper coach as him.

"I know you!" he said to her as he stuffed his backpack under the bunk and took off his shoes. "And I owe you a drink!"

The two spent the entirety of the 12-hour journey talking, allowing only one hour for a quick nap when neither could keep their eyes open and immediately picking up where they had left off the instant they woke. She was 27, born in Seoul but raised in the Bay area, the product of a Korean mother who had been swept away by the suave American consultant visiting the country on business in the mid-70s. Her name was Sun; he started to call her Sunny because of the way she emanated joy and happiness. They covered everything from their favourite books as children to the infinite potentials inherent in the universe. She had a dimple on her right cheek that emerged when she would throw back her head in laughter, that seemed to Conrad to hold within it the secrets to the universe. He spent the entire trip doing everything he could to keep her laughing.

At the kitchen table, Conrad's phone pinged in his pocket. Vanessa indicated that he could check it.

"Awww," he said to his phone.

"Sun?" asked Robert hopefully.

"No," said Conrad, putting the phone back in his pocket.

Sunny broke to him at Hour 8 that her dad had recently been diagnosed with cancer.

"Is it bad?" Conrad had asked.

It was, and that was the reason she was heading back home to San Francisco to be with him. "My father is an incredible man," she explained, snuggled into the corner of her bunk clutching the battered stuffed bear he had given her the day she was born. "Just as he was there to witness my entrance into this world, so it will be my privilege to be there to witness his exit."

And here Conrad paused in the retelling, misty and distant.

"So…" nudged Vanessa. "You're in love? Is that it?"

Conrad gazed at her, surprised that that had been her takeaway. "No," he said, clasping his hands in front of him as if in prayer. "Sunny is like a sister to me."

Robert stood up suddenly, having reached his Conrad limit. "Dessert anyone?" he asked, clearing plates from the table. "Ice cream maybe? I think we have chocolate."

Vanessa and Conrad ignored him entirely.

"How are you so grounded when you're so young?" Conrad had asked Sunny as morning light started to peek over the horizon rushing past the window of their carriage.

Sunny had taken a few seconds to consider, then replied, "Can I let you in on a secret?" Conrad had nodded, yes, of course, anything, and she had drawn closer to him.

"Well…" she had said, setting down the teddy bear and taking both of Conrad's hands in hers.

Robert slammed the freezer door loudly.

1999

When Vanessa was 23, she caught a chilling glimpse of her future.

Two years after graduating with a bachelor's degree in art history, Vanessa was working for the provincial government, impressing her seniors with her savvy internet skills hunting down people who had filed workers' compensation claims and then moved before receiving the payout. It was a surprisingly hideous job: often they hung up; occasionally they lashed out, leaving her shaken and numb; most of the time it was far more labour-intensive than handing out unexpected money should be.

"Good afternoon," went a typical call one Monday afternoon, "may I speak with George Francis please?"

"Speaking."

"Mr. Francis, hello, my name is Vanessa and I'm calling from the BC Ministry of Labour. According to our files you filed an injury claim in" – Vanessa checked her file – "1996?"

Vanessa could hear *The Jerry Springer Show* going in the background. A woman was screaming rapid-fire rage while the audience bayed like hounds on the hunt.

Vanessa kept going: "And I have some hopefully great news for you. If we can confirm your identity with a few checks, I can get your compensation payment out to you finally."

Jerr-y. Jerr-y. Jerr-y.

"Mr. Francis?"

"You're from where again?" asked George.

"The BC Ministry of Labour," repeated Vanessa patiently. "My name is Vanessa."

A puffed exhalation of air: George was smoking.

"Can I just confirm that you used to live at…" she started.

"Is this about my knee?"

"I'm afraid I don't have the details of your claim in the file, Mr. Francis, only that you filed in 1996 and were awarded…"

"Why has it taken so long?"

"It says on my file that the payment came back as undeliverable. Usually this is because the person moved home between filing the claim and preparation of the cheque."

Whoooaaaaaaa! roared the audience. A few whistles.

Vanessa rubbed her eyes. "Is that *The Jerry Springer Show* you're watching, Mr. Francis?" said Vanessa, angling to establish trust. "I love that show." (In truth, Vanessa found it puerile and degrading, and harshly judged anyone who watched it.)

"Mmm," said George noncommittally, distracted.

"Do you remember filing the claim, Mr. Francis?"

"Of course I do."

"Great. If we can just complete a couple quick identity checks, I can get your file off to the cashier this morning. Can I please confirm the address you were at when you filed your claim?"

George grunted. "How much is it for, the cheque?"

"I would be more than happy to discuss all the details as soon as we have confirmed your identity," assured Vanessa. "Can I please check the address you were at when you filed your claim?"

It was all going down on *The Jerry Springer Show* in the background: now a man was shouting over the woman, who was still shouting, and the audience had never really stopped shouting. Vanessa started to doodle random geometric shapes on her notepad to offset the need to throw the phone receiver through the window to her right.

"Mr. Francis? Is there a better time for me to call perhaps?"

"No," said George. "Who did you say you were again?"

And so on. The cheques ranged from less than a hundred dollars to a few thousand, for claims dating back years upon years, and she had yet to have a single person be happy that they had money coming to them.

As impressive and full of potential as her parents believed a job with the government to be, Vanessa was merely a temp, brought in to fill a desk without anyone needing to be financially responsible for her holidays, her healthcare, her future, or her general well-being. She was deployed into battle like a frontline medic, rushing off for a week here and three weeks there to stand in for a sick receptionist or address some urgent low-level administrative chore unwanted by any of the permanent staff. She was paid by the half hour, and in between timesheets she processed those folders, right to left, and got called names for money. Despite this, she was a beloved, cherished, celebrated temp – she assumed on the basis that she could spell her own name.

Vanessa worked in a cubicle surrounded by cubicles: only the top brass got offices anymore, but this was the public sector and even the offices were cramped pens not worthy of envy. The trend for the rest of the staff was to be clustered like little drone bees in rectangular honeycomb cells in the name of "facilitating creativity" and "maximising space efficiency," but really mostly just stripping them of the ability to make a phone call without twenty other people hanging on every word.

Some of Vanessa's colleagues had attempted to make their little cell homely: Monique next door had papered her cubicle walls with photos of beaming children on sunny days; Maria a few over went for holiday snaps and peppy mantras on colourful backgrounds. Vanessa's cubicle wall was empty save for the odd Post It note and a scattering of jobless thumbtacks: putting anything up would have been admitting defeat.

Temping had initially been a clever way to escape the emotional brutality of the service industry while Vanessa contemplated her existence before getting a Real Job. The Art History degree, while great fun for the most part, had not proven a reliable compass towards her destiny: the month before she considered being a professional fundraiser; a few months before that Marketing and Communications seemed a plausible option. Her parents obligingly kept setting her up for coffee dates with successful peers of theirs.

"You are an impressive girl, Vanessa," the contacts would all say, squinting at her approvingly. "You have a bright future ahead of you."

"Thanks!" Vanessa would reply, with perfect posture and a professional tone. "I've been really interested in [insert career path] for quite a while now but I'm not sure how to get my foot in the door."

"Networking," the contacts would say, tapping the sides of their noses with manicured fingertips. "It's all about who you know. Do you have a Palm Pilot? Get a Palm Pilot. Expensive but essential. Anytime you meet someone, put everything you know about them in there."

One contact showed her her entry: *Christopher's daughter. Art History. Temping. 23 (77?). Coffee 02/15. Cat: Whiskers.*

Vanessa found this blunt summation of her entire story and self profoundly depressing.

"That's a great idea," Vanessa would reply, as if she had the inclination and means to invest in a Palm Pilot on the way home. "I sure appreciate your time today, and if there's ever an opportunity with you…"

"Ha ha!" they would laugh, signalling for the bill which at least they would always pay. "Unfortunately, we're in the middle of downsizing but I will definitely keep you in mind should something come up!"

The year before Vanessa had wondered whether there was any point to doing a PhD or an MBA and hitting the snooze button on life one more time. It had been a long time since she wanted to be a popstar.

With George Francis eventually placated and his file ready to go to the cashiers on the next floor up, Vanessa had just opened the next folder when her colleague Marcus appeared at the entrance to her cubicle. "Knock knock!" he said merrily, miming an outsized invisible door. "Did you catch the rainstorm last night?!"

Marcus was a lifer in the department, with fifteen years served and counting as an administrator. He was a good guy with a wide mouth and a penchant for sweater vests. He was also the one responsible for signing Vanessa's timesheets. His cubicle was sparingly dotted with photos of his family back home, wherever home was – somewhere with lots of lawn and blue skies.

"It was brilliant," replied Vanessa, one finger marking a random place on the new file in an effort to appear busy. "I love a good thunderstorm."

"Nearly fell out of bed, the clap was so loud. Thought for sure it had hit the neighbour's house or something but no sign of anything this morning."

His bodyweight was making the cloth-bound partition between his world and hers wobble. Vanessa conspicuously glanced down at the file under her finger as though torn between chatting further and the profound lure of the work, then looked back up apologetically, sorry for being distracted, darn her commitment and professionalism.

"Anyway," said Marcus, "we're grabbing lunch at the Italian place if you want to join us."

She glanced at the clock. If she waited until 12:20, she could sneak out and put on her timesheet that she ate from 12:30-1. She might even be able to have a short nap in the stationery room later on, having recently been assigned guardianship of the only key.

"I'd really love to, Marcus," she said, "but I have so much work to do." (Her second lie of the day, and likely not her last.) "I'm getting really competitive about these aged files. This one's been open for five years!"

"We'll be in the food court next door if you change your mind," said Marcus amiably, wandering off to see if anyone else was up for lunch.

Vanessa glanced down at her folder. The ink was smudged where she had pressed her finger, on Harold Nguyen. He had not moved far and Vanessa quickly got him on the phone, following which it took her a good ten minutes to reassure him that she wasn't calling from a radio station prank show and that she was not one of those scam artists he had heard about on the news. Mid-call Jenny popped her head over the cubicle wall and mimed "eating?." Vanessa pointed at the phone and flapped her hand like a gibbering mouth. Just as she was on the brink of sending phone, computer, and desk hurtling through the glass window to the unsuspecting streets below, Harold consented to receiving unplanned money and Vanessa moved another folder to the left.

Later that week, Vanessa's boss called her into his sparsely decorated civil service office.

"There you are, our new superstar!" he greeted her, standing up to shake her hand and guiding her to the informal table and chairs in the corner. "How's everything going?"

"Good, thanks, Adam," she replied. She genuinely liked the man and his mild, people-centric management style. "Managed to close eight of the aged files so far this week, on top of the standard ones."

"That's great work. Everyone is very impressed, me included."

"Everyone has been very welcoming and helpful."

He offered her a caramel from the dish on his desk. "Some of those cases you're closing have been around for years. I don't know how you do it!"

"If I learned nothing else in my degree, I definitely became a master of Google!"

The two shared a brief, commiserating laugh.

"Vanessa," he said, "I'd like to discuss making you a permanent member of the team."

Vanessa was stunned. It was not joy she was feeling.

"You'd be on the Clerk stream, starting at Junior, but there's plenty of opportunity to develop within it, and given your skills I have no doubt you would rise quickly."

She sucked on the caramel and examined her fingernails. She really needed to stop biting them.

"You would continue doing the work you're doing now," he continued, "but we can definitely see if we can find other opportunities for you to really use your skills. Marcus says you like to write? I'm sure we can find you a task that would enable you to write. Maybe a report on cases closed or something?"

As Adam studied her, a grey gloom passing briefly over his expression.

"There's one thing to be aware of," he said gravely, pursing his forehead together as if to diffuse bad news with charm. "The way the government works, the streams don't really intersect: if you start in the Clerk path, you tend to stay in the Clerk path. Which is a very good path with a lot of opportunities for growth, it's … Well, I'm not convinced it's going to satisfy your… ah… aspirations…"

She didn't need to decide now, he ended, which was a very good thing as at that moment it was taking every fibre of her being to not stand up, flip over the table, yell "I am a Viking!" and make a run for the sunshine.

"Thank you so much, Adam," she finally managed to eke out. "That's really kind of you and I will definitely consider the opportunity closely."

Recently the messaging from her parents' professional contacts had been that temping was the new trend for businesses seeking to reduce costs and increase profits. Soon, they would say over their Palm Pilot contact lists, resplendent in their established careers, everyone would be hiring temps: they're convenient and inexpensive. Watching the colour draining from her dreams with every coffee meeting, Vanessa wondered whether she would know when it was time to give up.

"A Clerk role!" she squalled to Nick on the phone that evening. "A Clerk role! Not even Secretarial."

"Hilarious."

"Though at least it would be permanent? Which would be... good?"

"V, you are so much better than a Clerk role."

"It would be nice to have that security..."

"Security is overrated."

"Is rent overrated?"

"Hold out, V," said Nick seriously. "There's something amazing out there for you still. You just need to find it."

"Like managing a warehouse?"

She had hit a nerve. "Some of us actually have responsibilities beyond ourselves," he muttered.

"You do!" Vanessa seized to save herself. "You're doing what you need to do. I admire you, really, I do. Your life has meaning. Mine is so..."

"Don't take the job, V," said Nick.

2022

"I mean, Becca, it's insane. We're sat there at the kitchen table, and he's telling us this story of some half-Korean woman he met on a train in, like, Nepal or India or something – "

"It's always a woman," said Becca, sitting on the stationary bike to Vanessa's right.

The two had been at it for twenty minutes now. The sweat trickling steadily down from Vanessa's head to the collar of her T-shirt was about to gracefully merge with the band of damp beneath her breasts; Becca had a healthy sheen and a pink spot on each cheek. Around them, Beyoncé snarled above a pounding base beat about someone who had done her very wrong, and every now and then a great bellow and crash would sound from the free weights area.

"And the next thing I know he's passing out these pamphlets, and he's saying, 'Oh Vanessa, you're one of the smartest people I know, I'd sure like to get your thoughts on this.'"

"Religious conversion?"

"I don't think so. I didn't see anything religious on them, just lots of talk about self-fulfilment and manifesting your best life and making the world better."

Under the pretence of fiddling with the settings on her bike, Vanessa leaned heavily forward onto the handlebars to give her legs a rest. Becca increased her Level setting by two notches; Vanessa reluctantly picked up the pace.

"Was he selling anything?" asked Becca, her eyes fixed on a woman with two bright pink top knot buns doing deep squats twenty feet away.

"That's the thing… Yes? Sort of? This woman introduced him to some guy in San Francisco, who's, like, mentoring him or something."

"Mentoring him? Mentoring him how?"

The woman with the pink hair caught Becca staring and gave a slow grin over one shoulder before starting on a set of impeccable lunges. Becca slowly and unconsciously wiped an invisible streak of sweat off her jawline with the back of her index finger.

"Conrad's been taking these classes with this guy, and he's built up this… like, like, product base – there's a catalogue – and now he's looking for people that he can mentor… or something…"

Becca's pedalling slowed. Vanessa seized the opportunity to slow down as well.

"I don't understand?" said Becca, attractively furrowing her brow while checking her heart rate on her limited edition rose gold Fitbit and comparing it with the pulse in her neck. "Is it a business of some kind?"

Vanessa both nodded and shook her head, ending up with something resembling a shudder. "I'm not entirely sure. He says it's about his own self-improvement journey, but he gets a bonus whenever he signs people up to be mentored or whenever someone buys something. And I think he's under a lot of pressure to do so. He must have gotten at least six texts from people back in Utah during dinner alone."

Becca stopped cold in her stirrups.

"No. Is he?"

"Is he…?"

"Is Conrad in a pyramid scheme?"

"Or a cult, I'm genuinely not sure."

"Did he try to sell you anything?"

"Not really. There's a catalogue of all sorts of new age spiritual items that are available for purchase but he didn't try to convince us to buy anything. He showed us these geometric star crystals that he said would help detoxify our bodies from all the mercury we apparently ingest all the time."

"And did you buy them?" asked Becca, starting to pedal faster again.

"God no," said Vanessa. "I need all the mercury I can get."

"But he has to sign people up to make money? That is totally a pyramid scheme. Wild."

Becca stood up on her bike and started to pedal at top speed, triggering Vanessa to obligingly do the same. *Wooooaaaahhhhhh, we're halfway there!* sang Jon Bon Jovi from the speaker. BOOM went the weightlifters. The girl with the pink hair finished her lunges and passed by the line of stationary bikes with a crooked grin and hopeful side eye, but Becca was too enthralled in the recent news to notice or care. The girl disappeared out the exit with a subtle backwards glance.

"And you?" asked Becca. "How are you feeling about it all?"

Vanessa sat back down on the bike seat. "Sceptical, of course, except… I mean, he really seems different, Becs. He doesn't have that heaviness about him that he's had since that first trip to Thailand, you know? He seems… clearer…"

"Well that's good!" said Becca, settling back, "because he's been a real piece of work. You know what I mean, right? Like, I love him, but he's a lot sometimes. I'm glad that things might be changing for him at last."

"Yeah, no, he's… upbeat, full of life. Weirdly calm about everything. It's really nice, actually. We came down the stairs this morning to find breakfast on the table, with these fruity, vegetable-y drink shots that he said would help us focus our energies for the day."

"I bet Robert was loving all that."

"Based on all the faces he's been making, he's not buying any of it."

Vanessa's bike flashed. "Hey," said Becca, "how did you finish so much before me?"

Vanessa looked perplexed. "Oh! God knows. Maybe the shots work?"

***

"I haven't spoken to him yet," said Becca to Nick over Thai food later that evening, "but it all sounds really dubious to me. Lots of buzz words and self-empowerment speak, says Vanessa: Be the best you! Live your best life! Realise your wildest dreams, make thousands of dollars a month!"

Nick impassively watched Becca chattering away over her drunken noodles but clocked a glimmer of curiosity in his gut. He had an odd sort of respect for the randomness of Conrad's life decisions, feeling his own decisions unrelentingly banal.

"And people are calling and texting him all the time apparently – isn't that a bit weird? He says they're friends he's made doing the courses, who like him are now going out into the world searching for other people to pass the knowledge onto, and they're constantly in touch with each other, offering support and cheerleading and whatnot. It all sounds very intense."

"Is it a cult?"

"That's what Vanessa thinks, but I'm wondering about this catalogue of things to buy. It sounds to me like a pyramid scheme. I mean, he was in Utah after all."

"I thought those were illegal," said Nick. "Aren't they?"

"They're not illegal if they have a product to sell, which it sounds like it does."

"So what's your problem?"

Becca stopped with her chopsticks halfway to her mouth. She didn't really know what her problem was, only that her instincts were waving expansive fields of warning flags. She didn't like the idea that someone might be preying on her sweet, well-intentioned friend's desire to heal the world. She didn't like that his romantic nature might lead him to spending money he doesn't have on products that probably didn't work. And even though she absolutely thought Conrad was long past due to settle down and get a job, multi-level marketing was the absolute opposite of what she had envisioned for him. What if he lost all his money? What if he lost everything? She had heard stories.

"He has a degree in Economics, Becs," reminded Nick. "Conrad's no fool."

"That was a long time ago, though, Nick," said Becca, aggressively spearing a piece of mango from the bowl of salad. "Since then he's been off gallivanting around the world having these surreal adventures that have no purpose and no consequences. Maybe he doesn't know what real life is like anymore."

Nick snapped a prawn cracker in half.

"Conrad's like a babe in the woods for these people," said Becca with a plaintive whine. "I used to know a girl who sold makeup via an MLM and she had to work impossibly hard to make any actual money."

"Conrad could work hard."

"Of course he could," said Becca, "but will he? And will it be worth it? That's even assuming this isn't a scam."

Nick dipped half the prawn cracker in the remnants of his green curry. "Or maybe this could actually be something?" he ventured hesitantly.

"Maybe, but, knowing Conrad, how likely?"

"Maybe we should let him make his own decisions?" said Nick, bolder. "Live his own life without thinking we always know what's best for him?"

Becca opened and closed her mouth in protest. "Well I'll tell you one thing," said Becca, folding her napkin into her unfinished plate of food, "I'm not buying any of his products, not even to" – fingers making air quotes – "*support him*."

"Has he asked you to?"

"No," said Becca, making a pouty face, "I told you I've not spoken to him about it yet. I just…"

Nick could feel the air between them grow thicker.

"Can I get the cheque please?" he asked the server.

***

"I knew they would think it was a scam," said Conrad on Wednesday, over beers with Nick in their favourite bar. "This isn't sales like those other companies. I mean, yeah, there are things you can buy but you don't *have* to buy them if you don't want to. This is about education and emancipation. This is an entire lifestyle change!"

"They mean well," said Nick. "They're just protective of you."

"But they don't need to be protective," said Conrad. "I know what I'm doing. I'm not an idiot."

Nick tipped back the last inch of his beer and signalled to the bartender for another bottle.

"I gotta' tell you, man: before I met Sunny – she's the girl from the train – I was feeling so low. I'm going to be 50 years old in a couple of years, and what have I accomplished?"

"You've been to a lot of cool places?"

"I have, and it's been amazing and wonderful and a gift, but to what purpose? What meaning has there been in my life? I've been going along, doing what seemed right, assuming it was all going to lead to something, and then… what? What has it led to?"

"I hear you there, buddy," agreed Nick.

"But ReYOUvenate – that's what it's called: ReYOUvenate, which, I know, is kind of a dumb name but, man, it is something special, Nick. It has really awakened something in me. It's made me see clearly that I have been given all these gifts that are so much bigger than me, and I have been squandering them on backpacking and booze and women. It is my responsibility to share them with the world, to do my part to actually make the world better, and ReYOUvenate is giving me the tools and resources to do it."

"Sounds like it could be promising, Conrad."

"It really is. And it's not only a good income, it's an entire community. It has given me hope, Nick. It has given me actual hope and, man, I really needed that. I am in control, Nick. I am in control and I'm going to win."

Nick clinked his bottle against Conrad's. "Cheers to that, man."

Conrad tilted his head. "You know," he said, as if it had just occurred to him, "you'd actually be really good at it, Nick, with your language skills."

Nick's stomach gave a leap. He could use some hope too, he thought. "I'm no salesman."

"But it's not sales, that's the thing!" said Conrad enthusiastically. "We get paid to train and to teach – and you'd be amazing at that!"

Nick thought about his family, about the upcoming annual inventory weekend at the warehouse, and wondered if he had it in him to take risks anymore. It had been a long time since he had felt curious about anything.

"I don't know about that," he said, "but it does sound interesting."

"Look, I'm not here to pressure anyone, I'm here for a beer with a friend I've really missed. I'm just saying that I see your potential. I've always seen your potential, Nick, even if you haven't always."

Nick scraped some wax off the tabletop with a fingernail. "It would be nice…"

Conrad opened his arms wide. "Wouldn't it be, though? Believe in yourself, Nick."

"Would I need to do some interviews or something?"

"Not at all," replied Conrad, squeezing his friend's forearm. "Becoming a part of ReYOUvenate is like starting your own business, except that business is *you*. And once you're settled in, it's your business, entirely yours, and you can pass on that knowledge and create incredible opportunities to the people you love. How old is Hayley now?"

"Oh," said Nick, recoiling, "I don't think…"

"Make it about you for once, Nick. Haven't you spent your entire life working for other people, trying to make other people happy?"

"I have," conceded Nick.

"And where has that gotten you?"

"Nowhere I want to be."

"Exactly. Now enough shop talk. Let's enjoy the evening and have a couple more beers and maybe shoot some pool, and tomorrow I'll send you over some literature and we can talk more. You know me, I can't BS, but I'd really love to see if this is a good fit for you, Nick, because I really believe it could change your life. It sure has changed mine."

Nick swigged the rest of his beer. "Next round on me," he offered.

2000

When Becca was 24 and a half, she landed her first big gig.

Becca was a former child star, to the extent that Canadian kids could be. Impossibly adorable from birth, she landed her first commercial (for household wipes) before the age of two, blinked big bright eyes in bit parts as a toddler, and did a reasonably good made-for-television movie as an unusually mature eight-year-old. By 12 she was a feature performer in a terrible but popular public broadcast science series that involved her jumping up and down on a trampoline in a bathing suit while the grown male host talked meaningfully about gravity: when she was featured in a local newspaper for this particular role, the journalist gave her a lascivious wink and then gushingly called her "Canada's next It Girl" in the article. As her friends discovered sex and wasted their days hanging out in shopping mall food courts, Becca threw herself into dance classes, acting classes, singing lessons, modelling shoots, and amateur talent shows, eyes fixed on the non-negotiable end goal of global stardom.

It had not been an easy path. She went straight from high school into plentiful and poorly paid work in the theatre, co-founding a series of small theatre companies that blended unbridled youthful enthusiasm and meagre public arts funding to produce a seemingly endless stream of excellent work that played to eight people at a time. At 20 she won an award for her turn as the Red Queen in an amateur interdisciplinary rave-style immersive theatrical production of *Alice in Wonderland*, simply titled *Wonder Land*, in which she chopped cabbages in lieu of heads in a warehouse room with floors of genuine sod and go-go danced dressed as a flamingo.

To put food in the fridge, Becca bounced from menial job to menial job, from telesales to dishwashing to stuffing pigeonholes in an airtight room with documents streaming endlessly from belching printers. She dreaded the inevitable conversations with depressed managers about loyalty and commitment, but accepted it was the price she had to pay for a creative life and kept stubbornly at it. While her friends ached and moaned about their futures, Becca looked around at her life and felt sufficiently content.

When she was 21, an actor colleague got snapped up for a stint on a major soap opera, playing the torturously beautiful and much younger love interest of the show's ageing villainess. Becca sat with their mutual friends in the favourite bar for his debut, cheering raucously and drinking copiously, trying to swallow the jealousy and be happy for him. She awakened the next day with a terrible hangover and a fire in her belly: if he could do it, why couldn't she? Enough with the bit parts and the wanton dreaming, the big time was beckoning. She ramped up her auditioning, got new and subtly sexier headshots, and sought out an agent.

Not long after she turned 23, a major studio announced they would be filming a motion picture in the province and, to satisfy Canadian Content laws, had put a call out for locals to fill supporting roles. Becca dyed her brown hair honey blonde, got a spray tan, and went to read for the part of "Jessica," the advice-dishing co-worker of the female romantic lead. She made it to the third call back, performing an acapella version of "Killing Me Softly" in anticipation of a musical dream sequence, but lost out in the end to a brunette.

"Eh," she said another busser at the restaurant as they cleared up after an 18-person dinner party, "that's show business."

A few weeks after the audition, she received an email:

Dearest Rebecca,

I was impressed by your audition the other week and would be interested in working with you on a future project. You have an uncommon presence and charisma – real "star" quality. If you'd be open to discussing further, please contact my assistant, Margaret, at the number in the email signature.

Yours faithfully,

Charles J. Entwistle
Windfall Productions

Becca immediately called Vanessa at work.

"This could be it, V. Charles Entwistle is a big deal, very well-respected in the industry."

"And he's not…" asked Vanessa.

"Not…?"

"A predator? I mean, I'm sure he's not, but, like, you hear all the stories about casting couches and Hollywood starlets being asked to do terrible things for roles."

"Not Charles Entwistle, no. There'd be rumours. There are always rumours, but I've not heard anything about Charles Entwistle yet."

"Just stay safe, Becs"

Becca frowned. "Are you jealous, V?" she asked.

On the other end of the phone, Vanessa drummed her fingertips against a stack of pale-yellow file folders. "No, I'm at work so keeping my volume down. We're not supposed to make personal calls. Anyway, why would I be jealous? I'm happy for you."

"And this is what I've been working for my entire life."

"Exactly," said Vanessa, "so I'm not jealous. I'm genuinely happy for you."

"Good. I really need you to be happy for me because I'm really happy for me. This could be my big break."

"Drinks tonight to celebrate?" asked Vanessa, distracted by a colleague making the frantic hand signal for an impending coffee run.

Becca emailed back:

Dear Mr. Entwistle,

Thank you very much for your e-mail, and for your kind feedback on my audition. I really enjoyed meeting you too and will contact Margaret right away to set something up. Working with you would be a dream come true.

I am attaching my headshot and resume for your files.

Very much looking forward to meeting with you,

Rebecca

And then called Margaret to set up the appointment.

Becca met with Charles Entwistle at a café in Gastown the following week, stomach sore with nerves. Charles was already seated when she arrived, ostentatiously trendy in a metallic casual suit, flipping through a script printed on paper as blue as a robin's egg. He lit up when he saw her come through the door, like he was reuniting with an old friend, and was immediately on his feet with his hand offered out to her.

"Rebecca!" he exclaimed, "so nice to see you again!"

"And you, Mr. Entwistle," jittered Becca in reply, chagrined when he only managed to capture and limply shake her fingertips. "Thank you for agreeing to meet with me. I've not been here before – it's beautiful."

And indeed, the café was beautiful, like being transported to Europe – Austria, maybe, or at least as Becca imagined Austria to be. Charles had found them a table by a small open fireplace, allowing Becca the comfort of the curved dining chair while he took the bench strewn with dark red cushions pressed flat by a thousand bottoms. The firelight shimmered on dark wood panelled walls and subtle electric chandeliers threw comforting shadows, and only the slightest hint of modern-day Vancouver could be glimpsed through the gauzy curtains. The entire place smelled like cloves and dark, earthy coffee. Below the din of the other guests, Becca could make out the familiar strains of some piece of classical music.

"Please," he said, "call me Charles."

"Charles," Becca repeated, stringing her purse unsuccessfully on the sloping back of her chair before settling in with it pinched between her knees.

"I must apologise," said Charles, pouring her a glass of ice water and lemon water from a decanter without asking if she wanted any, "but I have a meeting right after this so we're going to have to be quick."

"Of course, not a problem at all."

He gestured for the server, then faced Becca dead on and made a tent with his finger. "Okay, Rebecca," he said with gravity, "tell me about you."

"Well," replied Becca, "I have been a professional actor for 21 years, since the age of –"

"Not that. All of that I can read on your resume. I want to know about the you that's *not* on your resume. Tell me, Rebecca, what is your favourite colour?"

"I like... blue?"

"Blue?" said Charles, stroking his dark goatee thoughtfully. "Blue, blue, what kind of answer is 'blue'? Which blue, Rebecca? Royal blue or peacock blue? Cobalt blue or electric indigo? Tiffany blue. Cyan. Pale summer sky blue. Turquoise. Never just blue, Rebecca, never just blue."

Becca tried to picture a paint sample card of blue shades. "Cobalt?" she chose quickly. "A rich, deep blue. Dark. Like the ocean."

"Good, said Charles warmly. "And your favourite singer?"

"Whitney Houston?"

"Not Mariah Carey?"

"No," replied Becca, with increasing authority but diminishing clarity. "Mariah is talented but Whitney has more depth."

"Correct," he said. ""Two lava cakes and a black coffee," he instructed the hovering server.

Becca felt a flare of anxiety. "Oh, I'm sorry, I didn't know we were eating so I had something before I left."

In reality Becca was hungry – a fairly normal state of being for a poverty-stricken actor whose work often depended on how she looked in her underwear – but she couldn't actually afford to eat there and wasn't sure of the protocol if Charles attempted to pay. Would that constitute a business expense or a date? Or was it perhaps another test? Was this the start of him coming on to her? Becca didn't find him entirely repulsive, even though he was easily thirty years older than her with a receding hairline and the first hint of a middle-aged belly, but his eyes were kind...

Charles genially dismissed her protests. "On me," he said. "I'll expense it, don't you worry. Would you like anything else to drink?"

"I'm good with water, thanks," she demurred, thinking of the calories she was now going to have to work off on the stationary bike.

The server – a young man with the dark parted hair and doleful eyes of a boy band singer – gave the slightest bow and disappeared into the back. He looked familiar; she wondered if their paths had crossed at an audition.

Charles contemplated her. "Why did you dye your hair for the film audition? I noticed on your headshot that you are in fact a brunette?"

Becca unconsciously grasped the tendril of hair falling over her right shoulder. "Uh, yes. Um. I guess to stand out more?"

"It doesn't match your spirit, the blonde. You have more depth, more gravitas. Blonde is too superficial for you. Too bombshell. Too Hollywood."

"Okay," nodded Becca, not entirely sure how she felt about being told she wasn't a bombshell. Was she not? Was she more girl next door? Should she go more bombshell?

He leaned back and surveyed her for a few moments, tugging on the hairs on his chin. "Though perhaps not the brown either. Too dour. Too plain. Too serious. Have you ever considered red?"

Becca considered. "I'd be open to it?"

"I think you'd really suit red. Red like Ava Gardner." He cocked his head. "Yes. Do that."

The cakes arrived: flat-topped pyramids sprinkled with cocoa, nestled against a small pile of strawberries. When she noticed Charles watching her closely, she brandished her fork like a small weapon and raised her eyebrows.

"Enjoy," he said, pleased with himself.

She pressed the edge of her fork against the top edge, and it collapsed into a pool of molten chocolate. So as not to disappoint, she made sure to pile up an enthusiastic forkful.

"Oh my god!" she cried out through a mouthful of warm cake. "Wow that's good!"

Charles took a bite of his, dropping his fork on the plate with a clatter applauding heavily. "Bravo Johann!" he cried in the direction of the kitchen, "you've done it again!"

The couple at a nearby table craned their necks to see what Charles and Becca were eating that was causing such a ruckus. Charles held up his plate to show them. "You won't regret it!" he said.

As Charles ate with the unbridled enthusiasm of a hungry teenager, cawing and groaning appreciatively, Becca rallied her confidence. "Mr. Entwistle..." started Becca, catching herself when he gave her a judging look. "Charles! You mentioned there might be a project coming up?"

Charles held up one finger while shovelling the remainder of the dessert into his mouth and wiping the muddy crumbs away with a white cloth napkin, all the while unselfconsciously eyeing the uneaten remainder of hers. "So," he said eventually, dropping the soiled napkin onto his empty plate, "here's the deal: I'm producing a national tour of *Evita* next year, taking in the big theatres across the country. Big budget, big style, bit glamour, high buzz – you get the idea?"

"Oh!" said Becca, "How wonderful!"

"Do you sing? Your resume says you sing."

"I do sing, yes. I've studied for seven years under Rachel Hanson."

There was no discernible click in his inner rolodex. He gave a minute shrug. "What voice do you have, would you say?"

"Big," she said, "I have a big voice. Very musical theatre. When I was in *Merrily We Roll Along* they had to turn off the drop mics because I could make them crackle."

"Ha!" he boomed. "A big voice. Good. Perfect. Range?"

"E3 to Bb5." It had been years since she had done a range test and she hoped that was still accurate.

"Perfect! We'll have to do an audition, of course, and I will need to hear you sing but if you can nail the vocal demands then I'm thinking about you for the lead."

"Really?!" stammered Becca.

"I saw her in you during your audition, right away. I wasn't even looking for her and then there she was: strength and vulnerability, co-existing. You don't tolerate fools. You know your power yet you are still searching for your authentic self."

"I... yes?" said Becca. She didn't feel particularly powerful but, if so, fine, she could feign that moving forward, no problem.

"That's what I want my Evita to encompass: she is in full control yet there is anxiety, there is humanity. There is greed and opportunism, and genuine love for Juan Perón but also maybe a little contempt and a little jealousy. My Evita is complicated and fluid, like fast and deep running water."

"It sounds like an exciting challenge, Mr.... Charles. I'm really honoured to be considered for it."

Charles lit up. "You have three objects in front of you: a loaf of bread, a toy car, and an elastic band. Which do you pick up?"

Becca worked hard not to goggle at him. She mashed her cake with her fork to distract herself from the panic, thinking desperately. "The... bread?"

"Interesting."

"Is that not right?"

"There's no 'right,' Rebecca," said Charles with a fatherly glow. "We're getting to know each other." He patted his stomach with both hands and then braced himself against the bench with both hands. "Would you excuse me for a moment?" he said, "I must visit the little boy's room."

Becca finished off her lava cake in stunned silence. As the server passed back from delivering the desserts to the neighbouring table, he whispered, "How's it going?"

"Good, I think?" she replied. "Sorry, have we met? You really look familiar."

"*Godspell* in, I think, 1997. We spoke briefly at the audition."

"I'm sorry, I..."

The server shook a lock of hair out his eyes. "Don't worry. I know how it is."

"Did you get *Godspell* in the end?"

"No."

"Me neither. Not even a callback."

"Charles seems to like you though."

"Do you think?" she whispered, her heart pounding audibly in her ears. She felt sick from the richness of the chocolate.

"He's one of our regulars and I've seen a lot of people in your seat. Trust me on this one: he likes you."

Charles returned and clapped the server on the back fondly. "The cheque please, my good man!" he said.

Charles' eyes were gleaming and dilated, which made Becca nervous – this had already been the weirdest and most intense meeting of her career – but she pasted on her best, brightest, most charismatic smile. Charles plonked himself down on the bench heavily and happily. "This was a very pleasant and productive meeting indeed, Rebecca. Very productive indeed. One last question for you and then I have to get to my next meeting"

"Of course," chirped Becca, bracing herself.

"You're on Captain Bligh's ship. Do you join in the mutiny?"

Becca felt on the verge of an out of body experience. "No?" she guessed, putting her cards on loyalty.

"Hmmm," said Charles, placing enough money to cover the cakes twice over on the table and standing up to gather his belongings. "Thanks for meeting me today. Margaret will be in touch to set up that audition."

And just like that the meeting was over and Charles Entwistle was gone in a cloud of expensive-smelling shampoo. Becca felt shell shocked and completely discombobulated, shooting the bemused server a look of helplessness as she slowly put on her coat. He patted her shoulder: "At an audition last week I was asked if I was allergic to spiders."

In the end Becca did in fact land the *Evita* gig, but in the chorus. She had one solo line – stepping forward and hollering "Votes for Women!!!" in the first act – which she performed with gusto in small regional theatres across the country eight times a week every week for a year, grateful for the paycheque. She was never entirely sure what had been the deciding factor against her not getting the role of Eva: having sung the role quite well in the subsequent audition, she suspected she should have mutinied.

"Your job is madness, Becs," said Conrad.

"That it is, my friend," she replied. "That it most definitely is."

2022

Vanessa had never hosted a dinner party in her life. She had in fact never hosted a party of any kind – not a surprise birthday party, not a college kegger, not even a semi-formal get together with friends and a scattering of hors d'oeuvres.

The fact she wasn't much of a cook was an even larger challenge. That was more of a "won't" rather than a "can't" issue: she was quite content cycling through the eight dishes she could make with minimal effort, week in and week out, with a determined repetitiveness that baffled her more innovative and experimental friends. Robert's complete lack of influence in this area was a big contributor to her inertia: as a bachelor, he had subsisted almost entirely on store-bought granola and Campbell's Chunky Steak and Potato, and as a married couple they had fallen comfortably into a peaceful pattern of 50% hodgepodge from the pantry and 50% delivery. They periodically attempted meal planning and batch cooking, usually related to a temporary surge of self-improvement motivation, but in the end entropy and pizza delivery usually won.

But for this event she had a vision, or at least of a vision of a vision: it was going to be big and creative and unforgettable. Her entire self-definition as a human being depended on the success of this dinner.

The last time they had seen each other, all in a group, was three and a half years earlier, in those casual pre-Covid days before lockdown, on a mild summer evening during a brief Conrad stopover. What had started as a low-key evening picnic on the beach ended with Conrad stripping to his boxer shorts and giving away everything on his person to a bewildered homeless person while Nick monologued about immigration and drug culture and Becca cried as several taxis drove by without stopping for her. The clever homeless man, once he had figured out what was going on, opportunistically demanded $100 for the return of Conrad's clothes – money Vanessa would never see again.

After twenty-five years of friendship, Vanessa could see the hairline fractures at the edges of the group's cohesiveness. They continued to operate as a unit in lengthy comment threads under Facebook posts and the occasional sporadic tweet, but saw each other in person in variations of one-on-one. Vanessa and Becca had their gym sessions and gossipy brunches; Becca maintained a semblance of closeness with Nick by allowing herself to be entertained by the same shadowy moods that put off Vanessa; Vanessa and Conrad instant messaged each other highly polished stories from their lives when he was off into the world and giggled over meals during his visits home, while Becca simmered jealously from the side lines. That last evening together, Vanessa had spent ten minutes watching the members of the group perform their usual roles of the malcontent, the freethinker, and the queen as if through a window, feeling the distance tugging at their bonds like a strong wind.

The rub, then, as she sat down at the end of the rosewood table in her dining room, with cookbooks, sticky notes, highlighters, and other office paraphernalia stacked high around her like protective walls, would be to find a menu that would feed, impress, *and* unite.

She brandished a pen. *Menu*, she wrote at the top of the first page in a fresh notebook.

She chewed the end of her pen absent-mindedly, studying the blank page, then added *The Dinner Party* quickly above *Menu*.

She pursed her lips, crossed out *The* and wrote in *Conrad's*.

She tore the page out of the notebook and scrunched it up into a tight ball. *Conrad's Dinner Menu* she wrote at the top of a fresh page.

She opened the nearest cookbook and started flipping through the sections with an appealing combination of enthusiasm and trepidation. She abandoned fish because it was too smelly, rabbit because it was too cute, pork because it was too intelligent. She contemplated lobster before remembering that she would need to either boil it alive or put a spike through its head. Mussels had a high food poisoning risk, she vaguely remembered – that was a no then. A graphic diagram of how to correctly skin some manner of self-caught mammal made her snap the book shut and rummage through the fridge for the remainder of last night's wine.

Damn it, she remembered as she sat back down and took a large swig, Becca's vegetarian.

She spent the next hour watching Facebook videos suggested by algorithm: Michael Jackson on tour, reality tv clips, funny pets, close call motor vehicle accidents, various years of Miss America being crowned, teen pregnancies. Every time a video would pause for an ad break, she would scroll down to the next. Mila Kunis speaking perfect Russian. Some trending Tik Tok dance. A white woman threatening to call the police on a Black family for using the shared pool.

Shameful, thought Vanessa, then saw the time. She went to refill her wine glass and called Nick for support.

No answer.

There were 547 unread messages in Vanessa's old Hotmail inbox, which she hadn't checked in many months. It took her twenty minutes to clear that out, as they were mostly marketing emails from businesses she hadn't cared enough about to give her actual email address.

"Robert!" she said when her husband stuck his head through the door, "come in and help me!"

Robert stayed suspended from the doorframe by one arm like a cheerfully grinning monkey. "Wish I could, honey, but I'm off to meet the boys."

"Please, I'm trying to come up with the menu for Conrad's dinner."

Had Robert flinched, or was she imagining it? His smile hadn't flickered.

Vanessa felt sorry for Robert when it came to Conrad. Although he had clearly accepted Conrad's periodic presence as part of the package of marrying Vanessa, they had never hit it off. There had been a moment at their wedding rehearsal dinner when Conrad was telling a story about reading erotic vampire poetry in New Orleans – "And they handed me this glass of blood to drink – of course it wasn't actual blood, though I'm not sure what it was…" – when Vanessa watched her husband glaze over and realised there was always going to be tension there. Things had not improved in the years that followed.

And then there was that silliness around her and Conrad, as if there was anything between them after all these years. There had hardly been anything between them to begin with, despite all the drama of their youth. Nick's dogged insistence on bringing it up constantly was starting to bother her and was plainly causing Robert stress. She resolved to have a word with Nick about it the next time they spoke.

He jigged up to her and planted a jaunty kiss on the top of her head. "I'm sure it's going to be great, whatever you decide on. You can do it. I believe in you."

"I need help!" she wailed as he withdrew from the room.

"Call your mother!" he replied, closing the front door behind him.

Vanessa tried to make a game of it: with her eyes closed, she stacked eight of the cookbooks, gave them a half-hearted shuffle, and selected one at random.

The Meat Cookbook.

If only Becca and her life choices weren't reducing the entire group's options so significantly, thought Vanessa resentfully.

"Health benefits of vegetarian diet," she typed into Google, killing another fifteen minutes reading headlines with only vague interest.

"Jason!" she exclaimed when reading was interrupted by a call from her brother. "Perfect timing!"

"Can't talk," said her brother, "Jess is waiting for me in the car. Just wondering if you'd gotten anything for mom and dad's anniversary yet?"

Vanessa had – a spa weekend at the hotel in which they'd had their honeymoon. She agreed to let Jason pay half and put his name on the card.

"You rock," said Jason as sign off. "Catch you later!"

To get the ideas flowing, she browsed the fridge for some cheese to go on crackers. Did they still have grapes? No. She cut up an apple.

"Oh Vanessa," said her mother when she called to ask them for ideas, "how are we supposed to know what you should cook?"

Vanessa put her head in her hands. "I'm not asking you to tell me what to cook, mom, I just thought you might have some recommendations given how often you entertain. God. Never mind."

She tried calling Nick again, and this time he picked up. He sounded out of breath.

"I'm the last person who would know how to plan a fancy dinner party, V."

"Well I can't exactly ask Conrad given that the party is in his honour."

"And Becca?"

Vanessa felt protective and petty all at once. "I think part of me needs to impress her on this…" she confessed. "I know. It's stupid. Please, Nick, I am actually begging. Help me come up with some ideas. I'm desperate. I don't even know where to start."

"Steak," said Nick.

"Becca's vegetarian."

"And?"

"*Niiiiick.*"

"Fine," he said, "ten minutes and then I need to get to work. Okay if I eat while we talk?"

Such was the severity of her situation that she lied and said she did not, and the remainder of their call was punctuated by munching and slurps that drilled into her soul.

"What's the theme then?" asked Nick. A soft drink or beer can popped open.

"Travel," declared Vanessa off the top of her head, having not decided until that very moment but ultimately pleased with her decision. "World travel, because of all Conrad's travelling. Unless you can think of something better?"

Vanessa could hear Nick laughing quietly on the other side of the phone. "STOP LAUGHING AT ME!"

"I'm not laughing, you ninny. Travel is a solid theme. Okay, um, what about... something from his favourite places that he's been?"

"Do you know what those are, though? He's been to so many, and I've not been paying too much attention if I'm being honest."

"Something from every continent?"

Vanessa made a pained noise. "And just what exactly is Antarctic food, Nick?"

"And you'd never be able to not have the full set, hey?"

"Never," said Vanessa. "That would totally defeat the purpose of the theme."

Nick brainstormed: Food laid out in the form of flags. Food in the shape of countries. Food named after countries. Food named after famous people from different countries. Food that spelled out his name: Cod. Oranges. Nickel...pumper... bread...

Just as Vanessa was giving up on Nick being able to help, the doorbell rang – Beethoven's "Ode to Joy" in alarming bonging boops. She and Robert had found it absolutely hilarious in the shop when they had first discovered it, but the ironic pleasure had quickly dissipated once installed and used a handful of times. Only the rarity of visitors had enabled its survival all these years.

"I'll let you go," she said as she hung up on Nick, checking her hair in the reflection of their 'This Kitchen is Seasoned with Love' wall art. "Someone's at the door."

It was Conrad, looking sheepish. "I was so excited this morning that I totally forgot my keys." As he brushed past, she noticed he was dressed in smart chinos and neatly buttoned shirt. Who was this man who only vaguely resembled her Conrad?

"The meeting didn't go very well," he said, hanging his coat on one of the wall pegs by the door and moving on without noticing it tumble to the floor. Vanessa replaced it on the peg. "I mean," he said, "it's all a learning process, this, and I'm still quite new to it. I'm sure it will get better."

"Was this..." Vanessa paused, searching for the right words. "... your new business? Rejuvenate?"

"ReYOUvenate. And it's not a business, it's a life transformation." Conrad plunked himself down in one of the plush chairs in the sitting room and put his feet up on the coffee table.

Vanessa gave him a look.

"Oops," he said, removing his shoes and tucking them behind the chair out of her line of sight.

"It didn't go well, hey?"

"People have such biases! They come into these conversations with their minds already made up, and they make every excuse to not confront the opportunity. It's so frustrating."

Vanessa felt awkward standing in the doorway. Both cross at the trivial distraction of having to console Conrad and relieved for the reprieve on planning the menu, she went to perch on the edge of the sofa.

"I mean," he said, turning his head towards her but staring downwards into space, "you see the opportunity, right?"

Vanessa blinked. "Yes," she said perkily, "sure I do. For you I mean, definitely I can see it for you. Not sure it's quite my thing…"

"You can relax," said Conrad, now gazing at the curtained window like a forlorn poet. "I'm not trying to sell you anything, V. I'm just… I'm feeling momentarily discouraged."

Vanessa fiddled with the brocade trim on the decorative cushion with the whimsical octopus print. It was her favourite. The brocade was coming loose on one corner – she made a mental note to get her sewing box out and snug that up when she had a moment.

"Well," she said, wanting to be supportive but actively dreading engagement on the topic, "what did they say?"

"They said it was a pyramid scheme."

"Isn't it, though?" asked Vanessa delicately. "Like, a legal one, of course, but… isn't it ultimately pyramid shaped? I mean, if you're trying to recruit people to sell for you?"

"ReYOUvenate isn't about sales, V. It's about education and self-enrichment, about using the tools around us to understand ourselves and our place in the world better, and to do better by the world."

"By… selling things?"

Conrad's expression hardened at the edges. "Do you call universities a pyramid scheme because they're trying to get people to attend classes? No. ReYOUvenate is a university, a big global university, with campuses everywhere and courses on loads of subjects and students going on to become teachers. But instead of studying Economics" – his disdain for the word was palpable – "we learn about how to become a positive force for change and goodness in the world."

Vanessa didn't say anything.

"You don't understand," Conrad said, standing up.

"Maybe I don't, not yet," said Vanessa, standing to meet him and resting her hand gently on his back in what she hoped was a maternal and not remotely sensual way, "but I can't wait to learn more about it. Just perhaps not right –"

Conrad's phone pinged and he glanced down at it.

"I have to get this," he said, standing up, "then I'm going to go lie down." And he was gone upstairs, the cloud of his frustration lingering in the air behind him. Vanessa replaced the octopus cushion where it belonged, between the hand-woven cushion from Turkey and the embroidered horse cushion from IKEA, and gave it a pat to fluff it up.

Her mobile phone rang in the kitchen.

"Vegan," said Nick.

"Sorry?" asked Vanessa.

"Becca – you said she was vegetarian but I think she's actually fully vegan now. That probably won't help your menu planning."

Vanessa chewed on her lip and felt momentarily despondent and martyred. Was she wrong for wanting to throw a nice dinner for her friends? Should this be so difficult?

"Thanks for letting me know."

She dropped the phone on the table and sank into one of the hardwood chairs, absent-mindedly chewing on her index fingernail.

The phone rang again.

"Yes, Nick," she answered wearily.

"In case you forgot, I don't eat garlic or onions," he said quickly.

"Okay," she said, hanging up on him and putting her head in her hands.

Why was she even bothering?, she asked herself, placing her fingers on her temples and rubbing slow circles. Upstairs in his room Conrad made an almighty bump doing goodness knows what.

She lifted her head suddenly. "No but seriously…" she said aloud to her empty kitchen. After all she had done for Conrad, to be told she didn't understand when she was trying very hard to and then have him stomp out of the room – *her* room, in *her* house, to go up to *her* guest room – like some hormonal teenager was unacceptable.

"And who doesn't like garlic?" she said to no one, punching at her phone to see if she had received any notifications since she had put down the phone. (She hadn't.)

Becca was less surprising, she conceded, rolling her eyes theatrically. Vegan or vegetarian or whatever she was now, because of course she was. If it were all the rage, Becca was all over it. Pop culture counterculture, Instagram subversion, that was their Becca.

Vanessa put both hands flat on the table and prepared to push herself to standing, thinking feverishly how ridiculous she had been to think she could do something nice for her difficult, ungrateful friends, when suddenly it came to her: the perfect theme for her dinner.

Vanessa.

The theme would be herself.

Ostensibly something more general, but deliciously, subtly, entirely about her for once.

Vanessa's stomach lurched with vindictive satisfaction. Let them think it was about Conrad's return. She was quite confident they would be too self-involved to notice, and so what if they did? It would serve them right for something to not be all about them for once.

With the grit and determination of a new world coloniser, she marched into the living room and started planting sticky flags in *Beyond Poutine: A Canadian Culinary Adventure.*

To start, an homage to her great-grandmother, whom Vanessa had been told had been one-eighth Anishinaabe: bacon-wrapped grilled wapiti with wild mushrooms and blueberries.

For the main course, a tribute to her Italian immigrant roots: pappardelle in lemon cream sauce with fiddleheads and smoked salmon.

For dessert, a mixed cheese platter purely because she didn't have the biggest sweet tooth, with a homemade partridgeberry chutney in a cheeky tribute to Wade, the sandy-haired acoustic guitarist from St John's to whom she had lost her virginity at the age of 16.

Vanessa sat back and surveyed her notes.

Wait, she thought, Becca the vegan. She reread the menu, tapping her pencil against her front teeth thoughtfully.

Eh.

2001

The first Becca heard about planes going into the World Trade Center was via an email from a friend who lived and worked in the city. "I'm fine," screamed the friend in writing, "I'm in New Jersey but I can see the smoke."

It was just coming on 8am Vancouver time and Becca was still half-asleep, sitting cross-legged in front of the computer with her coffee and absent-mindedly flicking through emails. Casting calls, a nudge from her mother to not forget her father's birthday dinner, a few chain letters that she casually deleted.

"Wait, what?" she said aloud, going back to the email from her friend.

I didn't go into the city today and I'm safe on the other side of the river in New Jersey. I hope and pray that none of your friends, colleagues or loved ones are in danger.

In case you don't have the news on: two planes have crashed into the World Trade Center in NYC, one of which was hijacked out of Boston. I was watching TV over breakfast and saw the news break. NYC is on what they call a "full terrorism alert." They say the State Department in DC just got hit by a car bomb. I could use a thousand exclamation marks but they wouldn't be enough to express anything.

I am sat on a hillside and I can see the smoke filling the sky. I don't know what's going on. It's horrifying. I just wanted to tell you that I'm not in NYC and I'm cancelling my plans to go into the city today.

Oh, God, one of the WTC towers just collapsed.

Becca shook her head as if to dislodge a buzzing fly and padded downstairs to the tv room.

And there it was, without even having to select a channel, on an endless, grotesque loop punctuated occasionally by the chatter of electrified, bewildered newscasters: planes going into towers, towers coming down, people running through the streets powdered like doughnuts with ash and dust, clouds of paper swirling like tumbleweeds in gutters, flames pouring from a gash ripped through the Pentagon, smoke churning above an oblong stream of charred earth in a deserted field.

"Pray for us," said a newscaster on one channel. "Good lord," said another.

"Wait. What?" Becca repeated, and she started to cry.

Are you watching this?!?!?, she emailed her friends.

They were, mostly. Vanessa, always an early riser, had been catatonically watching the news for nearly two hours by that point and had witnessed the towers come down in real time. Nick, having opted for an early start on the warehouse floor to get a head start on inventory, heard the news come shattering through the classic rock radio playing in the background and had spent the remainder of the morning huddled with a small group of colleagues in the staff room listening to it all unfold. Conrad was in bed with Simone – or was it Susan? – until nearly noon Vancouver time, oblivious, and woke up to a changed world.

Over the next hours, they wordlessly gravitated into each other's orbit: Becca appearing at Vanessa's door with bruised eyes; Nick swinging by Conrad's with a six pack of beer for shared television viewing. By evening they had congealed as a foursome on a bluff overlooking North Vancouver.

Conrad and Vanessa were on the hood of Nick's 1989 Honda Civic, Chester; Nick paced with closed eyes and clenched fists nearby. Becca sat on the grass by the edge, curled into a ball with her knees to her chest and her hair in her eyes. The warm evening air wrapped around them like a heavy blanket, the gauzy lights of the city blinking lazily at their feet.

"I mean," said Conrad to nobody, fiddling with his car keys nervously, "I don't understand how it's even possible."

The sentence shivered in the air between them, unanswered and unanswerable.

"Like," he said, "how did this happen?"

"I'm not surprised," answered Nick in an ominous tone.

"You're not?" asked Conrad, surprised.

"It's been a matter of time."

Becca lifted her head towards Nick with her eyes scrunched.

"No, I mean…" said Conrad quickly, shaking his hands in front of his collarbones like he was trying to cool himself down. "Like, how is it possible we live in a world in which passenger planes can bring down 110 story buildings full of people?" He was jiggling on his feet like an overstimulated toddler.

"Burning airplane fuel," said Nick matter-of-factly.

"No no... I mean... holistically...," said Conrad. "That this is a thing. That everything could line up and this could all be possible and this could have happened."

Nick spat into the dirt beside him. "Seems pretty straightforward to me," he huffed, kicking at the small puddle he had made. "Bunch of lunatics hijack some planes, lots of innocent people die."

Conrad spun his keys around the ring one by one, listening to them clink softly as they fell until Vanessa, who had until that moment been lying as if asleep on the hood of the car with her eyes closed, reached one arm over and snatched them from his grip.

"Stop it," she whispered, allowing them to slip from her fingers and drop into the grass beside the car.

"I wish I had been awake for it," Conrad mused. "I feel like I missed out. You all witnessed history this morning."

Vanessa let out a derisive bark.

"No, I mean," he attempted to defend himself, hands pressed against his chest like it was hurting him to breathe, "like, that moment. The world has changed and I... I slept through it, like it was just another morning, just another day."

Vanessa opened her eyes but did not look at him, fixing her eyes on an inky sky marred only by the blur of city lights. She noted the complete absence of planes and the uncanny silence of the city at their feet and felt a strong and sudden need to vomit. She wondered if 25 was too old to crawl into her mother's arms for comfort.

"What did it feel like, witnessing it?" asked Conrad.

Vanessa furrowed her brow. Her mind buzzed, full of thoughts and yet empty of them. It was as if every synaptic nerve ending in her brain was screaming all at once in an infinite number of pitches, filling the space and drowning each other out entirely.

"Like nothing," she tried. "Like everything had become nothing."

"Everything is nothing," muttered Becca from her ball.

"Like nothing mattered anymore," finished Vanessa.

"Be glad you didn't see it," said Nick brusquely. "Who needs to watch a bunch of people die?"

"It's wild," murmured Conrad. "50,000 people are in those buildings on an average day. 50,000! God only knows how many were there today! Could it have been 50,000? Imagine. All those people with dinner reservations for tonight, leaving the dishes on the counter to do when they get home, forgetting to take out the garbage. Poof. Plans. You know?"

Conrad looked around eagerly for any sign of engagement, but his friends were lost in their own thoughts: Nick standing with his toes poking over the edge of the cliff, hands in fists stuffed into his jean pockets; Vanessa like a corpse beside him with her feet resting on the front bumper; Becca unmoving in the grass. "To think," he concluded meaningfully, shaking his head slowly.

"What am I even doing with my life?" whimpered Becca, hiccupping. Her nose was running, mixing with the tears.

"Artists heal the planet, Becca," hushed Conrad, taking Vanessa's hand gently in his. Vanessa tried to recoil but he hung on tightly. He could feel her nails digging into the back of his hand. "We need you more than ever right now."

"Musical theatre," sobbed Becca. "I'm really doing the lord's work with that."

"You're giving people happiness," reassured Conrad, "by sharing your talents with us every day."

"And twice on Saturdays," said Becca with a cough that sounded like a sob. She stared over the glittering cityscape. "It's not enough. It's not enough. I need to do more, be more. I need to do something."

"It's too late for that," said Vanessa hoarsely. "There's nothing we can do. It's going to domino, even if it doesn't go into full-fledged war. They're already starting to call it 'a day that will live in infamy.'"

Nick bent down to snap off the head of a dandelion and threw it overhand towards the cliff edge, where it dropped undramatically to the ground by his feet.

"Ours is not a culture of forgiveness," said Vanessa. "We nuked Japan because they had the audacity of bombing Pearl Harbour. Eye for an eye, that's the rule. Make sure everyone is blind."

"Governments love war," agreed Conrad. "It's great for business and re-election."

Nick kicked a tree stump, flinched from the pain, and kicked it again. "The thing I want to know is," he said to no one in particular, "how'd they know who did it so quickly? Huh? Don't you find that suspicious?"

"They'd been watching them, I think," said Conrad, rubbing the back of Vanessa's hand with his thumb. She squeezed it for a few seconds, then pulled it sharply away when he added, "They may have even known it was coming."

"I bet there are more," said Nick firmly. "And I bet they're in Canada too, waiting for their turn."

Becca stiffened. "Don't, Nick," she muttered.

"Hey man," said Conrad, "let's not go there."

"We had, like, thirty thousand refugees come here last year, and hundreds of thousands more immigrants," continued Nick, oblivious. "Why? What's so bad in their home countries that they want to come here? Do we even know who all of them are? I've been reading a lot lately and we don't. I'm tired of the government rolling over and letting those people flood in here."

Becca snapped her head towards Nick. "Those people?"

Nick turned to look at her, his lips a thin, tight line. A gust of wind caught a lock of hair and flipped it upright briefly as they stared at each other. "Yes," he said, "*those* people."

Becca climbed to her feet, her eyes blazing in the darkness. "You'd rather we only let in fair-skinned PhDs from the Commonwealth, is that what you're saying?"

"If that's what it would take to keep us safe," sneered Nick, "then yes, but that's not what I'm saying and you know it."

"What *are* you saying then?" asked Becca.

"I'm saying that our government isn't doing enough to keep bad people out of this country. People shouldn't be allowed to come here just because they want to, especially those who make no effort to integrate. If they want to live their traditional way of life so badly, let them stay home. Truth is, I don't trust them and I don't want them here."

Over on the car hood, Vanessa made the sound of a falling bomb with her lips.

"Dude," said Conrad helplessly. "Becs."

"One step closer to the apocalypse," said Vanessa, rolling onto her side with her back to Conrad. "Let's go slaughter a few million people in another country to show them they can't hurt us without us hurting them back and be done with it. Then we can go back to our blissful fantasies of world superpower and economic domination."

Becca was visibly trembling, her entire torso squared off to Nick. "People DIED today, Nick!" she hissed.

"People were murdered today, Rebecca," growled Nick, "and who knows, next time it could be us."

"That's one vote for war," said Vanessa with a limp wave of her hand. "Who else is up for a little smash and grab in a third world country?"

Nick laughed – a booming, harsh sound that reverberated amongst the trees in the thick silence of the evening. "You two keep polishing your halos and ignore all the evidence that North America is a failed experiment in multiculturalism," he spat. "Oh la la la, let's all celebrate our cultural backgrounds and make no attempt to figure out who we are as a nation and what we stand for. 'America's a melting pot; we're a cultural mosaic.'

Bullshit. We're a powder keg is what we are. Only one side is going to walk away from this alive and I'll be damned if I let them try and replace us."

Becca took a step toward him, her arms tight to her sides. Nick took a step towards her, the muscles in his chest flexing as he pumped his fists.

Conrad slid off the car and walked toward Nick. "Nick, man, maybe cool it a bit. You're upsetting the girls."

"I'm not upset," said Becca defiantly. "This asshole couldn't upset me with his xenophobic bullshit."

"Are you calling me racist?"

"I've read your blog," she replied with icy cool. "Some interesting friends you've got commenting there lately, Nick. If it quacks like a bigot…"

Sensing the lunge before it happened, Conrad threw his body in between them and caught Nick in a bear hug. "Dude," he said, holding on tightly as Nick audibly growled at Becca over his shoulder. "Dude. Nick. Hey, let's take a walk, okay. Let's go for a walk."

"She can't talk to me like that," shouted Nick, straining against Conrad's embrace. "She has no right to talk to me like that!"

"She's hurting," hushed Conrad. "We're all hurting."

Behind his back he could hear Becca making small huffing noises. He couldn't tell if they were sounds of fear or rage.

"Don't do anything you'll regret," said Conrad loudly to both of them, leaning his full bodyweight against Nick.

"God," said Vanessa, still in a ball on the hood of the car. "This is so great. So what we need right now."

Conrad forcibly spun Nick in the other direction and steered him towards the trees. "We're going for a walk now," he said, not letting go of his grip. Beneath his hands, Nick seethed and trembled like an enraged animal.

"She can't…" said Nick.

"I know," said Conrad.

Becca watched the boys wander off into the darkness, immobilised by her fury. When she could no longer make out Nick's form, she bolted to where he had abandoned his denim jacket on the ground, snatched it up and with a mighty howl threw it overhand off the cliff.

"Fuck you, Nick!" she shouted, watching as the jacket got entangled in the branches of a tree ten feet away. "Fuck you and fuck them and fuck this and… and…" She lobbed a rock at the dangling jacket, then started throwing fistfuls of pebbles and dirt and whatever she could scrabble from the ground around her feet over the edge. "FUCK!" she concluded before letting her entire body go limp.

Over in the car, Vanessa didn't move. If she was hurting, she didn't feel it. She didn't feel anything. She wondered if she would ever feel anything again.

"Right," said Becca smartly, clapping her hands and brushing emotional dust off her jeans. "Okay so that's it. As soon as the *Evita* tour is over, I'm quitting acting and doing something to bring some good into the world." Her voice was raspy and sounded tired.

"Oh yeah?" mumbled Vanessa.

"Yes. I'm not sure what yet but I'll figure it out. Maybe be a teacher or something, try and sneak some education into kids before assholes like that get to them. Volunteer with refugees. Something. Anything. Just no more fucking dinner theatre."

Vanessa rolled over and off the edge of the hood, leaning against the car to prop herself up. "Sounds good, Becs, you do that," she said without intonation.

"And what about you, V?" asked Becca.

"Me?"

"What are you going to do? Surely you can't go back to work in that office tomorrow like nothing's happened?"

Vanessa shrugged and examined her fingernails. There was some dirt caught under the left thumbnail, which she attempted futilely to grit out with her teeth.

"Vanessa?"

"Yeah?"

"Are you okay?"

"Is anyone?"

Vanessa watched the city shimmer in the stillness below them. It wouldn't have taken much effort to pretend that nothing was wrong in all that quiet beauty. She closed her eyes.

"It's okay to be sad, V."

"I'm just tired, Becs. I'm just tired."

"That's okay too."

Vanessa blinked at the sky to stop the stupid, useless tears that burned in the corners of her eyes.

"Like, what's the point? What's the use, you know? All the consumerism, the territorialism, the hostility our culture embodies as tenets – I don't see how this is going to get better anymore. And I don't want to live in a world where security is that tight and where you see everyone around you as a potential enemy."

Vanessa wrapped her arms around herself in a futile attempt to self-soothe.

"I don't want to watch people falling headfirst to their death on repeat on my news," she whispered, and with that something inside of her jostled loose and she cried for the first time that entire day.

Becca rushed over and embraced her friend tightly. "It's going to be okay, V," she murmured.

"Is it?"

"It has to be."

"I'm not so sure."

The two women swayed together for a few moments, until Vanessa abruptly pulled herself free and aggressively wiped the tears from her face. The sudden withdrawal of connection left Becca feeling small and cold.

"I guess even the President of the United States felt pretty useless when he heard of passenger jets crashing into the World Trade Center," Vanessa said matter of factly, to break the silence. "Where are those boys? I want to go home."

No one spoke on the way back. Nick, sat rigid in the front passenger seat, gritted his teeth, and fumed over the things he wanted to say but couldn't, having promised Conrad to not stir the pot any further tonight. Conrad watched Nick from the corner of his eye, troubled by what his friend had said but unsure of what to do about it. In the back, Becca contemplated potential future career paths – immigration law, refugee centre management, at risk youth outreach – and bored holes in the back of Nick's smug, hateful head with her eyes. Vanessa watched a curl of Conrad's hair twist in the wind from the open window and concentrated on not screaming at the top of her lungs.

"Thanks for the lift," said Nick when they pulled up outside his house. When no one responded, he rubbed his jaw and gurned. "Sorry," he managed glumly before slinking towards his darkened front stoop.

Only when Vanessa had been dropped off and it was only Conrad and Becca left in the car did anyone speak.

"Forgive him," said Conrad. "He's not a bad person, he's just scared."

Becca looked up and away. "His fear is the problem," she said crisply.

"And we can help him see that," said Conrad, pulling into her driveway and reaching one arm back over the seat to try and take her hand. "We all need to make sense of it. This will be the single most defining moment of our entire lives. We need time to figure out what it all means."

Becca patted it as she got out of the car. "We'll see," she said, not hearing any of it. "Thanks for the ride."

Later that night Conrad forwarded Vanessa an email:

Hey V,

Check out what my aunt just sent me. It's super creepy if you ask me:

> *>>>In the year of the new century and nine months,*
> *>>>From the sky will come a great King of Terror...*
> *>>>The sky will burn at forty-five degrees.*
> *>>>Fire approaches the great new city...*
> *>>>There will be a great thunder,*
> *>>>Two brothers torn apart by chaos,*
> *>>>While the fortress endures,*
> *>>>The great leader will succumb,*
> *>>>The third big war will begin when the big city is burning"*
> *>>>Nostradamus, 1566*
> *>>>*
> *>>>New Century - 2001*
> *>>>Nine Months – September*
> *>>>45 degrees - New York is at 45 degrees latitude*
> *>>>The Fortress - The Pentagon*

Could this have been predestined? Was this supposed to happen?

It all makes you think!

Peace.

C.

Vanessa powered off her computer without replying.

2022

"Wapiti?" asked Becca, wrinkling her nose attractively. "Why not call it elk? Elk I've heard of."

Vanessa, third in the exceedingly long queue at the high-end butcher, kept her gaze benignly forward. "Because we're honouring First Nations Canadians with the main course and they call it wapiti," she explained calmly.

Becca fondled the end of her glossy ponytail and surveyed the butcher shop, which had opened recently in the neighbourhood to great fanfare. Effort had clearly been made to appear both Instagrammably charming and reassuringly immaculate. The entire left side of the long narrow shop was filled with country kitchen shelving units bursting with quinoa crisps and quirky chutneys, duck and quail eggs in tidy stacked boxes, extravagantly packaged chocolate bars with pink Himalayan salt, crystal ginger and wasabi infusions, an impossible array of mustards. This was all echoed on the opposite side by small baskets of crackers and impulse items dotting an immaculately polished display cooler with mounds of red, pink, and grey meat arranged in geometric patterns and pyramids. The polite queue of shoppers tucked brown-paper wrapped packages into reusable shopping bags and called the staff by name, saying things like, "What's good today, Bill?" and "Can you slice it extra thin this time please, Ellie?"

Becca watched a staff member drop the hindquarters of an animal back into its section of the display, where it shivered for a second or two before settling and peacefully bleeding.

"Do you want to wait in the car?" asked Vanessa, seeing her friend go ashen. "I won't be long here."

Becca shook her head. "I'm fine," she replied, giving Vanessa's shoulder a scratch of thanks. "I said I wanted to spend the day with you and I'm spending the day with you!"

Vanessa was now second in the queue. The woman at the front was selecting which precise strips of biltong she wanted pulled down from the ceiling drying racks.

"Bit of a weird place to bring a vegan," admitted Vanessa sheepishly.

"Ah," said Becca, examining a bin of flavoured rice cakes to take her eyes off the meat, "we're back on the dairy. I missed cheese and Max likes Greek yogurt with her granola in the morning."

"I told you it's the dessert course, right?"

But Becca wasn't listening. "And are vegans actually morally superior to vegetarians?" she mused aloud. "As long as you don't hurt animals, it's really more like symbiosis than exploitation, don't you think?"

The butcher was wrapping up the biltong now, taping it shut with a long, printed sticker.

"Plus it's totally possible to live ethically as a vegetarian as long as you stay organic and local and non-GMO and small farm all that stuff, so it's basically the same thing." Becca looked at Vanessa with an expression of combined horror and enjoyment: "Oh, except eggs - do you know what they do to male chicks?"

Vanessa, who had had poached eggs with her avocado on toast for breakfast that morning, did know. "Don't those sound good!" she said, pointing to the package of black truffle rice cakes in Becca's hand.

Becca chewed on her lip and tossed the rice cakes back in the bin a little carelessly for Vanessa's liking. If those broke, she thought, she would make Becca pay for them.

It was Vanessa's turn at the counter. The butcher was pink faced from the customer rush, diamonds of sweat beading on his forehead and dampening the top edge of his black mask. When Vanessa asked for two kilograms of wapiti loin, he was momentarily confused. Behind her left shoulder, Vanessa could feel Becca's smirk.

"Elk loin," sighed Vanessa in defeat. "I called early to check you had some in stock? Also, do you have thick cut bacon? 16 slices of that as well too please."

"Gross," muttered Becca.

"I know," said Vanessa. "Next time."

The meat quaintly bundled in brown paper and paid for, Vanessa turned to leave.

"Excuse me," said Becca to the man behind the counter, "is that meat my friend just bought at least free range organic?"

The butcher, who had moved on to helping the next customer already, flicked his eyes towards her without losing a beat in his practised customer patter.

"Come on," said Vanessa, grabbing her friend by the elbow and physically towing her away from the counter. "Sorry!" she called as the door closed slowly behind them. "Sorry! Thank you!"

Becca opened the door of Vanessa's new opaline Volvo SUV and hung unsteadily off the door bar to clamber into the passenger seat. "Sorry babe," she said, kicking off her shoes and twisting the rear-view mirror to check her lipstick situation. "I'm just watching out for you."

Vanessa stood with her fingers on the door handle and counted to ten slowly and with intention before getting in and starting the engine. "Which I appreciate, Becs," she said graciously, readjusting the mirror and shoulder checking as she began to roll slowly backwards out of the parking space.

"They put so many hormones and chemicals in meat these days and it's toxic for our bodies and for the environment," said Becca, tucking her sock feet up underneath her. "There's a woman about to step out!"

"I see her," replied Vanessa calmly.

"There was a study from Montreal a few years back that found dioxin levels 18 times higher than the internationally accepted limits! 18 times, V! Imagine all of that accumulating in your body over a lifetime and what it could be doing to you!"

Vanessa considered. "At least that's unlikely to be the case with the wapiti," she said. "That would be more the case with factory farming, no?"

"Oh no," said Becca with big, bright eyes, "it's all of it. I mean, maybe not to the level of 18 times higher but it's all of it: the entire meat industry. And all the hormones they're pumping into cows to make them gain weight faster are making little girls get their periods before they're ten!"

"Is that actually true?"

"Look it up, V! It's all over the internet and on some really reputable sites too."

Traffic was calm for a Thursday evening. Vanessa pulled up behind an idling Audi at a red light and watched a young family cross the street in front of them. A small blonde boy, his face, hands, and hair coated in something blue, was howling like an angry wolf.

"Oh hey," said Vanessa, "did you hear about Patrick?"

"The yoga instructor?"

"That's Anthony. Patrick is our neighbour – the older guy with the yappy dog."

"Why would I be keeping tabs on your neighbours, Vanessa?"

"Because his son works in your firm?" said Vanessa, but Becca was busy examining her ponytail for split ends and clipping them out with her teeth. "Anyway," continued Vanessa, "they found a shadow in his brain scan the other week. They think it might be cancer. It's not looking very good for him."

"That's awful," said Becca. "I bet he eats red meat."

"Oh probably," sighed Vanessa. The light switched to green, and the cars rolled forward.

"No, seriously!" said Becca. "The World Health Organisation has labelled red meat as carcinogenic. No joke."

"Red meat did not give Patrick brain cancer, Becca."

"Okay," agreed Becca, "maybe not Patrick specifically, but it's giving a lot of people cancer and yet the American Cancer Society keeps encouraging people to eat it!"

Vanessa wondered where the best place would be to buy fiddleheads out of season, if that were even something that could be done. She could replace the fiddleheads with capers if not.

"I've been doing a lot of reading recently and it all makes so much sense, V, when you start connecting things. Why would the American Cancer Society recommend that people eat a known carcinogen? It's illogical, right? Except who do you think is behind the big health organisations? Taco Bell, that's who. Kraft and Taco Bell and McDonalds and all those companies! Who don't want us to know the truth about meat, so they fund the health organisation in exchange for positive spin."

Vanessa took a sharp left on a red without slowing down and put her arm out to stop Becca from being thrown forward. "Sorry," she said.

"But if McDonalds is behind the health organisations, who, then, is ultimately behind the pharmaceutical industry who are funded by the health organisations? McDonalds, that's who!"

The slip road to the freeway was blocked up due to an accident. Vanessa checked her watch and turned into a residential street to try and get to the grocery store before it closed.

"They are making us sick in order to sell us the drugs to make us feel better, and they are making *billions* from it all. It's so clever, V. I'm not surprised they want to keep this from us. Can you imagine what would happen if everyone figured out what was going on and started eating good, natural, organic food?"

"You sound like Conrad now."

Becca was hurt. "This isn't some wacky new age nonsense, Vanessa, this is science. We have become too far away from how our ancestors lived and ate, and it is, in very blunt terms, literally killing us."

Coming up upon a cute little duplex on the right, Vanessa was briefly distracted by the tanned, rippling physique of a young man out mowing the lawn outside. She touched the brake pedal lightly to give herself a few more seconds of the view but managed to not crane her head as they passed.

"It's why I'm not getting the Covid vax," said Becca smartly.

Vanessa slammed on the brakes, nearly causing the car following to hit her from behind. She lifted her right hand in apology and pulled over to let him pass. He gave her the finger as he did.

Becca was watching her, bewildered. "Everything okay?"

Vanessa sat with her hands on the wheel. She had a simultaneous need to scream and to fight, to enter into debate and to run away, to fight back, and to give up. Her lips twitched with statistics unspoken.

"Vanessa?"

"That's… quite an intense opinion," Vanessa managed. She clicked on her indicator and slid back into the road.

"Oh V," said Becca brightly, "you have no idea how bad vaccines truly are. They are promoted as these life-saving jabs, but I saw a piece written by a doctor on Facebook that showed the links between vaccines and a whole bunch of really dangerous neurological disorders and it was truly terrifying. And now this untested," – making air quotes around the word – "'*experimental*' vaccine that doesn't prevent contracting or transmitting Covid, for a disease with a 99.7% survival rate? No way, I want none of it. I trust my immune system to protect me. It's done a great job so far."

Vanessa pulled a tight U-turn and heading back the way they came.

"Are we not going to the grocery store?" asked Becca.

"It's getting late and the shops will be closed soon. I'll finish the shopping tomorrow."

Becca's arms were folded across her stomach. "Are you upset?"

"I'm not upset."

"You don't want to talk about vaccines."

"No," admitted Vanessa wearily, "not really."

"That's understandable," said Becca as though speaking to a child, unfolding her legs and clasping her hands in her lap. "It's uncomfortable to face the reality that we've been lied to all our lives. It's uncomfortable to face the lies we tell ourselves because we're afraid of the truth."

"The truth you've learned via Facebook."

"Yes, and YouTube and a lot of websites that aren't controlled by those who want to keep us sick."

"Becca, please, can we talk about something else?"

"Can you afford to talk about something else, V?"

Vanessa's knuckles were white against the steering wheel, and she nearly clipped a cyclist passing on her left. She brushed her hair out of her eyes with one hand agitatedly. "Shall I drop you off at home?"

"Open your mind to it, V," insisted Becca. "They get away with it because you allow them to."

The car tangibly increased in speed as they hit a straight stretch of road.

"Check your mindset, Vanessa," finished Becca, staring at Vanessa intently.

The air in the car became thick and hot. Vanessa imagined reaching over her friend's lap, flicking the handle to open the door and, without slowing down, pushing her out of the car.

"Well," she said instead, "this was fun."

"It's okay if you want to get vaxxed, V," said Becca sullenly.

"Good thing too," replied Vanessa sharply, "since I am and intend to continue to be. In fact, I like being vaxxed so much I think tomorrow I'll make an appointment with the travel clinic and see what they can offer me. Maybe a nice yellow fever or a Hepatitis B. Ooo, maybe if I'm lucky my tetanus will be up for renewal. I live for a good tetanus shot."

Becca sat back in her seat and clicked the backs of her fingernails against the car window. "I get it," she said. "You don't want to hear it."

"Correct. I don't."

"I thought you'd find it interesting too, as I've always thought of you as an open-minded thinker."

Vanessa snorted. "Do you though?"

"Do I what?"

"Think of me. Think of anyone, ever, other than yourself?"

Becca's mouth was agape, her hands fluttering in her lap like dying doves. "I'm just trying to help…"

"Well you're not."

The radio was on at a nearly imperceptible volume, the drum beat tinny in the silence. Classic rock. Duran Duran maybe, Vanessa couldn't quite make it out. She thought about turning it up but reached over and snapped it off.

The wheels of the car made soft thuds as they crossed bumps and lines in the road. Every time Vanessa touched the brakes, there was a high whine that would need looking at sooner rather than later.

In a high, quiet voice, Becca whispered: "Have I done it again?"

Damn it, thought Vanessa, scrambling to hang onto the righteous anger. Fight me, she thought. Don't back down yet. I need this.

But Becca sat picking at her nail polish, forlorn.

She looks sad, thought Vanessa. She leaned heavily on the horn at a jaywalker up ahead who had more than enough time to safely cross and felt the last of the anger wisp away.

And though she tried to string out Becca's emotional turmoil as long as she could possibly bear, eventually she knuckled. "It's okay," she conceded.

They were magic words: Becca reinflated instantaneously. "I don't mean to be such a jerk all the time. You know that, don't you? I just get excited and I love sharing things with you because you're the smartest person I know. It's okay if we don't always agree, right? I still love you, and I know you still love me. We can agree to disagree on some things, right?"

Vanessa pressed her lips together to crush all the words left unspoken.

Becca clasped Vanessa's right hand and held it to her heart. "I'm grateful for you, babe. You keep me grounded."

They drove the rest of the way in that position, palms damp with shared sweat, Vanessa awkwardly trying to signal and turn with one hand. Only when they had pulled up in front of Becca and Max's glossy high-rise condo building did Becca finally let go.

"I hope we're still invited for tomorrow?" said Becca, dropping from the high seat onto the sidewalk and reaching back to collect her shoes and her purse from the floor.

"You're an idiot," said Vanessa.

"Takes one to know one," replied Becca. "Love ya' babe. Genuinely."

Halfway up the path, as Vanessa watched from the car to make sure Becca got safely inside the door, Becca turned back. "Oh, I forgot to mention: I'm gluten free now – will that be a problem tomorrow? That's not about chemicals, though. It gives me a leaky gut."

"Love you too," said Vanessa, grimly.

2003

When Conrad was 26, he shot a goat.

He had not awakened that morning with the intention of shooting a goat. Quite the contrary, dopey from yet another extended night dancing on a foreign beach with a blurry melee of other young foreigners, all he had had on his mind was breakfast.

He was in Thailand on a boy's trip, which had started as a generic two-week all-inclusive package holiday and had to date lasted seven weeks and counting. This was the eighth trip he had taken since graduating from university, and with each one thoughts of a life in Canada and a career in Economics grew increasingly vague and distant. Back home he sold overpriced khakis to shallow fools with too much money, and spent his breaks glumly watching the brainwashed world rush past; on the road he could feel the fresh air down to his very DNA.

The small fishing village in which he had found himself was a charming place, with obliging locals dotted in here and there among the hordes of tourists. The main street, extending at most a hundred yards up from the beachfront, consisted of a small grocery store selling postcards and fresh fruit warm from the heat, a surf tack shop and school, a battered missionary church of some denomination or other, and a handful of small restaurants with plastic stools and chickens pecking contentedly around diners' legs.

Conrad was staying in a hostel just off the main street, sharing one little room with three others for the price of a cup of coffee and a donut back home. He had been there for twelve days already, which, again, had not been in his plan. He had arrived in one night, liked the vibe of the place, and stayed. The owner of the hostel had taken to calling him "Conman" for the way he casually charmed the young women that passed through, with a not insignificant percentage of them eventually squeezing into his single bunk for a free night's accommodation. The next morning the owner would wink and bring the girls some fruit.

Last night had been typical of his evenings there, with the restaurants clearing their plastic chairs to make ad hoc dance floors that extended into the liquid darkness of the beach. Conrad danced and toasted and drank sweet beverages through straws, and watched the stars glimmer overhead with clarity he had never witnessed at home. By the time he had crawled into his bunk with a redheaded Kiwi named Bianca, he was certain he had found paradise.

The hostel owner met him outside the dorm the next morning with fruit for Bianca and a business card in hand. "Conman!" he whispered, "I have something for you."

Conrad glanced at the card: a delivery service of some kind, perhaps groceries.

"Other side," said the owner.

On the other side, handwritten, was a name and an address.

"Want to shoot a gun?" asked the owner, shooting two finger guns like a Wild West gunslinger. "A big gun, like in the movies. Automatic. M16. Browning M2. Big guns! My friend, he has a place."

Conrad, still half asleep, was struggling to follow, but the owner's enthusiasm was so palpable and charming that Conrad, sworn to always say yes, decided to go along with it.

Bianca was horrified. "Shoot guns!" she said incredulously, stuffing her toothbrush into her backpack. "No way, babe, I came here to surf, not kill."

"We're not going to kill anything!" said Conrad, feeling attacked. "I don't know, it feels like a life experience opportunity. How often does someone get a chance to shoot an M16 assault rifle?"

Bianca stood on her tiptoes to give him a light kiss on the cheek, smelling faintly of suntan lotion. "You do you, man," she said brightly. "I left my email address on a piece of paper on the bed, in case you want to stay in touch or whatever. Thanks for the place to sleep, and please pass on my thanks to the owner for the fruit platter. See you around, hey?" And she was gone without a look back.

Conrad studied the address on the business card. Eh, why not. He had nothing else planned that day.

"I'm going to do it!" he said when the hostel owner appeared during breakfast.

"Good!" said the owner, giving him two enthusiastic thumbs up. "You will never forget, Conman!"

By 10am Conrad was clambering onto a small bus empty save for the driver and two teenage boys seated in the very back.

"Hello!" one of them cried as Conrad got on.

"Hello," nodded Conrad, choosing a seat near the front.

"Hello!" called the other one.

Conrad glanced back over his shoulder. "Hello," he nodded again.

The driver said something sharply to the boys in Thai and they shrieked with joy and pressed their heads together. Conrad could hear them tittering for much of the way.

Conrad sank low in his seat and watched the countryside pass outside his window, interspersing swells of motion sickness with lurches of unease. When the bus passed a group of men in military clothes standing by the side of the road with large weapons slung casually over their shoulders, Conrad wondered whether surfing with Bianca wouldn't have been a better use of the day after all.

"Goodbye!" called the two boys in unison when the bus pulled up in front of a long, battered metal shed on a dusty yet verdant lot of land.

Stepping off the bus, the morning sun blazed oppressively down on his exposed skin and the air was thick with the smell of gunpowder. Conrad could already hear the occasional sound of gunfire: a heavy, foreboding noise that made the hair on his arm stand up on end. In the intermittent silence between bursts, there as a complete and uneasy absence of birdsong.

A grinning man in a garish Hawaiian-style shirt came bustling out of the shed, hands outstretched to clasp Conrad's. "Hello, sir, good morning!" he cried, his smile large and welcoming. "You are very welcome here!"

"Thank you," said Conrad politely, glancing around. "Are you" – he consulted the business card which had become damp and creased from being clutched in his hand all morning – "Frank?"

"I am Frank!" said the man. "You are a friend of Michael, sir?"

Michael must be the name of the hostel owner, realised Conrad. He had never thought to ask his name.

"I'm a guest at his hostel," stammered Conrad. "It's very nice," he added as an apology.

"It's very nice," agreed Frank.

Frank grasped Conrad by the elbow and began towing him towards the shed. Despite being over a foot shorter and many years older than Conrad, Frank was surprisingly strong. Conrad's feet dragged in the dirt as though he were unable to fully pick them up and walk properly.

"Can I get you something to drink, sir?" asked Frank as they walked. "Perhaps a beer? A cold beer? Very nice on a hot day!"

"Sure, thank you," said Conrad, thinking it early for a beer but powerless against Frank's all-consuming momentum.

"Bieh!" called the man to an older child watching from around the corner of the shed. The boy returned a few moments later with a cold bottle and passed it to Frank, gazing up at Conrad with enormous, curious eyes. Conrad fished a tiny maple leaf pin from his pocket – one of the hundred the Canadian government had sent him on request – and passed it to the boy, who took it with both hands and bolted.

"So!" said the man, handing over the bottle ceremoniously. "What would make you happy today, sir?!"

Conrad paused, at a loss on how to answer that. "I don't…" he began. "The owner of my hostel…" He caught himself. "Michael…"

They reached the door into the shed, and Frank held it open. Squinting into the darkness, Conrad could make out a few tables and chairs to the left, and what looked like metal horse stalls with closed doors to the right.

"Um… I guess… I mean, I don't really know…" said Conrad, stepping through the doorway.

What he had thought was a shed turned out to be more like a warehouse: long and wide, made of corrugated metal and beams. The floor was a hard rubber tile, red dust from the road outside tracking the common paths across the space. There were four white plastic tables in the open space, each with three or four chairs and a laminated menu propped up in a silver stand. At the far end, where the man had disappeared, a bar had been set up with neon brand lights and a small selection of familiar bottles. Fluorescent strip lighting diffused dimly throughout the space, with sharp rays of sunlight piercing through from small holes in the slanted ceiling.

Frank took a menu from one of the tables and handed it to Conrad. He realised with a jolt that it was not, as he had thought, food and drink, but rather a list of available weapons. The options were dazzling: Uzis, machine guns, assault rifles, battle rifles, pistols, even – Conrad blanched – bazookas.

"Uh," spluttered Conrad, "I guess an M16?" he said, selecting a weapon entirely on the basis that he had heard of it before.

"A classic."

Conrad touched Frank's forearm as the man started to leave, assumedly off already to collect the selected weapon. "Is it… safe?"

Frank laid his other hand over Conrad's and gave it a squeeze. Conrad could see dust collected in the lines around the man's eyes.

"Very safe, very safe," he assured Conrad. "Very popular with tourists and very safe. Don't worry, sir, I will take care of you."

There was meaningful pause. Conrad sensed that Frank was offering him the chance to walk away, which he found comforting. He didn't move.

"Please, sir, this way," said Frank, and without releasing Conrad's hand from his arm he started to move toward a horse stall about halfway down the length of the shed. Conrad followed obediently.

"Please, sir, sit," said Frank, nudging a plastic chair placed outside the stall. Conrad did so.

"Wait here, sir, please," said Frank, whooshing off to a door in the far end of the shed.

Conrad sat in front of a long stretch of painted plywood panelling, interspersed with six or seven rough doors. He could hear voices from the far end, by the entrance, but couldn't make out what was being said. And he waited, with his beer.

It was good beer, as it turned out.

Frank returned in a few minutes, brandishing a case. "Are you ready for fun, sir?!" he asked.

Conrad held up his hand. "Wait, um, sorry... How much?"

"Ah, don't worry, very affordable. Two US dollars per round, minimum ten rounds."

Conrad did a quick calculation. He had long since run out of the paltry savings he had managed to pull together over his last stint at The Gap and was now eating into his savings, but he had come this far and was loath to miss out on an experience. "Okay, uh, twenty rounds? To start?"

The horse stall door by the entrance opened, and two men in jeans and baseball caps came chattering out, followed by a different smiling local man.

"Dude!" one cried out to Conrad in a thick southern American drawl, fist pumping the air. "That was AWESOME."

"Yeah?" said Conrad. "Cool, great."

"What are you shooting?"

"M16?"

"Awesome. I went for the AK47. Wicked."

His friend shook the hand of his smiling local, who resembled Frank to such a degree that Conrad assumed they were brothers. "Thanks again, Joe," he said. "I'll never forget that."

"Please, sir," said Frank, opening a plywood door and beckoning Conrad to enter.

The horse stall was in fact a private three-walled chamber, open on the fourth side to a wide expanse of land dotted with targets, barrels, and other random objects. There was a low wall with stands, presumably for the guns, and a ledge for Conrad's beer. As Frank set up Conrad's chosen weapon, Conrad listened to the cicadas sing in the distant grass.

Frank took Conrad through how to hold the gun against his chest, warning him about the kickback and the noise. He explained the parts of the gun, showed him how to rest his index finger lightly on the trigger. He asked if Conrad had any questions; Conrad did not.

Frank's smile nearly reached his ears. "Ready?!"

Aiming carefully at a target in the distance, Conrad lightly tapped the trigger as he had been shown and fired a single shot. There was a flash of fire and smoke and an almighty crack that pushed the butt of the gun into his shoulder and echoed through his skeleton.

The surge of adrenaline was instant. Conrad's mouth fell open. He wasn't sure if he had hit anything and he didn't remotely care.

"Yes!" cried the man. "You like it!"

A second shot, CRACK, YES, MAN. Conrad couldn't explain it, but there was something primal about the noise, the pain of the kickback, the impact of the bullet into the dusty distance.

Frank rubbed his hands together. "Now are you ready to *feel* it?!" and he coached Conrad on how to shoot fully automatic.

Conrad had never experienced anything like it. The remaining bullets went so fast, BRRRRRRRRRTTTTTTTTT, and then it was over and he was holding his breath from the intensity of the raw power and the emotion.

He was a warrior.

He needed more bullets. Ten more, please. No, make it twenty. If he ran out of money his parents could send him some. Could he try other weapons as well?

Conrad spent the better part of an hour and over one hundred US dollars there before he began to feel sated. What an experience, he thought to himself as he lowered this gun. This is why we travel. This is living.

"All done, sir?" asked Frank, appearing soundlessly behind him.

"Yes, thank you," said Conrad, rushing forward to shake the man's hand gratefully. "That was incredible. I feel... amazing..."

"Powerful."

"Yes," exhaled Conrad. "Powerful. And humble. And... ahh... That was incredible."

Frank watched Conrad shuddering from the adrenaline. With a discerning look, he said: "You are truly a man who lives life, sir. Perhaps you are not quite done?"

At first Conrad assumed Frank was just trying to sell more bullets and was tempted.

Instead, Frank pulled out a single sheet of paper, laminate peeling on the corners, with pictures of animals: a chicken, a cow. "Perhaps something more?" he asked brightly.

Conrad recoiled. "Oh, no, I... I..."

"Shooting into the dirt is okay fun, like a child," said Frank. "You are a Man, sir. You are a Hunter."

Conrad waved his hands frantically. "No, really, I couldn't..."

"Totally ethical," hushed Frank, "I help you shoot. Quick and painless, very fun."

Conrad didn't answer.

Frank's eyes glinted knowingly. "Perhaps you're a little curious…?"

And, indeed, high on the rush and the discovery, Conrad was a little curious. Just a little, really not much at all, but in that momentary hesitation Frank saw and nailed down the opportunity for a sale. The next thing Conrad knew, a fat black and grey goat was being pegged into place out on the dystopian landscape beyond the half wall and a rifle was being set up on the stand.

Conrad could hardly believe he was doing it. What was he doing? Why? He should walk away, why wasn't he walking away?

"Come," Frank beckoned.

Through the scope of the rifle, Conrad could make out the features of the animal. A gentle face with wide yellow eyes and a long white beard. Short horns starting to curve back. Long straight back and shaggy hair on the belly nearly dusting the ground. Little black feet. Little black tail, twitching. Chewing on grass or something – was there grass out there? The goat was completely unstressed; Conrad in comparison was wound so tightly he would have shattered like glass if someone had touched him.

He wanted to explain to Frank that this was all a misunderstanding. He wanted to say that he had had an incredible experience that he would never forget and it was probably better to leave it all right there. He wanted to order another beer and maybe sit at one of those plastic tables and just sit and enjoy the moment.

Finger on the trigger.

Walk away, Conrad. You don't want to do this.

Frank beside him, smiling, still smiling, always smiling, business is good today.

Conrad, what are you doing?

Conrad, you don't have to do this.

Conrad, don't.

Conrad.

Conrad.

Conrad.

Conrad, what have you done?

The hostel owner met Conrad at the door like a returning hero, arms outstretched to receive the dazed Canadian into a back-slapping embrace.

"And so, Conman?" exclaimed the owner, holding Conrad at arm's length and surveying him. "How do you feel?"

Unable to offend the hostel owner, Conrad managed a head bob. "Yeah," he said. "Yeah, good, good."

The owner made a crowing noise and patted Conrad's cheeks with the flats of both hands. "Good!" he said, "Good! And next…"

Conrad managed to shake his head quickly. "I think..." he started but faltered and fell silent.

The owner seemed to understand, the happiness visibly draining from him as Conrad's chin dropped to his chest. The silence yawned between the two men standing in the doorway of the hostel, broken only by a bird calling "ow wow! ow wow!" from a nearby tree.

Conrad ate salad for dinner that night and moved on the next day, opting next for a major city in which to dance and toast and drink sweet beverages through straws.

2022

Six hours before her guests were due to arrive, Vanessa was raring to go.

"Don't be nervous," Robert had said as he kissed her goodbye that morning. "It's going to be perfect and you know it."

"Psssshhh," Vanessa had replied, wafting both him and the insulting idea that she could possibly be nervous away with her hand.

She wasn't particularly nervous: with her honour on the line, she had planned the dinner out fastidiously. Excited, definitely, and a little anxious that in her inexperience she would be prone to making stupid and unwitting mistakes, but in general she was comfortably confident and mostly just impatient to get started.

She unwrapped the wapiti loin, involuntarily shuddering at the unpleasant sensation of its cool dampness on her fingers, and dropped it on the cutting board with a sticky thud. Just as she was about to make the first cut, she set down the knife, rinsed her hands, and rushed upstairs to pull her hair back into a tight ponytail. Robert always teased her about how bad a mistress she would make on account of her tendency to shed like a sheepdog, and what an obvious way to ruin dinner that would be. As an afterthought, she tied Robert's "I like big buns and I cannot lie" barbeque-ing apron over her jeans and T-shirt.

She seasoned the loin pieces with liquid smoke and Worcestershire sauce and sprinkled them liberally with garlic powder and black pepper, before wrapping each piece with a strip of bacon and skewering the lot with the metal prongs she had borrowed from a neighbour. Far too early to start cooking, she popped them back in the fridge in a glass dish.

There wasn't a lot of preparation she could do for the pappardelle. She chopped as many of the ingredients as she could in advance and stacked everything on the countertop in matching ramekins: first in rows, then in a pleasing pyramid formation.

She fished out the crystal serving plate and silver cheese knives from storage and laid them out attractively on the kitchen table. From the fridge she collected the selection of Canadian cheeses, leaving them wrapped in a tidy row with labels facing upwards to come up to room temperature. The strong earthy smell of the Québecois Magie de Madawaska seeping from the folds of its wrappings made her salivate.

For the partridgeberry chutney, she sautéed red onion and chopped apples until the former were translucent and the house started to smell like Christmas. "Zest the orange" read the recipe; Vanessa had to first quickly google search the term and then zested and juiced the fruit into the pot.

After the orange came the shredded ginger and the berries. She had had to swap out the partridgeberries for cranberries when it turned out to be difficult to find partridgeberries in Vancouver out of season, but the recipe reassured her that that was fine. Nutmeg, fresh ground. Cloves, a pinch. Brown sugar, a few tablespoons for flavour. The smell was heavenly.

She popped on the lid and went to pour herself a triumphant glass of wine and have a sit down while she waited for the chutney to thicken.

It did not take long for the smoke to start.

"Damn it!" cried Vanessa, snatching the pot off the stove with her bare hand and dropping it in the sink, feeling the burn rise on her palm. She cracked the kitchen window with one hand while running cold water over the other, and stood for a good minute futilely flapping a magazine to shoo out the billowing clouds. Before long she was precariously perched on a chair punching the reset button on the shrieking smoke alarm repeatedly and to no avail, eventually resorting to removing the battery entirely in order to shut it up.

She surveyed the dry, blackened mass in the bottom of the pot, shame rippling over her chest and cheeks. According to the cookbook, she had forgotten the apple cider vinegar. No moisture – of course it would burn. She could have kicked herself.

She heard her father: "If only you had paid closer attention…"

She heard her mother: "Oh Vanessa…"

She heard Becca: "If it were me…"

"No," she said out loud, patting down the front of her apron and inhaling deeply. "Come on Vanessa. You're better than this."

She poured herself a very large glass of wine, straightened her spine, and grabbed her car keys for a replacement grocery run.

For her second attempt she resigned herself to meticulously checking off the steps in the cookbook as she put the ingredients in the pot. As the chutney began to bubble and thicken, and after her initial taste tests were positive, she even dared to put in the final, optional pinch of red curry powder, hot.

"What smells incredible?" called out Robert, who had snuck out of work early to help and was now standing in the doorway rubbing his hands together. "How's it all going?"

"Good!" she said, wiping off her hands on a dishtowel and presenting her cheek for a kiss. "The chutney's simmering, the wapiti is ready for the grill, and the pappardelle is ready to be assembled. I am feeling very accomplished!"

"Oh no, what happened there?" he said, spotting the charred remains still in the sink. He poked at the burnt fruit with a fork and whistled.

"I followed the recipe!" said Vanessa, flushing pink.

Robert held up a piece of unrecognisably charred fruit in wonderment. "Impressive work!"

Vanessa raged. That's what her mother always did – focusing on the one bad thing instead of all of the good – and she was tired and stressed and not going to accept it from Robert, not today of all days. She snatched the pot from his hand and started violently scraping its contents into the garbage bin.

"I made a mistake," she snapped at him. "People do that sometimes you know, even me."

Robert tried to take the pan from her but she fought back, her eyes wide and wild. Her eyes began to sting from the welling tears.

"I'm doing my best," she whimpered.

"Oh oh oh," said Robert, pulling her into an embrace. "I know you are." His warm breath ruffled her hair and she folded herself into the scratchy comfort of his sweater.

"This is important to me," she wept, "and I'm failing."

"You're not failing," he said, "not in the slightest."

"I am. I'm trying so hard but I'm failing."

"You're doing so well. Really, you are."

"The evening is going to be a total failure and I am going to look like a complete idiot in front of everybody."

"It won't be and you won't."

"I burned the chutney."

"It happens."

"And I burned my hand."

"Poor poor you."

"I didn't read the recipe correctly."

"Your second attempt smells amazing."

"I have no idea how to cook wapiti."

"That's why you have a recipe."

"Two of the courses involve meat and there are two vegetarians coming tonight," she confessed. "What kind of monster does that?"

"A monster with a Plan B for the vegetarians, I would expect," said Robert, resting his cheek on the top of her head.

She moved her head out and peered up at him. "I did it on purpose," she said.

Robert kissed her forehead consolingly. "They probably deserve it."

Vanessa laughed into his shoulder until the fear and unhappiness subsided and the ridiculousness of her reaction loomed up instead. "Thanks," she said, pulling herself from his embrace and wiping her eyes. "Phooo! Sorry, little stress break there."

Robert squeezed her upper arms. "How can I help?"

"You can set the dining room table with the good plates and the wedding silverware," she said, adding as an afterthought, *"Properly."*

Robert saluted smartly, planted a kiss on the top of her head, and disappeared into the next room.

She followed him in a few seconds later to supervise. "Smaller forks and knives on the outside! No, no, dessert utensils above the plate, fork pointing to the right and spoon to the left. And side plate to the left! Not there, up left. 10 o'clock. Two wine glasses each, plus one for water. The good wine glasses, Robert! Did you find the charger plates?"

Robert's kind, supportive grin never dropped.

"Is the white wine in the fridge chilling already?"

Robert's grin dropped.

"Robert, did you forget to pick up the wine?"

"Crap."

With Robert out collecting the wine, Vanessa laid out her pièce de résistance: a spectacular centrepiece of woven pine branches interspersed with red and white gerbera daisies and tiny paper Canadian flags, crafted to order by her favourite florist. It had cost her an absolute fortune but, seeing it now on the table, Vanessa was quite sure it was worth every penny. In the middle she tucked a small plastic goat she had picked up at the toy store, positioned so as to appear to be nibbling on a carnation.

And the rest was set dressing: alternating red and white cloth napkins, glittery pinecones scattered in a pretence of accident amidst the table's empty spaces, name cards printed in crisp Helvetica font – the official typeface of the Government of Canada, as Vanessa had discovered in her research and was therefore set on.

There was a bang in the hallway and Vanessa heard Conrad's heavy boots in the hallway.

"Don't come into the dining room!" she called out.

"I won't!" yelled Conrad, rushing past and up the stairs to the guest room.

Vanessa stuck her head into the hallway and yelled up, "Dinner's still at 8 though!"

"Yup!" he shouted down, shutting his door firmly.

2007

When Vanessa was 31, she became Mexican.

Nearing the 18-month mark as a Marketing and Communications Assistant at a public relations firm owned by a friend of her mother, Vanessa found herself once again questioning her future. Marketing was a fine job that paid more than she was arguably worth (and certainly more than her half-hearted commitment merited), but it lacked something: a fire, a passion, a sense of belonging. Like wearing someone else's clothing, it didn't fit her properly.

"Then why stay?" her friends would ask. "Why not look for something else?"

"I'm good at it," she would reply thoughtfully, "and I don't know what else I'd rather be doing?"

Desperate to distract herself from lurking feelings of failure, she dropped thousands of dollars at IKEA in one afternoon to completely furnish the two-bedroom apartment she rented in a rougher corner of town. Bolstered by her obliging credit card, she would casually concede to the allure of meals out, knickknacks that served no practical purpose, new art for her walls, stuffed vine leaves for dinner. Debt had become a normal, comfortable reality for her, an annoyance that went hand-in-hand with living a life resembling the one she wanted. Rent, utilities, student loans, credit card minimum payment: all the unavoidable and therefore unemotional monthly cost of living. She shared none of her parents' ambition to get out from underneath it, feeling so effectively mired by the combined totals that what was one more dinner out?

And, indeed, if one dinner out made absolutely zero difference, how bad could a frugal trip to Mexico be, looking at the situation holistically?

"V, no," said Becca, judging over post-yoga smoothies.

Right on, V! said Conrad, via email from an ashram in Bangalore.

"Oh yeah?" said Nick, with one ear fixed on some conservative pundit frothing convincingly about "the other side of the climate debate."

Her parents sighed and moved money out of their savings account in readiness.

Mexico as a tourist destination was a whim on her part, inspired by a beautiful man with long eyelashes she had met at a bar in downtown Vancouver. As she lay tucked into the crook of his arm later that evening, listening to his heartbeat while he regaled her with stories about hiking the smoking volcano that nestled up to his city, she realised she knew nothing about Mexico.

"It has mountains?" she asked. "I think of it as desert and little sand-coloured houses. Ponchos. Tequila."

"You need to get out more," said the man.

With his lips against the soft skin of her shoulder, he made her promise that she would come visit and properly get to know his country. When she received an email from him a few weeks later informing her that he was now seeing someone, she wept self-pityingly for a few hours and then decided that this was all a sign from the universe to be bold. He may have been a casual hook up, but he had been right: she did need to get out more.

Eight hundred additional dollars in debt and two weeks' holiday from work later, she was standing at Benito Juárez International Airport primed for adventure.

As the taxi driver loaded her unnecessarily large suitcase into the back of the vehicle - in the absence of knowing how to pack, she had opted for two of everything – she found herself struggling to breathe from the visceral happiness and anticipation. Or, she wondered, recalling her preparatory research, was that perhaps because of the city's famous air pollution?

Right out of the airport, Mexico City was everything Vanessa had hoped it would be: noisy and colourful and chaotic and absolutely nothing like Vancouver. Vanessa spent the entire drive to the hostel flattened against her window like a dog on a road trip, taking in every billboard, every shopfront, every truck painted rainbow colours in religious veneration. The city was a strange and enthralling combination of historic decadence and mass urban decay, of poverty and thriving life, with the thumb prints of Spanish colonialism slowly being subsumed by graffiti and crumbling concrete. It was so *real*.

Whenever they stopped at a red light and people flooded the intersection juggling or selling refreshments, Vanessa was in wondrous awe. She was delighted by a family of acrobats entertaining the waiting cars but when the family came wandering past her driver told her to keep the windows shut and not make eye contact. Vanessa thrilled with fear and curiosity, wondering wildly what could possibly happen if she were to tip them a few pesos for their talents. Would they demand more or get aggressive? Were they armed? Was there more behind the face paint than poverty and determination? She shivered from the exotic danger of it all.

"Where are you from?" the driver asked her as they pulled away from the intersection.

"Canada. Vancouver."

"Ah, beautiful! I would like to visit Canada sometime. Very cold!"

"In the winter," laughed Vanessa.

"What brings you to México?" he asked, peering at her through the rear-view mirror. From the stem swung a sizable crucifix with Jesus in writhing agony and a single infant's shoe. His eyes in the reflection were warm.

Vanessa blushed. "A guy, sort of. He has a girlfriend now."

"This is not true! Que tonto. Okay, we have a deal, I am now your boyfriend."

Vanessa tugged on her hair and tittered. "I was supposed to be visiting him, but I decided to be brave and come anyway."

"Good for you," said the driver. "And you are very welcome."

As the driver began a passionate and practiced monologue of places to do and things to see, Vanessa watched the city slide by and slipped into thought. What an adventure she was on, coming here all alone. She needed this. She *was* brave.

"Do you like Frida Kahlo?" asked the driver, his eyes fixed so enthusiastically on her through the mirror that it seemed impossible he was maintaining control of the vehicle.

"Oh! Sure?" said Vanessa, having heard of Frida from that Salma Hayek movie that she had meant to see.

"Visit her house, the Casa Azul. Take a boat ride in Xochimilco. And food, you must try all the food. Mexican food is the best food in the entire world. There is a restaurant in the Centro that serves pozole that…" and he was off again, like a child listing off the Christmas presents he had received.

As they reached the hostel, however, he grew grave. "Güera," he said while hefting out her suitcase and placing it on the sidewalk. "Cuidaté, okay? Just be careful."

"I know," said Vanessa absent-mindedly, appreciatively scanning the outside of the hostel. It seemed clean and welcoming.

"This is not Canada…"

"Mmmhmmm."

She was glad she had stumped up for the private room, as she was exhausted and really looking forward to a good night's sleep.

"Bienvenida a México, güera," said the already-forgotten driver. "I hope that you enjoy your holiday."

And he was gone. She realised too late that she had forgotten to tip him, and then had to look up in her Lonely Planet book whether tipping was even expected in Mexico.

Over the next few days, Vanessa touristed hard. She joined a small group of hostellers – three Australians, two Brits, a South African and another Canadian – and the eight of them wandered the city and saw all the sites recommended by TripAdvisor. She was enthralled by the pulse of the city – fast, vibrant, a bit hungry – and by the urgent prioritisation of religion and community, which she contrasted haughtily to the lazy and entitled consumerism of home. She lingered in markets savouring the calls and the smells, failing to resist the temptation of colourful trinkets and souvenirs. She particularly enjoyed the temples, and the descriptions of beating hearts pulled from chest cavities and heads bouncing down staircases running thick with blood.

"And all while Henry the Eighth was on the throne," commented Geoffrey, one of the Brits.

"Wow," said Vanessa, "so uncivilised for being so recent!"

Vanessa was particularly affected by the hustle of the locals: she loved how every street corner had a food stand and a busker and someone selling flags, though the sight of a man without legs dragging himself by his fingertips on the filthy floor of the subway car in order to polish people's shoes for a few coins did make her feel somewhat uncomfortable.

"You don't see many people begging here," she mused to Randolph, the South African. "Not like at home. There you see all these young, healthy people sitting around asking for money, but here everyone works. They might only get a few pesos, but they will work for those pesos rather than go on welfare. I respect that. It's really very noble of them."

Randolph ordered everyone another round of Don Julio and they toasted the city while their bellies burned warm from the drinks.

What Vanessa liked most of all about being in Mexico City was the attention she received. On the tall side even in Canada, she was a blonde Amazonian towering at least a head above the average dark-haired man on the subway in Mexico. Heads turned as she walked by. Men would whistle and shout unintelligible things at her in rapid Spanish. Sometimes she was followed, which she liked less but secretly still found exhilarating. She had been relatively invisible in Canada; here she felt like a supermodel.

"No graçias," she would say with a shy, coquettish smile as men – usually older – would approach her with jewellery dangling from their arms. "No más pesos."

"Please, please," they would chorus.

"Welcome," a teenager with patchy facial hair said to her while she was perusing fruit in a market, and then, when she smiled back, asked "Do you like porn?"

"I'm sorry?" she replied, shocked, as one of the Australians grabbed her arm and pulled her back to the group.

"Pinche gringa!" a young man yelled as he passed on his bike. Vanessa waved thanks.

The day of her departure loomed with palpable and rising grief under her sternum. On her last night, she and her hostel group – now down two Kiwis and a South African but up an American – decided to join the crowds in the big central square to celebrate the Mexican Day of Independence, few of them knowing anything whatsoever about the day or the event. The square was a throbbing, swaying mass of compressed humanity and tactile experience. Vanessa and her friends were jostled, bumped, and fondled as they pushed their way through the crowd towards the National Palace, aiming to get the best view of the President's speech. The smell of roast corn and sweat hung low in the warm city air.

At 11pm, or shortly thereafter – the group had had a few warm beers laced with lime and chilli by then – the President of Mexico appeared on the balcony of the National Palace. The people in the square below simultaneously inhaled.

"¡Mexicanos!" yelled the president, "¡Vivan los héroes que nos dieron patria!"

Vanessa understood nothing past "Mexicanos" but was dancing happily to the pulsation of the crowd when everyone around her rose up to reply in one bellowing, primal, visceral bellow: "¡Viva!"

The power of it made her freeze on the spot, her arms still held in the air.

"¡Viva Hidalgo!" shouted the president.

"¡Viva!" shouted the crowd.

Oh, thought Vanessa. OH. She brought her arms down to shoulder height, fingers resting lightly on her shoulders.

"¡Viva Morelos!" he howled.

"¡Viva!" the crowd howled back.

Oh my god, thought Vanessa, now hugging herself, once again unable to breathe. She was quite certain this time at least it was not the pollution either.

"¡Viva Josefa Ortiz de Domínguez!"

"¡Viva!"

"¡Viva Allende!"

"¡Viva!"

"¡Viva Aldama y Matamoros!"

"¡Viva!"

"¡Viva la Independencia Nacional!"

"¡Viva!"

The all-encompassing roars of life, the vendors bellowing for sales, an endless ocean of faces, and suddenly Vanessa felt a shot of clarity strike her like a punch to the sternum. She had never been one to believe in destiny, but she had never felt this strongly about anything before in her life. She didn't entirely dare to believe it would be possible but how could it not be given how strongly she was being called to it?

"¡Viva México!" bellowed the president.

"¡Viva!" whispered Vanessa.

"¡Viva México!" he shouted again.

"¡Viva!" said Vanessa conspicuously.

"¡Viva México!" he cried a final time.

"¡Viva!" cried Vanessa rapturously, accompanied by half a million of her new compatriots, starting to cry from the sheer personal profundity of the moment.

Within an hour of arriving home the next day, she had called each of her friends in turn to announce that her destiny was clear at last and she was going to pursue a graduate degree in Latin American Studies come September. She had found her path. She had never been more certain about anything in her life.

Good for you!, wrote Conrad.

"Sounds interesting," said Becca and Nick.

Wow, wrote her Gastown lover, in what would be his very last email to her.

"Okay," said her parents, brainstorming who they might know in that field to whom to introduce their daughter.

2022

Conrad met Becca for lunch on the afternoon of the dinner party, after leaving a vague and alarming message on her phone saying that he needed to talk. Becca, slammed with work but wanting to be there for her friend, managed to carve out 20 minutes for a takeaway sandwich (breadless for her please) in Sunset Beach Park and the two sat cross-legged on a bench overlooking the water in the summer sunshine.

"Thanks for meeting me for lunch," said Conrad. "And for buying lunch."

"My pleasure. You sounded stressed on the phone," she said, attempting and failing to spear a lettuce leaf with a dull wooden fork.

Conrad picked a sundried tomato out of his sandwich with his fingers and tossed it into his mouth. "Yeah," he said, "I guess I have something on my mind."

Becca stirred her sandwich-salad with her fork and wished she had given into the garlic mayonnaise at the shop. Her and Max's healthy eating initiative was going well and had reduced their carbon footprint by an estimated 6% according to a website Max had found, but she was bored of colourful, bland, and fibrous. Some nights she would sneak downstairs and eat butter with a spoon, just to put something in her mouth with empty calories in it.

"What has Vanessa told you?" Conrad asked, squinting off into the horizon and sucking tomato oil from his index finger and thumb.

Becca decided to play dumb: "About what?"

"I know you've spoken," he said balefully. "I talked to Nick."

"About your new business you mean."

"Yeah."

"Not a lot. She said it's mostly about taking classes, and, um, crystals or something like that?"

Conrad nodded slowly. "Something like that," he said, before falling ominously silent.

Becca covertly checked her watch, torn between wanting to help and needing to work. Just as she was about to nudge him, his phone chirped. He didn't move.

"Are you going to check that?" she asked lightly.

"I know who it is," he replied. He fished out the phone and showed it to her. *You can do this, buddy!* said the text. *I believe in you!*

"That's Andrew," said Conrad mournfully, picking at his sandwich without eating anything. "It's always Andrew."

"Who's Andrew?"

"My Student-Teacher-Leader."

Becca raised a quizzical eyebrow.

"My mentor at ReYOUvenate. He believes in me."

Becca bit her tongue so hard she could faintly taste blood. "We all do," she said.

"Not Vanessa," whispered Conrad. "She thinks I'm an idiot."

"Oh no. No no, she's not said anything like that. Not to me at least and you know Vanessa: she would have said something."

Conrad picked a curl of dry skin off the side of his thumb with his teeth. "Do you think I'm an idiot?" he asked.

Becca shook her head vigorously. "Not at all, no! You're just..." and she trailed off noncommittally, landing on, "Are you okay?"

"I don't know... Some days, yes, better than I've ever been, and others... Running your own business is hard, Becs."

"Oh, absolutely it is, yes."

A grey and white speckled pigeon came bobbling over in the hope of lunch, which Conrad dutifully obliged with a chunk of crust torn from his sandwich. Within seconds there were three pigeons, two seagulls, and a squirrel all circling hopefully. Becca tried unsuccessfully to shoo them away with her foot.

"Can I make a confession?" asked Conrad, staring in the opposite direction.

Becca felt a surge of what felt like happiness but which lay considerably closer to ego. The intimacy shared between Vanessa and Conrad had always perplexed her: Conrad was too flaky and Vanessa spent far too much time sulking for their connection to be anything but the echoes of their previous romantic explorations, and yet theirs was the tightest connection. Surely she, Becca, with her stable career and relationship, was the more logical cornerstone of the group.

"Of course, Conrad," she replied with flawless grace and empathy.

Conrad stared blankly out at the water. "I feel like shit, Becs," he whispered, as his body folded in on itself and became half its size.

"Oh Conrad," she murmured for lack of knowing what to say, putting down her salad and awkwardly rubbing his back. She was startled when he slid sideways and into her lap like a small child. When she spied a couple staring and whispering, she shot them her most withering, condescending look. 'What?' she challenged them with her eyes, 'haven't you ever lost your shit in a park in the middle of the day before?'

"I'm scared, Becs," he said wetly to her pant leg.

"Of what, honey?"

"That it's all a lie," he whispered. "That it's never going to be enough. That I'm never going to be enough."

Becca, feeling his pain in her sternum, attempted to lean forward and wrap herself around him like a protective burrito but found the position far too uncomfortable and resumed her perfect posture. "Oh honey, shh, shh, that's not true, you are enough," she soothed, slowly rocking him while he hiccoughed and choked in her arms like a colicky baby.

"This world is sick, Becs."

"It sure is," she hushed.

"I don't know if I have it in me."

"Shh shh, of course you do."

I am killing this, she thought to herself.

"How did you do it?"

"Do what?"

Conrad sat up and blew his nose spectacularly into one of his napkins, which he then placed with care on the bench between them. Becca did her best to pretend she wasn't fixated on it.

"You know," he said, "believe in yourself when no one else did?"

Conrad didn't notice her grimace.

"Sometimes I worry that I'm not going to be good enough at this."

"I'm sure you're great at it."

Conrad started to flicker with life, his eyes wet but bright. Becca was enjoying the flush of relief of having clearly said the right thing.

"No one is great at things when they're starting out. You just need some more practice, that's all. Some practice and some learning and a positive mental attitude, and then you'll be flying."

"That's what Andrew says," sniffed Conrad. "Success mindset."

"Sounds like Andrew knows what he's talking about."

I'm amazing at this, Becca thought to herself.

"Andrew says you make your own luck by working hard," said Conrad. He was watching her intently with the expression of a golden retriever seeking praise or treats.

"Exactly." She attempted strong eye contact but found the intensity of his gaze uncomfortable and only managed flickering and brief. "And you are nothing if not tenacious," she said to the beach.

"Andrew says that too. He says I have an impressive work ethic."

Becca watched a toddler stomp down a sandcastle like a tiny Japanese monster. She imagined the feel of the cool, damp sand between her bare toes and wiggled her feet in her pinching suede calf Louboutin pumps. This had been a good, productive lunch break.

"He says that if I keep trying, keep working at it, success will come to me. He says this is my calling, that we are part of a bigger plan." He patted his cell phone in his pocket. "He believes in me."

"That's good," said Becca, her mind starting to travel back to the work waiting for her back at the office.

Unconsciously detecting her drift, Conrad took her hand and pulled her back to his conversation. He looked her right in the eye. "Andrew says I am gifted," he said. "Am I gifted? Do you think I'm gifted, Becca?"

Becca bobbled her head briskly and unconvincingly. Being an agony aunt had never been her speciality and she was reaching her limit. "Oh yes, yes, I've always thought that about you Conrad. Very... gifted. Very... bold. Very bold."

Conrad peered at the sky and blinked hard a few times. "You're right. I am gifted. They don't know what they're talking about. I'm an amazing person. "

Just then a seagull lunged for her salad and soared off with the entire box. "Damn it," she exclaimed, jumping to her feet and half-heartedly chasing a few steps after it.

Conrad, who was brightening by the second like a dawning sun, benevolently held the scattered remains of his sandwich out to Becca like an offering. She put one hand up: "No, thank you, I'm fine. I was mostly done anyway."

Besides, she thought, there were cookies in the kitchen.

"Thanks for this, Becs," said Conrad. "I really needed to talk."

The curiosity got to Becca. "Have you talked to Vanessa about how you're feeling?" she fished, feigning nonchalance.

"No," said Conrad sullenly, "I can't. She doesn't understand."

"And I... can?"

"Well, yeah," said Conrad. "You know what it is to forge your own path."

Yes, thought Becca, I definitely do know that. She had worked hard for everything she had.

"I've realised recently," said Conrad, his entire body tense with emotion, "that I've been running all my life. From something, to something, it's never been entirely clear: I've just been running. And it's been great, don't get me wrong, it's been so great a lot of the time, but it never actually did anything to quell the agitation, the sense that this" – here he waved his hands, at the skyscrapers and the joggers bouncing past and at Becca's smart Holt Renfrew suit – "can't be what life is about."

Becca patted the front of her jacket defensively. She really liked what she was wearing, and she had bought it on sale.

Over on the other bench the couple were watching again, far less shyly this time, but Becca let them have this one. She would be ogling too if she were them.

Just then her work phone buzzed in her pocket. She wrapped her fingers around it.

"What I've learned, Becs," said Conrad, "is that satisfaction will always elude us if we go looking for it."

"Absolutely," she said, distracted by who could be calling her during lunch. The deadline wasn't until 4, wasn't it?

"And do you know why? Because contentment can't be found in external things, that's why. Contentment is a product of the *soul*. Of our interconnectedness. Of our shared humanity and identity. We don't need *things* to be unapologetically ourselves."

"Sure," she said, now both curious and distraught that her phone had stopped ringing.

"You get it, don't you, Becs!" he said, sliding uncomfortably close to her. "I knew you would."

After a momentary pause, his hand hovering with his fingers inside his jacket, he brandished a ReYOUvenate brochure from his inside pocket. "Have a read when you have a spare minute. It might be the most important change you make in your entire life."

Becca unconsciously took the brochure, pasting on the same gracious expression she gave *Our Voice* sellers when walking past without buying a magazine. "Rejuvenate YOU!" blared the front cover in jagged blue text, partially obscuring an image of a taut and serene older white woman in lotus position holding a badly-photoshopped orb containing what appeared to be the entire universe. Examining more closely, Becca thought she could detect a faint glow emanating from the woman's sacral chakra.

"Did you know you can make money without playing the capitalist game?" said Conrad excitedly, mistaking her silence for interest. "Like, *lots* of money, plus you'd be making a real difference in the world, really making the world better."

Becca realised with horror that she had allowed the entire conversation to go on too long and was now in swampy territory.

"This is great, Conrad, thanks. I will definitely have a look at this." She fumbled to her feet and brushed invisible crumbs off her suit to make it clear to Conrad that his time with her was now over.

"Yeah?" asked Conrad, eyes bright and smile huge. "If you have any questions…"

"Definitely," said Becca through her teeth, checking the missed call notification on her phone. It was one of the recruiters that regularly called her to see if she needed any hiring support services.

"I'm sorry, Conrad," she said, waving her phone, "someone's trying to call from the office and I think it's important. Can we talk more some other time."

"Tonight maybe?" he offered. "At dinner?"

Oh no, she thought.

"Yes, maybe," she allowed in her desperation to escape. "So nice to see you today. The seagull and I thank you for lunch." And with a peck on his cheek she was off, as fast as she could walk in her teetering heels.

"Becca!" he called after her at her retreating form, "I knew you'd get it!"

She ducked her head, waved one hand back over her shoulder, and disappeared around a corner.

Conrad shimmied with satisfaction. He had only set out to get basic reassurance from someone he respected, but instead may have signed up his second recruit in the space of days. He pulled out his phone to text Andrew the news.

2010

When Nick was about to turn 38, his father died.

It was not altogether unexpected: Bruce was well into his 70s and profoundly unhealthy. Like many of his generation, he smoked, drank, never took any exercise, and bragged excessively about all three habits. He spent his retirement tinkering on automotive restoration projects that rarely progressed to completion and muttering about the failed experiment of multiculturalism in Canada. Despite their many similarities, he and Nick were not close.

Nick's mom, Helen, had died many years earlier when Nick was in his first year of high school. That had been even less of a shock – four years prior she had found a lump in her armpit and the entire family had huddled together to witness the slow but steady decline – but her death nonetheless shifted the dynamic of the family immediately. Bruce retreated to his garage; Nick and his older brother Matthew were left pretty much to their own devices. By the time Matthew had finished school and packed off for a distant life in Toronto, the family had deteriorated to the point of awkward ten-minute phone calls on Father's Day, Christmas, and birthdays.

News of Bruce's death came via a call from Matthew on a Wednesday evening, as Nick and Nancy were washing up after dinner. Nancy saw the notification on Nick's phone and by its unscheduled rarity knew instantly that something was wrong. She listened from the kitchen table, cupping her tea with both hands.

"Matthew?" said Nick with mild concern, answering the phone.

"Nick," clipped Matthew efficiently.

"How are things?"

"Good, you?"

"Good."

"Sorry to call you out of the blue but, ah, dad's dead."

Nick felt as though a hole had been punched through his chest and yet there was no pain, no emotion. He rested his weight against the edge of the counter, the fingertips on his left hand finding and worrying a piece of food that had dripped over onto the underside.

"When?" asked Nick.

"This morning. Heart attack by the looks of it, out in his garage beside the car he was working on."

Nick shook his head fiercely to clear the conjured image, like a human Etch-a-Sketch.

"What's going on?" mouthed Nancy from her chair.

"Dad's dead," mouthed Nick.

Nancy covered her mouth with her hand.

"How do you know?" Nick asked his brother.

"The neighbour called me."

"Which neighbour?"

"The one across the street."

"Alice?"

"Alice, yeah. The garage door was open and she saw him go down. He was gone by the time the ambulance got there."

Nick closed his eyes, lacking the energy to deal with the news. Upstairs Nick heard five-year-old Anna shriek in distress over something her older sister was doing to her. That they were even in the same room was an issue: they were both supposed to be doing their homework in their bedrooms. He should probably get up there and sort it out.

"Dad must have given her my number at some point, for next of kin purposes."

It was a slap in the face. "She didn't call me."

There were several seconds of suspended silence on the line, broken when Matthew audibly signalled to someone else in the room that he was nearly done with the call. "No idea, bro," he said. "Anyway, the funeral's a week Friday, at Bradford & Sons on Royal Oak."

Nick grappled about for pen until Nancy tossed him one from the drawer beside the fridge.

"Time?"

"2pm."

"Do we need to do anything?" Nancy whispered to Nick.

"Do I need to do anything?" asked Nick to Matthew.

"No," replied Matthew, sounding distracted. "Dad had it all sorted out and paid for and the neighbour knew where to find the paperwork for the funeral home."

"Okay," said Nick.

Upstairs Hayley shouted, "Oh you are *so* going to get grounded!" and Anna started to cry loudly. Nick wondered if he could hang up, but he could feel Nancy's eyes on him.

"Are you going?" Nick asked, partially turning his back on Nancy to protect himself from her penetrating gaze.

"Yeah, we'll be there. We're looking at flights for Thursday."

Nick pursed his lips. "We have a guest room," he offered, feeling it the right thing to say but unsure whether he hoped his brother would accept or decline.

"Thanks, but I'm fine at the Travelodge," replied his brother. There was a pang in Nick's gut which he swiftly buried. "Anyway, gotta' run."

"Yep," said Nick, and the phone went dead.

Nancy stood up to give him a hug, but Nick unconsciously took a step away. She took his phone from him instead, setting it gently on the counter.

"Are you okay?" she asked, caressing the back of his hand with her thumb.

"Yeah. It was bound to happen sooner or later."

"It's okay not to be okay, Nick."

Nick patted her hand affectionately before withdrawing from her touch. "I need some space to process I think."

"Okay. I'm here if you need to talk."

"Thanks," he said, turning away, but as he reached the door to the kitchen, he put one hand on the doorframe and paused. "Nance?" he said to the hallway.

"Yeah?" replied Nancy, poised at the counter on high alert like a hunting dog.

Why was I not his next of kin?, he wanted to ask her. Why does Matthew not want to stay here? Why did he get no part in the funeral planning? Why is it so hard to talk to Matthew when he really needs his brother right now? Why does he feel simultaneously sick and sad and angry and nothing?

"Lasagne and garlic bread for dinner?"

"I'll make a green salad," she said, proud of him for trying.

The next week passed in an emotionless blur, though with no discernible changes other than Nick spontaneously leasing a brand-new black Land Rover with tinted windows after spotting it on the lot and deciding to take it for a test drive. Nancy said nothing when it appeared on the driveway; the girls on the other hand were highly approving, with Hayley declaring it "extra."

On Friday, dressed in sombre black, the family piled into the monstrous vehicle and drove in silence to the funeral home. Quite a few people were there already when they pulled up, and a single bagpiper throttled out something familiar as they entered. Matthew was standing by the door with his partner, Allen, a bubbly Nigerian-Canadian social worker with a face like a lighthouse in a storm.

Allen spoke first, capturing Nick in a tight hug. "I am so sorry for your loss, Nick," he said sympathetically, his hand on the back of Nick's head. "Your dad was a special man."

"Thanks Allen," said Nick, sinking briefly into the sensation of feeling enclosed and safe but swiftly pulling away as soon as Allen relaxed his grip.

"Matthew," he said as his brother took a half step forward and extended his hand.

"Nick, good to see you," replied Matthew, shaking hands a little brusquely under the circumstances.

Anna, watching shyly from behind her mother, said rather loudly, "Who's THAT?"

The brothers unconsciously mirrored each other: hands in pockets, feet askew, chins dropped. When they made eye contact, words unspoken clamoured for release but remained trapped by 35 years of scar tissue.

"That's your Uncle Matthew, Anna," said Nancy to her youngest, "and this is your Uncle Allen."

"Hello Anna!" said Allen, dropping to his knees to shake her hand from her level. "So nice to meet you!"

Anna giggled flirtatiously.

As people started to file in, the brothers formed an unenthusiastic receiving line. A stream of well-intentioned friends and strangers clutched their hands and made genial, generic statements of condolence and support, and the brothers would nod and politely and repetitively say thank you, thank you, yes he was special, yes it is very sad. Occasionally someone would ask for a photo with them, as though as the descendants of the deceased they had become safari trophies for a vacation album. Nancy hovered nearby, wrangling the bored girls and monitoring Nick's emotional state; Allen whipped about ensuring people were seated safely and had everything they needed.

Nick found all of it borderline unendurable and was relieved when the officiant signalled that everyone should please take their seats. Ushered unwillingly to the first row by Allen and Nancy, Nick pinched himself into the corner furthest away from the polished pine coffin at the front of the room and made himself as small as possible.

"Welcome friends and family," said the officiant beneficently, placing placed a discrete, black-bound book on the podium. "What a great honour and privilege it is to be here with you all today to say farewell to an extraordinary man. I know Bruce would be truly proud to see his loved ones gathered together and supporting each other at this difficult time."

Nick made a noise, disguising it as a throat clearing. Nancy rubbed his back reassuringly.

"Bruce left very specific instructions regarding the proceedings, right from the bagpiper who greeted you on your arrival all the way to" – checking her notes – "the poem that Charlotte is going to read for us shortly. I hope his family will gain some comfort knowing that he leaves us in the style he desired."

Who's Charlotte?, thought Nick, looking around but unable to name more than a handful of people dotted around the room. He spotted his brother standing at the wall on the opposite side of the room, arms crossed rigidly across his stomach. Was there any sign of emotion in his brother's expression? Was he sad? No, Nick couldn't see any trace of sadness. Matthew's face was entirely blank, devoid of expression like a store mannequin.

"I didn't have the privilege of knowing Bruce," continued the officiant benevolently, "but speaking with the people who loved him best over the past week has left me with a very clear impression of the person he was."

Nick wondered who she had spoken to. He glanced at Nancy but her face was open and smooth.

"He was a proud and quiet man, with a deep passion for vintage car restoration and…" – checking her notes – "hockey."

The crowd murmured softly.

"Bruce was a lifelong fan of the Vancouver Canucks – ah, excellent choice! – and said once that his greatest achievement was being in the stands when Pavel Bure scored his double overtime goal in Game 7 against the Flames."

Somebody said, "Boo Flames!" with a choking noise at the end. A soft titter undulated through the gathered crowd.

"Bruce may have been quiet, but like a river he ran strong and deep," the officiant said sombrely. "He found true love in his wife, Helen, who left us too early but will be waiting on the other side to welcome him, and he was so proud of his two boys, Nick and Matthew" – here she gave a pause and a nod, first with Nick, who immediately looked away, and then over to Matthew, who dropped his head – "and the life partners they have chosen." Nancy and Allen smiled sadly. The crowd bobbed and nodded their heads in sympathy.

Nick suddenly felt a strong and illogical need to laugh. He lifted his right hand to cover his mouth and appear mournful, but he could feel his lips curling.

"At this time," said the officiant, "I would like to invite anyone who would like to say something to come up."

127

A petite man with unkempt tufts of white hair held up his hand. "Please," said the officiant, stepping back from the podium.

The man held onto the back of a chair to pull himself to standing and limped painfully to the front. His eyes were red rimmed beneath thick glasses that made him look like a startled owl.

"Well Bruce," wheezed the man towards the coffin, "I always figured it would be me first, what with my health and everything, but here we are. If I'd'a known, I woulda' asked you to put that '66 Pontiac Beaumont in your will for me!"

The crowd tittered.

"Who's that?" whispered Nancy. Nick had no idea.

"But I mostly wanted to come up here and say thanks for being a good friend all these years when my Laura died and Cooper left for Montreal and moving into the home and all. You didn't talk much, Bruce, but you always understood me. I'm sure gonna' miss you."

Someone blew their nose loudly.

"And that's all," said the man matter-of-factly.

"Thanks Jonno," said the officiant. Nancy glanced at Nick but he shook his head again: no idea. "Anyone else?"

What followed was a parade of ten, maybe twelve, sniffling loved ones, all clutching the podium with both hands to steady themselves and waving handkerchiefs, and utterly and entirely anonymous for Nick. None of their stories resonated, none of their descriptions fit the man Nick knew – he wondered briefly if he had ended up at the wrong funeral. Only when a well-preserved woman in her 60s, with her hair styled like an old Hollywood siren, stood beside the casket did Nick feel a flutter of recognition.

"I think that's Alice," he whispered to Nancy.

"The neighbour?" she whispered back, looking the woman up and down approvingly.

Alice shuddered. "Bruce," she said softly, placing a gloved hand on the top of the casket. "My Brucie."

Nick and Nancy audibly gasped. Nick tried to make contact with his brother but, based on the pure shock smeared across his and Allen's faces, they hadn't known either. Anna peered back and forth between her parents trying and failing to understand what had just happened.

"My Brucie, my Brucie," moaned Alice, "remember the time you said to me, 'Alice, it's all downhill from here'? You were wrong, Bruce. It kept getting better with you." She gazed at the crowd and dabbed at her eyes delicately with a vermillion kerchief that perfectly matched her lipstick. "As I'm sure you all know, I met Bruce during a house viewing. I used to joke that he was the reason I bought the house. There he was tinkering away at one his little car projects in his driveway, wearing this white tank top that showed off his muscly arms –"

She gave a playful shimmy and the crowd chuckled and shifted in their seats.

"– and I thought, that's the love of my life right there. I don't know how I knew, but I did, I knew. Took him weeks to say more than 'Good morning' to me, until one his lawn mower wouldn't start and he had to come over to borrow mine. April 12th, 2002. And that was it, we didn't miss a day together after that. Not a day, imagine that. Bruce taught me more about love and living in six years of marriage than in my previous 60 combined."

"Six years!" whispered Nancy in shocked delight. "Marriage!"

Allen whispered something into Matthew's ear.

"Bruce," finished Alice with a sob, "I waited my entire life for you and I will wait the rest of my life to be with you again if that's what it takes. I am my beloved and my beloved is mine, forever." As her knees began to buckle, two younger women rushed to the front to help her back to her chair and cocooned her protectively with their arms.

Once again Nick felt that bubbly pressure beneath his sternum, felt his cheeks lifting, his lips curling.

The officiant stepped into the space with her hands primly folded. "It is clear that Bruce lived for his family, and so, in honour of that love Charlotte here would like to read a poem she has written."

A girl of about ten years stepped up, with not a hint of insecurity or shyness.

"Who's that?" asked Anna loudly. Nancy hushed her and apologised to the people sat around them.

The girl flicked her long brown braids behind her back and began to read:

Majestic and strong, like the ocean
Quiet and still, like a tree
Hands in constant motion
Heart as deep as the sea

How do you say bye to an ocean?
How do you say bye to a tree?
When those hands have ceased their motion
And that soul has been set free

Grandfathers should be immortal
To never be far from our side
For today when you walk through that portal

I am losing my best friend and guide

But though right now we're saying goodbye
It's true you'll never be far
For although today we'll cry
You'll always be in our hearts

And then she stepped back into the crowd and curled up into Alice's lap. Nick could feel Hayley grow hostile beside him. "Why didn't I get asked to read a poem about grandpa?" she sulked to nobody in particular.

Nick's pulse was racing, and he began to giggle.

"Thank you, Charlotte, for sharing your beautiful poem," said the officiant. "I think it perfectly captures how much Bruce meant to everyone who knew him and why he will be deeply missed."

"Excuse me," said Nick to the crowd, stepping away and walking quickly towards the front door. He could feel eyes watching him, curious and empathetic, until he broke out until a flat out run. They would just think he was overcome.

On reaching his Land Rover, Nick put one hand on the sun-heated hood to balance himself and completely lost control. He laughed so hard he barely had time to draw in oxygen between extended howls. He convulsed until he was bent in two and the tears streamed from his eyes. He howled with laughter until his throat and his sides ached from the pressure. He laughed about oceans and trees and greatest achievements, he laughed for being proud of his sons, he laughed for the final days in the hospice watching his mother's body start its final failure and his father's helplessness. He laughed about a bagpiper – a bagpiper, when they weren't even Scottish! – and Alice the neighbour being there when he went down and being his stepmother and knowing Matthew's phone number but not Nick's. He laughed about poor Charlotte and her poem, and jealous Hayley seething beside him.

He laughed until he suddenly stopped and he was calm again, like someone had switched off a faucet.

There it is then, he thought to himself.

"Nick?" It was Nancy, coming up behind him softly.

"All good, Nancy," he said. "Where are the girls?"

"Still inside. The service is still going."

"Hayley's very jealous," he said.

"Yeah," she replied, "she really is. Do you need a moment?"

"Nah, I'm fine. Let's go back before people start wondering about us."

He squeezed her hand a few times on the walk back and managed to maintain his composure for the remainder of the service and the interment.

2022

At almost exactly 6pm, Vanessa's phone rang. Knowing Nick's tendency to cancel on large social events at the last minute, she let it go to voicemail three times before picking up.

"No," she answered.

"Vanessa, it's Nick. I'm so sorry, but…"

"You are not cancelling on dinner, Nick. It is 6pm. I will see you in one hour."

"It's just –"

"No."

Nick made an aggrieved noise and then everything went curiously silent: Vanessa had been put on mute. She gave Robert the signal to pour the Pinot Noir into a carafe to let it breathe and waited calmly for the line to click live again.

"Vanessa –"

"Not tonight, Nick. I don't care what's up, you're coming."

The line went that curious silent again. She tapped her fingers against the countertop and began drafting her line of verbal attack. She would die on this hill if it came to it.

The line clicked back. "Can I speak to Conrad, please?" asked Nick quietly. "His cell phone is off."

Vanessa felt the impatience bubble in her chest like a grade school science fair volcano. Robert, stood in the doorway to the patio, gave two questioning thumbs up. "I hate them all," she mouthed. He shook his thumbs up at her in enthusiastic optimism.

"I'll go check," Vanessa said to Nick. "I'm busy and I'm hanging up. If he's there, he'll call you back. Regardless, I will see you in an hour."

She could hear the music blaring from her upstairs guest room from the downstairs hallway, and had to knock three times, hard, before Conrad appeared at the door.

Vanessa caught her breath. The man in front of her had clearly come home via a salon and spa: his hair was styled to perfection in that perfect space between casual and debonair, and his skin glowed from a close shave and exfoliating facial. Streaks of grey at his temples and dark-framed glasses she hadn't known he wore inferred scandalous things of university professors and scholars she had loved before. The scent of his cologne was wafting in from his room and it was heavenly. He could have been mistaken on the street for a Hollywood star.

"Oh," she said, reflexively holding out her own cellphone to him. She tried to remember how many glasses of wine she had had while getting ready: it must have been more than she realised, for her head was spinning.

"Nick needs to talk to you but your phone is, um, off, apparently."

She thought she could feel Robert at the bottom of the stairs.

"Thanks V," replied Conrad, flashing that devastating smile of his. "Yeah, I turned it off so I can focus on tonight and be 100% present in the moment. I'll call him now."

He watched her walk backwards slowly, up to the moment in which she misjudged distance and stumbled into the banister railing, half-toppling sideways and tripping down the first few steps. "Can't wait for dinner!" he called to her disappearing form.

Conrad could hear the distress in Nick's voice from the second he answered. "Conrad, I'm in trouble, man," said Nick. "I need the money I gave you."

"You okay, buddy?" Conrad asked with genuine concern, perching on the arm edge of Vanessa's velvet wing chair.

"I just need it, okay?"

Conrad, who had received detailed training for this exact and expected scenario, considered his options and potential responses. "That's not really possible," he started with, "but whatever the issue is, we can work through it together."

He could hear scuffling on the other end of the line, as though Nick were moving the handset from side to side.

"Are you in trouble? Because I can help you if you're in trouble."

"I'm fine," replied Nick quickly. "Can I get any of the money back?"

"If you need money, I can loan you some, no problem. No interest, pay me back whenever."

"I gave you five thousand dollars yesterday."

"You did," agreed Conrad, "to start your business. And it's been invested, just as we discussed."

"Already?"

"Yes," replied Conrad evenly, "I signed you up for those courses and that conference you said you were interested in. The series about manifesting, remember? Your welcome pack and catalogues will arrive early next week, like I told you, and then you can start recruiting and start making money. I heard they're even going to throw in a bathrobe."

Nick made a strangled sound.

"That's a really big deal, Nick. They only usually give those to their top sellers."

This was true: Conrad was himself still working towards the much-coveted ReYOUvenate bathrobe, though Andrew had given his special dispensation for Conrad to offer it to his recruits in exceptional circumstances.

"They clearly see something in you too, like I do, and they want to encourage you."

"I want my money back, Conrad."

"It's not possible, Nick, I'm sorry." Line now clearly drawn, Conrad shifted tactics to restore confidence: "But you won't regret this, I promise. The universe has a plan for both of us, Nick. Trust it and give it time. I know it's scary but you and the universe are co-creating something really special right now and it's going to reward you beyond your wildest dreams when it all comes to fruition."

Conrad could hear Nick breathing heavily on the other end of the phone. "How long was it before you started making money?" he asked dully.

"Not long, not long at all. Right away, really. Not, like, thousands of dollars right away of course but you'll get more out the more you put in. You should have your original outlay earned back in maybe a month or two. Three months, tops, I promise, if you're willing to put in the work. Do you want me to set up a one-to-one coaching call with Andrew?"

Nick did not reply.

"I know how you're feeling – I was really scared when I started out too – but he's been doing this for a while now and can explain better than me what an opportunity it is."

Conrad watched Vanessa's neighbour across the street leave the house to walk a small, bouncing brown and white spaniel.

"You're going to be an amazing leader and really help people," said Conrad to the heavy silence on the other end of the phone. "I can't wait to tell everyone that I somehow managed to snag *you* for my team. This is huge for me. We are going to have so much fun together!"

"Can I sell back any of the product?" asked Nick. "Maybe I don't need to start with any of the supplements. Maybe that crystal wand thing? I don't even remember what it's supposed to do."

"Oh sure, sure," said Conrad, remembering his training, "though I would recommend against it if at all possible. The warehouse will need to charge you a restocking fee – you understand – and it can end up being a pretty big chunk of the total. Much better to really push to start selling as soon as possible, so you don't just not lose money but you actually realise profit as well. I think you pass the wand over pain points, if I remember correctly – I'll read up on it tomorrow and we can do it together. And the supplements, my god Nick, they will change your life, seriously."

Nick felt all the fight drain out of him like a fatal haemorrhage.

"Nick?"

"Yeah?"

"What's caused all this? Are you in trouble?"

That scuffling noise again. "No," said Nick, "No trouble. I've been talking to Hayley about all of it and she has some questions I guess."

"What a clever girl, watching out for her dad," said Conrad.

In the background, Conrad could hear a female voice say something. She sounded exasperated. "I'm just–" said Conrad to the woman before the line was briefly muted.

Conrad waited patiently, chewing on his right thumbnail. I've done the right thing, he said to himself. I owed it to him to share this opportunity with him, and he signed up of his own free will. It will be fine. It will be more than fine: it will be great, for both of us. This is just the beginning.

Hayley took the phone. Conrad felt his heart sink: now 22, Hayley had never warmed to Conrad. In general he tried to avoid her; when their paths crossed, he often felt like he was about to be challenged to a swordfight.

"I'm sorry but I have to ask: are you scamming my dad?" she asked bluntly, not even saying hello.

"Definitely not!" cried Conrad, horrified at the very idea.

"Is my dad going to lose all his money?"

Conrad began to pace. "I mean, anything can happen in network marketing, Hayley, but I'm here to make sure your dad gets the support he needs and doesn't get burned."

Hayley blew the sound of her distrust down the phoneline.

"Hayley, give me the phone back," Nick said in the background.

"How do the commissions work?" asked Hayley. "What would my dad need to do to earn full commission? Is that even possible? How many people does he need to sign up in a month? What happens if he doesn't? And crystals, really?!"

Nick took the phone back. "Hayley, go pack your bag. Your mom will be here any minute." The sounds of her protestations faded into the distance.

"Sorry about that," said Nick quietly.

"If would help, I can talk to her and make sure she understands that this is a legitimate business opportunity?" offered Conrad, relieved to have escaped so quickly.

"It's okay, I can talk to her," said Nick. "I thought she'd be more supportive, if I'm honest. Based on what you were telling me, I thought maybe she might even be interested in it herself."

The pain in Nick's voice cut into Conrad like a razor. I've done the right thing, he repeated to himself. I've done the right thing.

"Right, okay, well, if that's it then that's it I guess," deadpanned Nick in defeat. "See you at dinner."

It will be fine, thought Conrad. They'll all see and they'll understand. It will be great.

Downstairs, Vanessa's phone rang again. This time she didn't make Nick wait.

"What?"

"I'm coming," said Nick.

"Yes, you are," said Vanessa, "but I'm glad to hear you know it too now."

"Can I bring anything?"

Vanessa laughed with relief. "You're asking half an hour before, Nick? A bottle of wine, maybe, or whatever you're drinking."

"Red or white?"

"Either. Can't wait to see you!"

"Yeah, it'll be fun," agreed Nick, distinctly sounding like he expected the complete opposite.

2011

When Becca was 35, she was called to the bar.

It was standard for Becca to slip into melancholy after a show closed, so no one paid any attention when she took to her bed following the end of the *Evita* tour in December 2001. As the days passed and she showed no inclination to rouse herself, both she and her friends wrote it off as logical that an extended tour would merit an extended period of rest. When her agent asked if she should continue sending Becca audition notices, Becca responded brightly that she "was going to take some time to really focus on me" and then began hiding from the woman's calls altogether.

"I'm totally fine, I swear," she would reassure her friends when they called to check in on her. "I'm really enjoying the downtime to do some thinking and make decisions about what I want from life."

This was a complete lie: something was wrong and Becca knew it. Post-show crashes usually meant sleeping and weeping, but this time Becca was struggling against an agitated dissatisfaction and listlessness. She spent her days prowling the limited confines of her apartment like a bored polar bear in a zoo, peering suspiciously at the world going by from the folds of her curtains, rearranging her pantry cupboard such that all the labels faced outwards, by size of object, and then by colour of label. She couldn't put her finger on what exactly was wrong, flagging it only as a general sense of existential ennui: a pervasive but wordless sense that she had taken a wrong turn somewhere and it was too late to correct her trajectory.

"I wonder," she started hesitantly during a phone check in from Vanessa, "I wonder if I made a mistake by not going to university."

Vanessa audibly scoffed. "And what good has it done any of us? Nick studied English and he manages a warehouse. Conrad studied Economics and is folding jeans at the mall. I studied Art History and I have absolutely no clue what to do with my life. Super return on investment, all of us."

"I suppose," sighed Becca, shifting a can of baked beans so that the orange was appropriately positioned before the red soup cans.

"Besides," said Vanessa, "is academia really your thing? I mean, face it, Becs, you got through high school on charisma and extra-curricular credit."

Becca crawled back into bed for another week. The duvet on the couch began to release a sweetly sour smell that both repulsed and comforted her.

Becca observed that Monday to Thursday on her favourite soap opera was a frustratingly repetitive lead up to a surge of actual narrative progress on Fridays, but was at that point sufficiently invested in Zombie Charity's plot to kill the Tabitha's living doll and loyally stayed put.

Do you regret going to university? she messaged Conrad via MSN Messenger.

No? he replied after a few moments of silence. *Not totally?*

Becca (12:13)	*But you do regret it a little?*
Becca (12:14)	*Conrad?*
Becca (12:15)	* You have just sent a Nudge! *
Becca (12:18)	* You have just sent a Nudge! *
Becca (12:21)	* You have just sent a Nudge! *
Conrad (12:26)	*Back. Sorry. Had to go buy more internet time.*
Conrad (12:27)	*Regret.*
Conrad (12:27)	*Maybe a little.*
Conrad (12:27)	*Mostly because I'll be paying off my student loans when I'm dead.*
Becca (12:28)	*Ha*

Becca inspected the fingernails on her right hand. The seam of her acrylics were almost halfway up her nails and were visibly lifting at the sides. Beneath the stubborn remnants of chipped silver polish on her left thumb, Becca could make out small spots of dark – was that staining from the nail polish or was that mould? Becca frowned and put her thumb in her mouth to try to clean it off.

"Are you okay?" her friends kept asking.

"I'm fine," she kept reassuring them.

"Should we come over?"

"Soon," she would promise. "Just working through some things and need to concentrate. All good."

In the kitchen, the dishes started to pile up and sprout white fluffy tufts on leftover bits of food. As the freezer emptied out of portion-controlled pots of high fibre, low fat batch cooked meals, Becca discovered ramen and

Kraft Dinner from the corner shop. She developed a particular taste for canned ravioli in sweet iridescent red sauce, sprinkled with black pepper when she was feeling up to it.

"How's the life planning going?" asked her mother on the other end of the phone.

"So good," replied Becca. "Pages of notes, lots of ideas."

"I'm proud of you, Rebecca," said her mother. "You're working so hard to realise your dreams. You've always been such a hard worker."

"Thanks, mom," said Becca, eyeballing an eye-wateringly garish scarf on The Shopping Network with vague interest.

"If you need anything at all, just let me know."

"That's great, mom, thanks," said Becca. She had never worn a scarf before and wasn't sure if she would in the future but there was something appealing about the unapologetic exuberance of it.

"You know I'm always here for you and I'm sure your dad would be happy to help too if he could put down that child he's dating for a moment."

"She's 38, mom," said Becca impassively, deciding spontaneously against the scarf when it was displayed on a 60-year-old model and made her look dowdy and awkward.

"She's 16 years younger than him. Compared to him she's a child."

"She has a PhD in Biomechanics."

"And she hasn't birthed any children unlike your old mother here so everything will be all nice and taut still. He'll like that."

"Bye mom," said Becca, hanging up without waiting for a reply and turning up the volume on the television.

When bathing became optional, Becca started to wonder if she was maybe getting too deep. The hair growth on her legs, under her arms, between her legs, felt alien and unnatural: she spent hours caressing it with her fingers as one would distractedly pet an animal. Whenever she caught a waft of body odour, she would feel an odd surge of accomplishment.

Rock bottom was hit when Becca's one-eared rescue cat, Vincent, pooped on the pillows on her bed in blatant retribution for an overripe litter box. Becca noticed the deposit when going to grab another pillow for the couch and stood for at least a minute contemplating leaving it where it was: she had taken to sleeping on the sofa anyway, it didn't smell terrible, and she couldn't be bothered to go get a bag from the kitchen.

Starting to think she might need a little help, with the cleaning at least, she worked herself up to inviting Vanessa over for a glass of wine one evening.

"Oh god," said Becca as she opened the door to her own Greek chorus of benevolent disapproval, "you told the others."

"Becca," said Conrad softly, his soft curls, doe eyes, and fresh beach tan making him look like a benevolent angel of empathy. He stepped forward to embrace her just as she took a step back to hold the door open for the group, and rubbed his thighs to distract himself from the wave of rejection.

"This is an intervention," proclaimed Vanessa, brandishing a bottle of wine in each hand, "Vanessa-style."

"For what exactly?" asked Becca, feeling touchy about the intrusion. "I invited you over for a glass of wine"

"For those roots, to start with," replied Vanessa, gesturing at the dark gap between Becca's scalp and where her hair suddenly became a brassy blonde. "Seriously, that is not okay. I'll pick you up some dye tomorrow."

Becca snapped an elastic from her wrist and pulled her hair up into a messy bun. "I'm giving it a rest from the bleach," she said. "It's good for it."

"I don't mind your hair like that, Becs," said Nick apologetically from the back of the pack. "It's kind of cool."

As the trio squeezed their way past into the apartment, they all in turn paused, gaped, and gathered themselves. Conrad and Nick, accustomed to Becca's immaculate tending of home and self, could not take their eyes off the mess. Encircling an embedded Becca-shaped dip in the sofa was a halo of potato chip bags, empty cans of Diet Coke, and discarded tissues. A near-empty tub of ice cream had tipped over on the coffee table and the small puddle left to congeal into a hard lump. There were cigarette butts on every surface, in every vessel.

"You smoke now?" said Nick, shocked.

For Vanessa it was the smell that hit her: a pungent potpourri of stale air, body odour, cat litter, and rotting garbage. "Oh honey," she exhaled, breathing through her mouth. She set the bottles of wine down on a side table and cracked the windows, letting in a fresh breeze and a hopeful trill of birdsong. Vincent let out an ecstatic *mrrrrrp!* and bolted outside.

Becca hastily collected some of the garbage, muttering about having been caught by surprise, didn't know they were coming, was just in the middle of something.

"It's okay, Becs," said Conrad gently, taking an empty Diet Coke can from her hand. "We're here to help, not judge."

"You don't need to do this," said Becca. "Honestly, it's not as bad as it seems. I've had a lot on my mind and just haven't been prioritising cleaning."

"Clearly," said Vanessa, "and that's why we're here. We're your friends and you need help."

For the next few minutes, the trio busied themselves with tipping things into the black garbage bag Nick fetched from the kitchen while Becca stood uncomfortably in the corner of the room and watched. Conrad stuffed her duvet into the washing machine and doubled the soap. Throughout they chattered superficially: This is my favourite flavour of potato chip too. Was she done with this partially eaten muffin? Conrad, tell her about that weird woman you saw on the bus yesterday.

"I've always really liked this coffee table," said Vanessa, grinding off the dried ice cream with a damp rag. "Where did you get it?"

When the room was in some semblance of order, Vanessa as de facto leader gave the signal. Conrad and Nick positioned themselves on the two plush chairs, Conrad folding his legs underneath him while Nick perched on the edge with his knees together and his hands on his thighs. Vanessa handed out wine glasses and gestured solemnly for Becca to sit on the sofa beside her. Once everyone was sitting, the wine was poured with all the ceremony of a Japanese tea ceremony.

"So," said Vanessa with gravitas.

Becca looked around helplessly.

Nick picked up one of the notebooks stacked on the side table, failing to notice Becca wince, and flipped to a few random pages. It was a dizzying melee of brainstorming, personal diarising, lists and comparisons, sketches, and doodles. Lines connected thoughts. Ideas intersected and contradicted themselves. Question marks and exclamation marks ended phrases that were underlined and circled and crossed out. If the content led in any singular direction, it was not obvious: it was as though Becca's brain had completely exploded, spattering the pages with mental gore.

"Cool," he said, gingerly placing the notebook back on the stack.

"I've been trying *The Artist's Way* to get the ideas flowing," Becca tried, by way of explanation. "They're my morning pages. Freeform thinking."

"Ah," said Nick supportively.

Becca studied the group. Vanessa looked hungry, her lips a tight rippling line of concern and judgement. Nick looked as though he would rather be anywhere else but there, and frankly Becca didn't blame him for that – her own flight instinct was raging. Conrad looked safe but sharing concerns with Conrad was like throwing coins in a wishing well: it might feel promising at the time, but in the end she would just be a few pennies poorer. She wanted to yell 'Hey, what's over there?' and bolt out the window like her cat or make up an elaborate and superficial story to diffuse interest and distract suspicion, rather than tell any of them anything about what had been going on in her head lately.

But surrounded by people who had dropped everything and rushed over with wine to the moment she had cracked open a window of opportunity, each of them currently radiating love towards her like dysfunctional Care Bears, Becca surrendered.

"Okay, fine," she said. "It's not a big deal, really, but I'll tell you if it will shut you up and because it was really sweet of you all to come and to… help tidy up a little…"

She took a deep breath; the other three held theirs.

"Deciding to quit acting has been harder than expected, and I'm struggling with what to do now," she admitted.

Vanessa looked momentarily shocked, then delighted, then compassionate. Nick and Conrad landed and stayed on shocked.

"You?" asked Vanessa. "You've always been the one of us who did know."

Becca flicked an imaginary piece of lint off her shirt. "I *did* know."

She drained her wine glass in the ensuing silence, her friends waiting expectantly for more. Nick leaned forward and massaged his knees. Vanessa's eyes were as big as saucers.

She lifted her hands from her lap helplessly. "I've wanted to be an actor since I was a kid, and I've been an actor since I was a kid. And now… what? Who am I if I'm not an actor?"

"I mean, *Evita* only just ended, Becs," said Nick.

"But I'm done," said Becca. "I'm done with the only thing I ever wanted in my life… and I no longer know what I want to be when I grow up. And that is…" – exhalation – "super scary."

"Do any of us?" asked Conrad.

"Yes, exactly," said Becca, "none of you do. None of you know what you want and somehow you're all okay with that."

Her three friends considered that statement with pursed lips and furrowed brows. Nick looked sombre, his jaw muscle flexing.

"Well sure," said Vanessa, "but isn't that pretty standard? I don't know anyone our age who knows what they want, not really."

Conrad agreed. "I mean, I know what I want but it's not a job title or an industry, it's more, like, the *qualities* of a job."

"Exactly!" said Vanessa, "I don't really care what my title is or what they pay me, I just want to be happy. I want a job which gives me purpose, where I feel valued…"

"Something challenging," added Conrad, head bobbing. "Flexible. Creative."

"Where I am a part of something bigger than me."

"Rewarding."

"And those qualities could exist in any number of career areas so it's a matter of taking the time you need to explore the options and find your path."

"26 years old and still searching for myself," said Becca with a trace of bitterness.

"It's totally normal to feel lost," said Vanessa.

"Absolutely," piped up Nick softly.

"I'm not sure we ever do find ourselves," mused Conrad, "or if that should even be our goal. Maybe the goal is to *stay lost*."

Becca stared at an invisible spot on the warm vanilla wall of her living room, somewhere over her friends' shoulders, to distract herself from rolling her eyes. She could feel them watching her intently and on some level she was grateful. What she wanted to say was, "Thank you for being here for me right now," and maybe even as far as, "but that's not what I need right now." However, caught in the undertow of all the thoughts that had gone months without an audience, what she said was, "Do you ever actually hear yourselves?"

There was silence from the group.

Becca squinted over at them, words fighting each other on her teeth and tongue. Vanessa looked thunderous underneath the visible exercise in self-control. Nick sat with his head down, gazing into the depths of his wine glass. Conrad's bewilderment was so pure, so naïve, so infuriatingly adolescent, that Becca wanted to throw a cushion at his head, hard.

"I love you guys, truly, with all my heart," she said to them, "but all this… this *drama*… she is tiring."

It was as if someone had sucked all the air out of the room. The offense lurched Vanessa off the couch to standing behind the boys' chairs, her eyes wild with outrage. Conrad sat opening and closing his mouth. Nick remained unmoving, staring hard into his glass.

Becca, in comparison, was feeling more like herself than she had in a very long time.

"We're just trying to help," said Vanessa in a clipped tone.

"Are you though?" asked Becca. "Find your path? Stay lost? What kind of ridiculous, decadent, self-indulgent thinking is that? You guys love to talk about what you want from life, but there's never any decision or action taken, ever. No wonder you're all lost."

"That's not fair, Becca," said Vanessa, crossing her arms in front of her chest.

"Yeah," said Conrad, tears visibly glimmering.

"Talking about who you want to be when you grow up. I've never understood that and yet," Becca grimaced, "somehow here I am with you."

Vanessa made a grab for the open bottle of wine. "Refill, anyone?" she said sharply, holding it high like the Statue of Liberty's torch.

No one else moved.

Becca looked at the top of Nick's bowed head thoughtfully. "You I have respect for, Nick," she said.

Vanessa choked. "Wait, sorry, did you just say you respect Nick, out of all of us?"

"Hey," said Nick, snapping his head up.

"Nick's doing something," said Becca, "It might not be what he's always dreamed about but at least he's doing *something*."

"And Conrad and I are just wasting our lives, is that it?"

"That's not what I'm saying, Vanessa," said Becca, judgements crashing and booming inside her, only held back by the seawall of her reluctance to cause actual harm to her friends. "I mean that he's getting on with things. He's not sitting around wasting time. I'm just saying…" She faltered, passing her hand across her brow. "I'm just saying…"

"What are you saying, Becs?" asked Conrad, his forehead creased with non-comprehension and hurt.

The wall of words inside her collapsed, her fight gone. "I'm saying it will be fine," said Becca. "I just need to make some decisions."

She picked up a nearby cushion and began fluffing it back up vigorously.

"It's going to be more than fine, actually, because it's in my control to make it happen."

The fluffs grew faster, harder.

"I just needed some time and I took that time and now that time is up."

The fluffs were becoming strikes.

"It will all work out, I *just* need to get *over* this *stupid, waste*-of-*energy…*" she said, punching the pillow to the rhythm and ending with a direct blow that made her friends flinch, "*FEAR.*"

And then, with her friends watching on in wonderment, Becca began to pummel the cushion with both hands. She punched until her shoulders ached and her hands burned from the friction. She punched until she was gasping for air and everyone could smell the odour wafting from her hair and body. Months of dread and uncertainty poured from her fist into its fabric, causing miniscule pieces of leftover food and dandruff to drift down onto the couch. Only when the pillow split neatly along a seam, scattering a few clouds of white cotton fluff, did Becca stop.

Gently she touched the debris field on her lap with her fingertips.

She turned to her stunned friends, her face progressing from horror to wonder to contrition, and finally to composed calm.

"So my idea," she said smartly, placing the cushion back on the couch with a pat, "is to go into law."

The idea rippled through the room like someone had thrown a boulder into a lake. Said aloud for the first time ever, Becca was pleased with how it sounded.

Conrad was the first to react, ever willing to stay in the moment. He lunged over to the couch beside her and wrapped his arms around her rigid shoulders. "Wow! Oh my god, Becca, that's so cool!"

Becca looked at Nick, her eyebrow arched.

"Why not?" said Nick with a reluctant half-smile of someone impressed yet not surprised. "You're the most driven person I've ever met."

Becca looked over at Vanessa who was fixated on running her index finger in circles around the edge of her wine glass.

"V?" she started by way of apology.

This was a common détente. The two men knew their best option was to keep still and quiet, which they both now did. The only sound in the room was the footsteps of the people who lived upstairs.

Vanessa could feel Becca's gaze boring into the top of her head. She tried to rally her anger and offense – how dare Becca say something so hurtful and then go back to making it all about her! – but there was undeniable logic in Becca's proposal and Vanessa disappointingly felt more curious than cross.

"Law?" she asked, trying to keep her tone cutting and judgmental in order to not completely give in. "Isn't that super difficult?"

"Well, I'd have to do a bachelor's degree first anyway, so you never know. As you said, V, academia isn't really my thing."

"I didn't –" started Vanessa, tensing.

But the battle was over. "You were right, though," Becca said softly. "It's not. This is very new to me. And if I'm going to do this, I'm going to need you guys…"

Conrad placed his hand on Becca's pyjama-clad leg. "We got you, Becs," he said solemnly. "For this, for anything else, forever."

"You bet, Becs," agreed Nick.

Everyone turned towards Vanessa. Becca's uncharacteristic need for validation was blatant, raw: Vanessa found it entirely disarming. To think, Becca needing *her* validation.

Vanessa held up her glass of wine. "To Becca," she said, "Class of… I guess 2012?"

"To my fully funded life in Thailand!" added Conrad.

"To showing us all up as usual!" threw in Nick.

Nine years later, to celebrate passing the bar exam, Becca leased herself a Lexus.

2022

Up in his room with the door open, waiting cross-legged on the bed for everyone to gather before he made his grand entrance, Conrad heard Nick arrive with characteristic precision at the crack of seven.

"Come in! Come in!" said Vanessa grandly. Her monarchical flourish reminded Conrad of when she had played Ranevskaya in a poorly attended production of Chekhov's *The Cherry Orchard* in high school. It had taken twenty years for Vanessa's numerical age to catch up to her behavioural age, he thought. Middle age suited her.

"Nice hair!"

"Thanks."

"Coat on the hook unless you want to keep it on, and first door to your left for the sitting room. We'll move into the dining room when everyone else is here. Ah, you brought wine, you doll."

Robert now: "What can I get you to drink, Nick??"

Nick's voice, lower than usual and raspy: ""Maybe a glass of water?"

Conrad chewed nervously on the nail of his left pinkie as he eavesdropped.

"You bet," replied Vanessa spiritedly. "Yes, that door there. Sit anywhere you'd like."

Footsteps.

Robert, hushed: "Does he seem okay to you?"

"Seems fine?"

"Not… low?"

"Nick's never the life of the party, Robert," she replied. "Now go put this in the fridge, will you? And get Nick some ice water."

Up in the guest room, Conrad ran his hands over the coarse fabric of his khakis and paced the length of the room a few times. Waiting upstairs with the people gathering below made him feel like a Christian preparing to face lions in the arena. He did a few lunges and forward bends to release the stress, swirled his hips around in a wide circle, practised his positive face and his interested face and then his patient and empathetic yet persuasive and powerful face. He was back at his post in the doorway to eavesdrop just as Becca and Max came clattering up to the door 20 minutes later.

"They're English garden-themed!" said Max, presumably about a bouquet of flowers.

"Ah," he heard Vanessa reply with the glittering facade of gracious reception, "for a Canada-themed dinner. How non-conformist! Nick's already here in the sitting room, first door to your left."

"Robert," she called, "Max and Becca are here!"

Oh god, thought Conrad with a thrill of apprehension, can that be everyone already? Best to give it a few more minutes. Let them all settle.

"Can I get you a drink?" asked Robert.

"I'd love a glass of red," said Becca.

"White for me, if there's one open?" said Max.

"On it." Robert's voice receding into the kitchen.

"Where's your washroom?" asked Max, coming dangerously close to the bottom of the stairs, from which point she would have been able to see Conrad by the door. He ducked quickly out of sight.

"End of the hall."

"So much gold! Very flashy."

Some bustle, some superficial chatter – "your wine, Becca" – and then they had clearly all gone to sit down in the living room as Conrad could hear no more from anyone.

Right, he thought, one minute more and then game on.

Conrad tiptoed down the stairs and to the side of the doorway to the sitting room, and then in one sweeping gesture manifested in the doorway like a magician at the triumphant end of a trick everyone saw coming.

"My friends!" he cried jubilantly, as though he had not seen any of them for years, much less most of them earlier that day.

"Ah!" cried Max delightedly, disentangling herself from Becca where they had been canoodling on the couch. "This must be the famous Conrad!"

Conrad pulled her into a vigorous bear hug, which was enthusiastically reciprocated. "We're nearly family now, Max," he said into her hair. "Family don't shake hands!"

Behind them, Becca stood up in anticipation, as uncomfortable with the instantaneous intimacy between her partner and her friend as with the space Max had left beside her. Conrad flashed her a dazzling grin over Max's shoulder.

146

And then it was time to make the rounds. Conrad had been prepped by Andrew about how best to do this: he needed each person to feel seen by him, to feel special and safe in that environment, so they would open their heart chakras to him. This was best done with a personalised comment addressing something unique or interesting, said with emphatic familiarity to draw attention to the bond between them. He would also hug them each because he was by nature a hugger and it felt appropriate under the circumstances.

"Becca," exclaimed Conrad, holding her at a distance by the tips of her fingers and giving her a top-to-bottom style check. "Look at you, you delicious thing."

Becca, who had spent a fair amount of time on her hair and makeup that evening, held out the side of her floaty lilac dress for a neat curtsy and a furious blush. "Why thank you, Conrad. You're not looking bad yourself."

"Robeeeerrrrrt," he double-finger-gunned his host, "very dapper with your pocket square there."

Robert's hands floated self-consciously to his jacket pocket, but the smile was genuine. "It was Vanessa's idea…"

"It makes you look like James Bond is what it does. Très élégant."

Robert blushed. Two down, two to go.

Nick was going to be more challenging. Slumped with his glass of water in an armchair, he was positively ashen. His thinning hair was gone, shaved back to a shiny scalp, and the effect was dramatic. There was, however, hope: sporting a tan sport coat and his best jeans, Nick had put in his equivalent of Becca's level of effort.

Conrad beamed out waves of positive, loving energy and light as he approached Nick. "And there's our Nick!" he said, grabbing his friend by both hands and physically pulling him to his feet and into a reticent and very brief hug. "Loving the haircut. Very Charles Xavier!"

"Yeah," said Nick, sitting back down and rubbing his shiny pate.

"It's very slick," said Conrad. "And the upkeep is going to be a breeze, I'm absolutely consumed with jealousy. Think of all the money you'll save on haircuts!"

"Heh," said Nick, feebly. "Yeah."

Good enough.

"And Vanessa," said Conrad, extending his arms in rapturous reunion with someone with whom he had bickered over leaving empty dishes in the sink not more than an hour previously. "Our gracious and beautiful hostess. Thank you for making this happen tonight, inviting us into your beautiful home – yours and Robert's of course – and bringing the whole family together after all this time."

Vanessa's smile was wide and bright but forced. "You always did know how to make an entrance, Conrad."

"Especially now with Max joining us and making our little family truly complete."

Becca wrapped her legs around Max's and nuzzled her neck.

Sum up and seal, thought Conrad.

"Imagine, all of us here right now, together, after all these years, after all we've been through. Becca the actress-cum-lawyer. Vanessa the academic. Me, the entrepreneur. Nick, the..." Realising his hands were empty, he raised an imaginary drink. "Nick, the life-changer."

And suddenly the air was thick with tension. Everyone could feel it. It slunk across the floor and seeped into the cracks in the furniture. It wrapped around their throats and made sipping their respective drinks of urgent, desperate importance and focus.

Nick shot Conrad a furtive glance, which Becca caught. "Oh Nick," she said with dawning horror, "you didn't..."

"Did what?" asked Robert.

"For how much?" asked Becca.

"And what if he did?" asked Conrad.

Nick coughed twice and everyone swivelled to stare at him. "Excuse me," he croaked, wanting nothing more than to crawl into the sofa cushions and disappear.

Vanessa, sensing the danger to her perfect evening, stood up quickly to draw attention away from Nick. "Well, I for one am hungry," she said, snatching up empty glasses. "Appetisers in half an hour, if that works for everyone? Yes? Yes? Half an hour? Yes? Great. *Robert?*"

Robert solemnly headed out to the grill.

Eyes were starting to slide back towards Nick.

"And Max," continued Vanessa wildly, "this is your first time here with the whole group. I'm so glad you were able to join us. You are very welcome."

"Your home is beautiful, Vanessa," said Max gamely, taking in the immaculately styled sitting room. She held up one of the pillows: "Is this artisanal? Wherever did you get it?"

"You've got a good eye, Max. That particular one is just IKEA but the rest are handmade, bought at an artisan fair on the Island a couple years back."

"Glad to see you have at least some IKEA in here," teased Conrad limply. "What kind of Gen Xer are you without a house full of the stuff?"

"Oh it's there," said Vanessa, sick fear stirring in her stomach. "Billy bookcases are the STIs of the furniture world. You can never be entirely free of them."

"A friend of mine left hers beside the road," said Becca, her cheeks pale, "and the next day they appeared on her doorstep."

"A friend of mine used his for firewood one Christmas," said Max, grasping her partner's hand in support, "and the next day they were back in her office, good as new."

"A friend of mine traded his for mid-century vintage teak," said Conrad, starting to enjoy himself again, "and the next day the they had metamorphosed into medium-density fibreboard Billies."

"A friend of mine," said Nick, but then faltered and fell silent.

Vanessa gave a wry laugh. "We don't have much anymore," she admitted, "but it's there. Anyone need a refresh on their drinks?"

2013

When Conrad was 38, he scrubbed his sins away.

The initial months back home following the goat experience in Thailand in 2002 had been viscerally uncomfortable for him. Wandering streets that had once whispered to him of safety and belonging, Conrad now heard only dissonant noise and deadening silence. Nothing fit anymore: everything was too big, too bright, too loud, too harsh. He was pinned between skyscrapers, searching for the stars in a sky muddied by light and population. He wanted to rend his t-shirt and primal scream into the capitalistic abyss.

"I can't do it anymore," he declared to his friends one evening on the beach. "My soul doesn't belong here; it belongs to the world."

Conrad spent Nick and Nancy's wedding ceremony daydreaming about jump dancing with Maasai warriors in Kenya. He spoke longingly to Vanessa while on a run along the seawall about needing to see the sunrise from Uluru surrounded by the spirits of his too-long-disconnected ancestors. He raved to Becca while they studied Emily Carr paintings at the Vancouver Art Gallery about a "Monastery Experience" in Nepal in which he would actually get to live amongst the monks in their search for unification with the universe.

"Don't you see?" he would ask his friends every few months.

"Of course we do, Conrad," his friends would say with feigned enthusiasm.

He crafted his life into a dutiful cycle of sacrifice and reward in which six or eight months of backbreaking work back home – stranded and disconnected scanning the Northern forest tops for signs of smoke, planting trees in British Columbia, working in the oil sands of Alberta – would be exchanged for the funds and freedom required to spend the remainder of the calendar year exploring the world and himself. With every trip, every country, Conrad sought a truth and meaning far beyond anything a life in economics could have ever given him back home.

The realisation that he needed to go back to Thailand came to him between bouts of being bent double over a metal bucket as part of an ayahuasca ceremony in Costa Rica. As he lay by the fire listening to the sounds of musicians, exhausted from a violent round of purging, he was visited by a vision of the big, brown, trusting eye of his goat. The regret and remorse for what he had done came crashing down onto his chest. Conrad clambered to his knees, sweating in the jungle heat and weeping profusely, trembling hands raised to the sky, pleading for forgiveness from the universe and pledging that he would restore the order he had unintentionally broken.

On his next work stint in Canada, he made his plan. Although he wouldn't be able to restore the life he had callously taken, it was obvious that his debt and therefore his penance was to animals: specifically, elephants, as the sacred and much-abused guardians of the planet. He had the sense that with their enigmatic intelligence they would be able to understand his pain and absolve him of it, if he could be allowed to serve them.

He found a sanctuary in the north of Thailand that offered the opportunity to live and work alongside a small herd of rescued elephants for three weeks for $2500, not including flights – a bargain, he thought, for such an unparalleled opportunity for personal redemption and cosmic equilibrium. And in this way in the summer of 2012 Conrad returned to the country of his greatest crime.

The tears began when the pilot announced their descent into Bangkok. He closed his eyes and sent out a small prayer to his tragic goat: "This is for you, my friend. Forgive me."

The entire country around him seemed to ripple as he stepped from the air-conditioned airport into the heat of the city, perhaps surprised and impressed by his courage. Waiting on a bench for the shuttle that would take him to his absolution, he watched Boomer tourists with fanny packs and white socks and sandals stream from airport to taxis, noses buried in their *Fodor's Guide to Thailand*, and thought what human tragedy it was that they would go home falsely believing that this was how to know a country. He felt less judgmental towards the younger people clearly there to party, having been one of them once, though to each he sent a wish that they would find meaning in their journeys.

"Are you waiting for the shuttle to… Sakdisith?" asked a moon-faced girl of about 20 in a thick Australian accent. She shook her head and checked her notes. "Sak-dis-ith-thi... Sakdisi-th-th-ee... Ha, I don't know how to say that, do you? The elephant camp, I mean. Is this where we wait for the shuttle?"

Conrad made space on the bench for her.

"Great," said the girl, the happiness radiating from her like light reflecting off a disco ball. "I'm excited about this, aren't you? I've been wanting to do this my entire life. I had a stuffed elephant named Horton when I was a kid – you know, after the book – and I've been totally obsessed with them ever since I was born almost. I can't believe I'm going to finally meet one! It's my birthday present to myself. What about you? Are you super excited? Have you ever done anything like this before?"

When a young couple appeared, the girl leaped to her feet. "Here for the elephants!" she cried. "Are you here for the elephants?"

"We are," replied the woman, clinging to the man's hand. American, noted Conrad. He adjusted his backpack so the maple leaf was clearly visible.

"I'm Beth," said the moon-faced girl, holding out her hand.

"Renée," said the woman, "and this is Matthew."

"Hullo," said Matthew amiably.

All three turned to Conrad expectantly and waited.

Conrad held his head high but kept his eyes lowered in humility and grace. "Conrad," he said.

"Wait!" cried Beth, waggling her finger at the couple, "are you guys here on your honeymoon? You are! I knew it! I could just tell, the way you're holding onto each other like you'll never ever let go! Did you just get married? Love is so beautiful! I can't wait to get married someday."

Conrad disliked them all. This trip was not about fun and friends, and the din of superficial chatter and selfies on smartphones would be distracting to his important self-journey. When three petite British girls with an excessive pile of bags teetering on two luggage carts joined the waiting group, Conrad made a big deal of checking his phone on airport Wi-Fi to avoid any further engagement. He never would catch their names and considered that well accomplished. That he would earn a reputation among the group for being reclusive and rude didn't bother him in the slightest.

The Ṣakdiṣithṭhi Elephant Sanctuary was built on a sprawling plot of land dotted with cozy bamboo cabins for sleeping and one large communal hall. Each of the guests were allocated a comfortable-looking floor mattress in one of the cabins, with a locker for their valuables. Toilets were a combination of standing and Western-style, Conrad spotted with some relief, having never mastered the squatting. An abundance of insects of all possible shapes and sizes rattled mindlessly against the screens loosely slung over the open windows.

The pink-cheeked owner and host met them at the gate. "Welcome, everyone, to the Ṣakdiṣiththi Elephant Sanctuary," she said in a strong English accent while everyone was tumbling out of the bus and scrambling to collect their bags.

Sak-seeth, chanted Conrad to himself, drilling the phonetics into his head. It was of critical importance he got this right. *Sak-seeth*.

Beth had her hand up already. "Beth, I'm Beth," said Beth. "What does the name mean?"

"Sacred," said Laura. "Holy. Divine." She opened her palms to the sky and gazed up towards the heavens.

"Oh," said Beth excitedly, "about the elephants, right? Elephants are totally sacred."

Laura flicked her thick brown braid over her left shoulder. "Thank you for your invaluable contribution to protecting these majestic – yes, as Beth correctly said, *sacred* – creatures. The donation to the sanctuary you made with your enrollment fee will enable us to continue our important work into the future."

Beth beamed.

"Most of our elephants here are rescues, saved from lives of starvation," – Beth flinched – "neglect," – Beth gasped – "and terrible abuse." At this point Beth emitted a sound of such human suffering that Conrad worried she might collapse right in front of him. He put a warm hand on her shoulder for comfort, which she grasped at wetly.

"Here, at last," smiled Laura, "our elephants can live out the rest of their lives, loved and cared for as they deserve. And this" – now she clapped her hands together as if in prayer and shook them at the semi-circle of enthralled foreigners – "is where you all come in! Over the next two weeks, you will have the chance to learn about and live among our elephants, to really get to know them, and to play an essential part in their lives."

Yes, Conrad thought to himself. Perfect.

"The staff will take your bags to your cabins in a moment and dinner will be ready at 6 in our dining hall. But am I right in thinking that, before anything else, you might want to meet... *the elephants*?"

Beth let out a high-pitched squeak. The other fifteen volun-tourists gathered on the path tittered amongst themselves, eager and impatient. Conrad, who had on the bus felt tendrils of jetlag drawing him to a nap on arrival, was suddenly brightly alert and slightly giddy.

"Shall we?" smiled Laura, sweeping her arm towards a nearby paddock.

Beth started to cry with joy.

The elephants – twelve of them in total – were some distance away and separated by a sturdy metal fence, each accompanied by his or her stone-faced keeper – "their mahout," explained Laura. Laura stood on one of the lower railings and waved her arm at the mahouts, who tapped gently on their respective elephant's shoulder with a bull hook. All but the largest elephant jogged confidently forward with trunks raised and mouths open; the largest held back, watching the herd closely, her ears flapping gently. Along the railing, the tourists with their smartphones formed a line of elephant paparazzi.

"Oh my god there's a baby!" cried Beth, now actually sobbing.

Tucked close to and behind the largest elephant, Conrad could make out a smaller form.

"That's Daaet," smiled Laura. "It means Sunshine. He's our little monkey. He's just had his first birthday."

Beth began to rock on her feet, the tears and snot dripping from her chin.

Conrad was less interested in the baby, feeling instead a distinct pull towards the largest elephant. "What's her name?" he asked, pointing, his hand shaking slightly.

"That's Mali," replied Laura proudly. "She's the matriarch."

Mali. Mali. Sacred Mali. *Sak-seeth* Mali. She was the reason he was there.

"Don't forget to tag us in your social media posts!" smiled Laura to the chittering, clicking group. She passed Beth a tissue.

Life on the elephant sanctuary turned out to be a lot of hard work: the group spent the majority of their time digging trenches in the humid heat of the afternoon, chopping and preparing the unfathomable amount of food required by the herd on a daily basis, scrubbing out water troughs and scooping poop, as well as painting and maintenance of the site itself. Quality time with the elephants was more limited than Beth and the other guests had perhaps hoped, but Conrad was calm and devout. He considered the labour his offering to Mali, to whom he would gravitate every time they had an interactive experience.

When he finally got to feed her, Conrad fixed his gaze on the dirt by her perfect toenails and held out bananas one at a time like an offering. He tried to make meaningful eye contact with her after she had delicately tossed the last one into her open mouth, but she was watching something in the distance, and he had to make do with studying the bristles covering her trunk and head with reverence.

Little further progress was made during an elephant bathing experience. Conrad changed into his red swim trunks and waited by the side of the muddy pond for the mahouts to finish fishing out and throwing patties of poop at the giggling group. After Mali had lowered herself onto her belly in the water with a contented rumble, Daaet by her head, Conrad stepped forward and ceremoniously scooped handfuls of muddy water over her back. Elsewhere in the pond the others were shrieking and scrabbling, having water fights, and pushing each other down into the mud. Conrad whispered, "Disrespectful," but Mali just closed her eyes and laid back on one hip.

"I feel like I'm living in the past," said one of the British girls later that evening when a mahout went riding by on the back of an elephant.

The days came and went, and some of the other tourists were starting to lose their enthusiasm. The three British girls began appearing for work less and less frequently, preferring instead to stay in their cabin or loll about in hammocks taking selfies. At the halfway mark of their allotted time on the preserve, newlywed Matthew started complaining that he had pulled his back scrubbing a water trough and shortly thereafter after both he and Renée packed up their lockers and left.

"I mean," mused Beth over noodles and vegetables, "shovelling poop maybe isn't the honeymoon for everyone?"

For Conrad, life outside the sanctuary seemed impossibly distant: all that mattered was today and Mali. However, despite all his ministrations, his offerings and his labour, as their days at the sanctuary drew to a close, he still hadn't had his moment of connection with and absolution from Mali. He had scrubbed her back with a broom, splashed her with warm lake water, fed her extra sugar cane, tolerated Daaet's reckless bumbling with the tolerance he reserved for the bothersome children of important colleagues, but every time he gazed into her eyes, hoping for a spark of recognition and understanding, he felt... nothing.

On their final evening, Laura caught him leaning against the metal fence alone and in thought.

"Not ready to leave, Conrad?"

Conrad ran his fingers through his hair to deflect from wiping away a tear. "I bet you get that all the time."

"We do," said Laura tenderly. "How do you think all this happened in the first place? I came for a month and never left."

The evening air was warm and sweet. His eyes burned with tears.

"I hope you got something out of the visit at least?" she asked gently.

"I guess I was hoping for something more."

"A connection with one of the elephants."

"Yes. Is that stupid?"

"You're not the first to want that. But these things can't be forced, Conrad. Elephants are complex, intelligent animals."

"But still... I thought..."

"Tell me."

"It's embarrassing."

"I guarantee I've heard it before. I've probably thought it before."

Conrad turned to Laura and met her gaze. "I felt something... you know, when I saw Mali on that first day."

Understanding settled on Laura's sun-baked face.

"Ridiculous, I know."

"It's not ridiculous. She's had that effect on people ever since Daaet was born. It's as though she became the mother of us all somehow."

Proprietary jealousy gnawed at Conrad's heart, mingled with shame and anxiety and guilt. He stared towards the green mountains in the distance. He felt the metal railing burn hot under his forearms, the setting sun on the back of his neck. In the distance, he could make out the shapes of the elephants in the trees – Mali would be among them, Daaet running headlong in circles around her. Hot shame prickled his cheeks.

"I'm here if you need to talk, Conrad," said Laura, touching his back lightly as she left to go help with dinner.

And then the bus was there to pick them up.

Waiting for his plane home at Suvarnabhumi Airport, Conrad felt strangely placid. On one hand he felt as though he was abandoning a path half-walked; on the other, reflecting on three weeks of labour, he was certain had made a lasting difference in the lives of those elephants. He fiddled with the string bracelet he had bought at the sanctuary's gift shop on the way home and thought of Mali. Would she miss him? Probably. She might not have made a big show of connecting with him but there had definitely been something there between them and elephants have great memories.

A middle-aged woman wandered past in an elephant print sarong, the pale outline of sunglasses faintly visible through her sunburn. Conrad felt sorry for her.

2022

At Vanessa's signal, which might as well have been a brass gong for the profound pomp of it, the guests shuffled from their places in the sitting room to seek their places around the dining table. Becca, following closely behind Nick, poked him once in the back as they walked and hissed, "Do we need to talk?" but he gave no indication that he had heard her.

"Please," said Vanessa grandly, half-bowing as she exited the room, "find your seats while I go get the appetisers!"

The group milled around the table, checking and rechecking the immaculately printed seating cards which were set out as so:

```
            B      M
    V                     R
            N      C
```

"Here's me!" said Conrad, plonking himself down with an expectant look around. "Who've I got on either side? Robert and... Nick!"

Beside him, Becca noticed Nick place one hand on the back of his chair but hesitate to sit.

"Actually," said Becca with a near-imperceptible headshake, "would it be possible for us to swap, Nick? Only I've not seen Conrad for so long, it would sure mean a lot to get to sit next to him."

"Of course," said Nick with a flash of relief, and so it became:

```
            N      M
    V                     R
            B      C
```

"Oh," said Max unhappily, "now I'm not sitting next to you anymore, Becca."

"Not a problem," said Robert, "I don't need to sit at the end. Becca, why don't you and I swap so you and Max can be together?"

"You are such a doll, Robert," said Becca, and so it became:

```
        N       M
  V               B
        R       C
```

"You're right next to me, buddy!" said Conrad, slapping Robert on the shoulder as he went to sit down.

"Indeed," said Robert waly. "In. Deed. Unless… given how much we've seen a lot of each other, what with you staying here and everything, if anyone wants…?" He swapped his name card with Vanessa's, and so it became:

```
        N       M
  R               B
        V       C
```

"As it's your reunion," he explained to Conrad, who was looking bereft, "it makes more sense for you to sit next to Vanessa than some generic plus one."

Becca reached over and rubbed the back of Conrad's hand. It was oddly, incredibly soft. "Oh my god, Conrad," she said, stroking the skin, "what do you –"

Vanessa entered, carrying two small plates of salad. When she saw the revised seating plan, she stiffened.

"I spent so long figuring out the seating plan, you guys…" she whined.

"This way works better," said Becca firmly.

"But it's standard practice that the hosts sit at either end of the table!"

"I know," said Robert, "but Max and Becca wanted to sit together…"

"Which they were."

"And since you and Conrad are old friends, it made sense for you two to sit together." Robert smiled without teeth, giving him a strained and unnatural air.

Becca, watching quietly from her safe seat behind the table, thought she saw a Vanessa block an impulse to lunge at her husband. That would be one way to make the evening more interesting, she thought.

"Fine," said Vanessa instead, lifting her chin. "I'm glad you all are happy. That's the most important thing."

To Becca's disappointment, the salads were for her and Max: a few shards of iceberg lettuce, eight halved baby plum tomatoes, a few slices of cucumber, and a sprig of parsley on top for decoration.

"Sorry, you two," Vanessa said, too showily to be completely credible, "I completely forgot to think about a vegetarian appetiser so I hope these will do. Can I get you some salad dressing?"

Becca sucked in her cheeks. "We're just grateful you thought about us at all, V."

"It's our fault for being the troublemakers with the special diet," said Max, grasping Becca's knee tightly under the table. "Salad dressing would be lovely, though, please."

Out with tremendous fanfare, then came the wapiti: grilled to perfection by Robert, nestled in a salad of warm greens and wild blueberries, the bacon wrapping crisp and wafting an inconceivably delicious smell. Conrad lightly pounded his fists against the table in anticipation.

"Bon appétit!" proclaimed Vanessa, her head majestically high.

Becca, munching resentfully on her iceberg lettuce while the others exclaimed and cheered and raved about their proper appetiser, couldn't stop herself. "Fun fact," she said, spearing a piece of dry cucumber – when had Vanessa prepped this? yesterday? – "did you know that the chemicals used to make bacon are a Group 1 carcinogen? And red meat is a Group 2A carcinogen?"

"I did know that," said Robert, nodding receptively.

"Wild," said Conrad, "so we're basically eating cancer-wrapped cancer." He took an appreciative bite.

"I'm not saying don't eat it, of course," continued Becca, "especially as Vanessa's gone to such trouble for you all tonight, but I'm happy with my salad is what I'm saying."

Vanessa shot her a withering look. "I'm glad to hear it," she said. "I do apologise again."

"Also –" started Becca, but Robert was on his feet.

"A toast," he declared, grasping his wine glass and holding it high. "To Conrad, for having the guts to pursue his wildest, craziest dreams."

"To Conrad!" they all chimed, clinking obediently.

Conrad beamed as they all sipped.

"So when are you going to give us the dirt on your new venture?" said Max. "Isn't that what tonight's all about?"

Conrad wiped his mouth with his napkin. "Well," he said coyly, "I mean, I've talked to most of you about this week, so I've rather ruined the big reveal."

"But we've only heard bits," said Becca.

"And we have so many questions," added Max.

"Plus tonight is in honour of you and your big life transformation," said Vanessa, "so, go on, take the stage and tell us everything."

Showtime.

Conrad took a deep breath to centre his energies and remind himself of what Andrew had said: if they love you, they will support you.

"So, as you know, I'm a businessman now," he said, struggling to remember the exact phrasing of the pitch he had pre-scripted for this very moment. "A business owner. I've started my own business. Like a franchise but not because I'm not beholden to anyone, just myself and the universe. I'm making money, or I'm going to make money, but money's not the goal. I'm not doing it for the money."

"Right, okay," interrupted Robert, "and maybe I'm being obtuse but what is the business exactly? You sell crystals? Or classes? Or...?"

"Not sell, not sell," said Conrad quickly. "I don't sell anything. I provide opportunities for people to become their best selves."

"Okay, but...," said Robert. "I'm sorry, I've been trying but I don't understand."

Max and Vanessa agreed. Becca peeped over at Nick who was glumly picking at his wapiti.

"Well," said Conrad, "okay, to put it simply: ReYOUvenate is about education. They offer seminars all about spiritual oneness and how we can improve our sense of purpose and our relationships through self-healing. But it's not like a religious cult or anything like that: nothing's mandatory, no pressure, no donations or minimum spends. You just pick the seminars you're interested in and enrol in them – that's it! And there are loads of weekend events and an annual week-long conference where the Student-Teachers can meet the Chief Visionary Officer, Frank, who's such a nice guy and clearly gets it, you know? He's put in the work and has made it happen. You should see the pictures of his house! He's really inspirational."

"And you're absolutely sure it's not a cult?" asked Becca, seriously but under the pretence of teasing.

"I promise it's not. Cults are belief systems in which everyone worships some charismatic leader, like Waco or those guys with the Kool Aid, whereas this is genuinely a business. ReYOUvenate isn't trying to tell you how to think, it's simply providing opportunities for you to explore how you already think and start harnessing that power. And the result is a solid, authentic, anti-capitalist business."

"Sounds great," said Robert unconvincingly, "but how exactly is it a business?"

"And how is it an epiphany?" asked Becca.

Conrad was finding his stride, building his confidence.

"Well," explained Conrad, pausing periodically to chew and swallow. "All these years, all those trips, they were always in search of something. Coming out of university, everything felt dark: no jobs, no mortgages, no healthy human relationships. We'd all gotten so angry – you guys remember. And so I ran, seeking attention, stimulation, something. I did everything I could think of to make my life a worthwhile tale and squeeze some meaning out of it, but I always ended up back here, no further along, no closer to satisfied."

"Here as in Vanessa's dining room?" asked Max.

"Not literally V's dining room, I mean, but here, in Vancouver, with you guys. And that felt like a failure somehow – not being with you guys, of course, but me, in myself. I felt like a failure. I had this image of myself and no matter what I did I couldn't live up to it. And then I found ReYOUvenate, and they showed me that I *am* enough, and have *always* been enough, and that the meaning I've been searching for is here, with you, in Vancouver, maybe even in this dining room, who knows? And now I've come home – for good this time – all thanks to what I've learned from ReYOUvenate."

Becca watched a frustrated fly buzz behind the window sash, repeatedly bashing its little body against the glass in a desperate but futile attempt for freedom. Wordlessly she went to crack the window open and discovered a fine layer of dust on the windowsill after running her finger along it.

"Okay," said Robert, still not following.

"It all sounds very positive," said Vanessa, with a vocal uptick at the end that suggested a degree of uncertainty in the fact. She gave his hand a supportive squeeze.

Max was openly unconvinced. "But how do you make money?" she asked.

It was, however, Nick who answered: "You get others to sign up," he said quietly.

Becca tried again to connect with Nick but again no response. Conrad had recruited him then, she was sure of it. The poor fool. She should have known he was vulnerable.

"Yes, sort of," said Conrad, waggling his head eagerly at Nick. "Like, okay, my Student-Teacher-Leader is Andrew, who's this great guy from California. He's been doing it for several years now and is doing really well: he's manifested a huge house and a great car and this incredible wife, Megan, who's a vet and a semi-pro tennis player. He has been working with me to help me select my courses and pick up a few things to help with my physical healing – like, Vanessa, you tried the Vegetable Vibration smoothie and you liked it, didn't you! So as payment the company pays me a small bonus. Like a finder's fee, sort of. The money-making part of your business comes when you in turn start working with other people and helping them with their self-work, you see? Everything they do earns you a bonus from the company!"

"So it's a pyramid scheme," said Max pointedly.

"No, no," said Conrad automatically, "those are illegal. It's a way to make some money doing something you'd be doing anyway: working on yourself and helping others. The money is totally incidental, just a by-product so you can survive in this capitalist society that continues to trade our lives for food and rent."

"How much of a cut do you get?" asked Robert.

"It's not cut," said Conrad. "It's a *bonus*. Everything Student-Teachers invest in themselves goes to themselves and their business."

"If someone gave you, say, five hundred dollars," said Max, doing calculations in her head, "what bonus would you get from the company?"

"Well…" replied Conrad, "it would depend on…"

"If someone gave you five thousand dollars," interjected Nick ominously, "how much of a bonus would you get then?"

Becca nearly threw up. "Five thousand dollars!" she cried, horrified. She had a strong and sudden inclination to strike Conrad across the face, she felt so protective of Nick and so betrayed to have been duped into friendly support of this absurdity.

As Nick sat on the end of the table like an angry, melting snowman, Conrad went on the defensive. "Some new Student-Teachers *do* decide to properly invest in themselves from the get-go by signing up for the full Induction Weekend and Product Sampler Package. They wouldn't have been obligated to do this, at all, ever, but as the saying goes, sometimes you have to spend money to make money."

"You did NOT, Nick," said Becca. "You don't have that kind of money."

"He'll earn it back in a couple months, if not sooner," promised Conrad, "and in the meantime he's signed up for some really interesting online classes on things like – um, Nick, what did we choose…?"

"Positive Psychology," said Nick.

"Positive Psychology!" exclaimed Conrad. "That sounds good, doesn't it, with all the pain and anger our Nick has been carrying with him every day for the last while? Don't you see how emancipating that will be for him? Just imagine what he will be capable of when he manages to free himself of that weight!"

"And how much of a bonus did that earn you?" challenged Becca, baiting him for a fight.

Max had her hand over her mouth. "Who has five thousand dollars to spend on vegetable juice and chanting?"

"Not much, Becca, I swear, and I don't get anything until next month anyway." Conrad was visibly panicking now, his forgotten wapiti in a gelatinous pool of bacon fat on his plate. "All of which I'm totally going to invest in our team business, and I'll be there for him with all the support and encouragement he could ever need for as long as he wants to be a part of ReYOUvenate."

"This is disgusting," said Becca, removing her napkin from her lap and dropping it on her salad bowl dramatically. "You can do whatever you want with your life, Conrad, but don't drag Nick into it."

Nick looked up finally. "He didn't drag me into anything," he said. "I chose this."

"No you didn't," said Becca. "You got conned. You got conned, Nick."

Robert grabbed Vanessa by the elbow and forced her to her feet. "Vanessa, shall we start thinking about the main course?"

"I didn't con anyone," said Conrad.

"What a great idea, Robert," said Vanessa, starting to collect plates. "Becca, I don't suppose you'd be willing to help me out in the kitchen for a few minutes. Only I've got to get the pasta on and –"

"Pasta?" asked Becca sharply. "I told you I'm gluten intolerant, V. Leaky gut. I told you that."

"It's gluten free pasta," Vanessa snapped, "because all I seem to ever do is listen to you talk about what you need and what you want and what you think."

"Vanessa –" said Robert, but she had left the room.

"I didn't con anyone," repeated Conrad.

"More wine?" asked Robert.

2015

Two months after Nick's 43rd birthday, his wife left him.

The previous six months had been rough for the family, starting with Nick getting laid off from his job due to company downsizing.

"It's a tough economic climate right now and the mining companies are getting shy about large equipment purchases. We're seeing it hit our bottom line pretty hard. You understand, right?" explained Nick's line manager, Douglas, after calling him into his office one afternoon to break the news to him.

Nick did not understand. "Is this about my job? Douglas? What are you talking about? Am I being let go?"

"We've had to make some tough choices," said Douglas with genuine remorse. "This isn't easy for me either." He picked up his stapler and fiddled with it, snapping the staple drawer open and closed repeatedly.

Nick stared down at an oily black smudge on the right leg of his trousers and licked his thumb to rub it out. Almost imperceptibly, he had begun to rock in place. He felt physically sick.

Douglas looked chagrined. He put the stapler down and tented his hands on the desktop. "I'm sorry, Nick, genuinely," he said.

"Nineteen years, Douglas. I've been here for nineteen years."

"I know, Nick, and I regret more than anyone that it's had to come to this."

"Isn't there anyone else who started more recently? Wouldn't that make more sense?"

"We've considered this at length, and unfortunately it does make the most sense to trim the fat in the middle-level management."

"Trim the fat?"

"If I'm being honest, you're expensive, Nick. You're good at your job, there's no question about that, but, as a manager, you're expensive and there isn't a lot about your job that we couldn't spread among other people in your team. This savings – and I promise it's not just you being affected by this – will make a huge difference to the future survival of Franklin & Co."

Nick pinched at his mouth with his left hand. "What if I took on more responsibilities for the same pay rate? Would that help?"

"I'm sorry, Nick."

Nick felt as though the walls of the office were closing in on him. "I have a family to support, Douglas."

"There are other jobs out there, Nick. Better ones, even, for a man of your skills."

Nick made a small choking noise. "I have an English degree," he said quietly. "I have an English degree and nineteen years' experience working in a warehouse. In *this* warehouse. What other jobs are out there for me do you think?"

Douglas ran his thumbnail against a minor scratch on the desktop.

"Please," begged Nick. "Douglas, please. Nineteen years, Douglas." He could feel his eyes stinging and stared hard at the ceiling to avoid tears. "Nineteen years."

"I'm sorry, Nick," was all Douglas could say. He put his thumbnail in his mouth and begged the universe for the conversation to be over.

"Is it me?" asked Nick quickly.

"No, no, absolutely not. As I told you, it is simply a question of reducing surplus overhead."

Nick rubbed his hands back and forth across the tops of his thighs until the friction made his palms hot. "Is it because of what happened with Carl? Because that was a misunderstanding, but I apologised and we're okay now. It was just a joke. I don't have any problem with his lifestyle choices. I'm not a bad guy."

Douglas pursed his lips. "I know you're not a bad guy, Nick. You're a great guy." He stared at the phone, willing it to ring and interrupt. "If you'd like to speak with Human Resources, I can set something up for you."

Nick pitched forward in the chair and pressed his fists into his eye sockets with such force that Douglas could see the Nick's eyeballs straining under the pressure. It was so disquieting, he had to avert his gaze. He tried to remember his training on responding to workplace violence in case Nick were to suddenly snap.

Nick was closer to collapse than snapping. He scratched his fingernails hard through his wispy hair, leaving welts on the skin. The pain gave him something to concentrate on other than the wellspring of emotion that he was in absolutely no way capable of managing. His mouth hung open, as if gasping for air.

"Hey," said Douglas, attempting to break the tension. "Hey."

Nick's entire body was trembling. A thin sheen of sweat had broken out across his forehead, and his eyes were wild and unfocused.

"It'll be okay, Nick, I promise," said Douglas softly. "We'll take care of you. You're safe."

Nick's eyes rolled towards Douglas, looking but not quite seeing. Douglas took it as a sign of progress.

"You will get a severance package commensurate with your years of service. Eight weeks I think it is for you, in fact – that will be a nice chunk of change, right? And I will of course give you a glowing reference, and if there's anything I can do to help you find another job then I am there for you."

Buck up, champ, said Douglas's eyes.

Nick grew still. His mouth closed, then his eyes.

"So when's my last day?" he asked bleakly. "From when am I unemployed?"

Douglas shuffled a few of his papers and laid them out in a neat pile in front of him like a protective barrier. "We were thinking at the end of the month," he said in his calmest, most positive manner, "so you can enjoy your severance pay over the summer. That should give you some much-deserved time to play golf, right?"

"I don't golf," said Nick. His skin had gone ashen but the sweat had stopped.

"Whatever it is you like to do then, Nick: garden, take long walks, spend time with your girls, learn to play an instrument. Just enjoy the paid time off. You've earned it."

Nick stood up and slipped his hands into his pockets. "Okay," he said, with his eyes still closed. "Are we done?"

"I think so. Unless you have any further questions?"

"No," said Nick, "I don't have any further questions. Can I go?"

Douglas looked sad. "Yes, Nick, you may go."

Nick turned on his heels like a soldier and slipped out, letting the door slam behind him. Several of his team members looked up as he grabbed his coat from the staff room and walked out of the building just after 2pm on a Monday afternoon but no one spoke – his expression told the entire story. He spent twenty minutes in the cab of his pickup howling and beating the steering wheel with his hands before he could see well enough to drive home.

By the time he got home, the anger had overtaken the initial horror and grief.

"Assholes," he growled over dinner, smacking the roast chicken leg around his plate and sending a baby carrot skidding across the table towards Anna.

Nancy brought him another beer from the fridge, cracking it open and sliding it in front of him in consolation. "Language," she said. "We'll be fine. We have a solid savings account and, with your experience and proof of loyalty –"

"Loyalty, what a load of bullshit."

"*Language.*"

"What a load of *crock* then. Nineteen years I worked for them and this is what I get. Tells you all you need to know about the kind of people they are, choosing profits over people."

"Exactly, who needs them? You'll find something else."

Hayley, 15 and in the early stage of her social activist phase, flapped her fork around happily. "I read that they urgently need people to work with refugees arriving in Canada, helping them get settled and registered with doctors and all that."

"I'm not sure…" said Nick, mindful of the politics of his Facebook feed. He had not accepted Hayley's friend request.

Anna, nearly 10 but still very much a child, lit up with the endless possibilities of Nick's future employment prospect. "Maybe you could go play NHL hockey like you always wanted?" she suggested earnestly.

Nick gazed at her with an aching need to seal her in a box before the world could break her too.

"Now there's an idea!" said Nancy approvingly, scooping up the girls' dinner dishes. "Anyone up for dessert?"

"Me! Me!" cried the girls in unison.

Nick speared a couple green peas on the tines of his fork and imagined they were the tiny popping heads of the senior managers at Franklin & Co.

He didn't try to find something quickly: after serving his final weeks with catatonic negligence, he retreated to the sofa in the family room to binge watch crime documentaries on Netflix. As the days passed, his mood increasingly soured: shock became depression, depression became bitterness. Something inside him that had hung on through the years had been snuffed out: the sense of life having an innate order, a fairness, a balance, a return on investment. He had never begrudged his life until that moment, even if it hadn't unfolded the way he perhaps would have chosen had he been free to truly choose. He had had responsibilities and he had risen to them, and all he had expected in exchange was to be okay in the end. He had had a deal with the universe and the universe had reneged on it.

Before long bitterness changed into emptiness.

At first the girls would join him – more often Anna than Hayley, who was increasingly distracted by the throes of being a teenager – and sometimes all three women, curled up with him and against him, feet tucked under his legs for warmth. For a while he would change the channel to something they all wanted to watch, but as his mood slipped so did his ability to concede anything. Hayley stopped coming first, deciding herself "over it," and then Nancy began making excuses to be busy in another room or elsewhere. Only Anna hung on stoically, putting up with a steady stream of police dramas about brutalised women and children in her unshakeable dedication to supporting her father, and then having nightmares afterwards.

"How about something lighter tomorrow?" attempted Nancy one night as she rocked her sob-wracked daughter back to sleep. "At least when Anna's there?"

Before long Anna stopped coming too.

When the spectre of money problems loomed, Nick got himself a job delivering parcels for Amazon. The days were long and tedious, stopping 150 times a route to drop off overpackaged boxes for people too lazy to go to the mall, but he was accountable to no one. Driving suited him: there was something about the mindless physical labour of it that he enjoyed.

Nancy was both surprised and unconvinced that he got as much out of it as he professed to. "It seems like such a waste of your skills and talents! Wouldn't you rather…?" she said one evening as they got ready for bed but dropped the subject quickly when something dark flickered behind his eyes.

This was the point when she began making plans to leave, unsure of exactly when but no longer if. Nancy had always respected Nick for his uncomplaining commitment to doing what needed to be done, but she could not shake the sense that, in allowing him to sell out his soul, she was putting her own at risk. As she covertly collected clothing, jewellery, and photos into suitcases hidden in the closet in the guest room, she watched and waited for a moment in which he seemed strong enough to not be finished off entirely by her decision.

That moment came one morning while eating breakfast with the news on in the background. After six months of gloom and rage, Nick seemed almost happy.

"That Nobel Prize woman won the election in Burma," he said brightly.

"Myanmar."

Nick munched contentedly on his Shreddies, eyes glued to the screen. Nancy fumbled with seam on her dress for several seconds before sitting down beside him.

"Can we talk?" she said softly.

"Sure, babe," he said, clicking the remote to mute the television and turning to face her. A tendril of milk leaked from the corner of his mouth as he chewed. "What's up?"

Nancy studied his face. He had grown old without her noticing. There were deep creases around his mouth and lacing across his forehead, and his hair was going grey.

"It's been a tough year for all of us, and I've been thinking..."

Nick's eyes unconsciously flicked back between the television screen and her. He was only half listening, she realised.

"I was thinking it might be best if I... went to stay somewhere else for a while," she managed, every word agony. "Give you some space."

The penny dropped. If a great fiery chasm could have cracked upon the kitchen floor beneath the feet of his chair, he would have happily thrown himself to his certain death. All he could hear was the delicate clacks of his breakfast cereal settling into the milk.

He turned back to the television and clicked on the volume.

"Nick?" asked Nancy. She tried to touch his arm but he jerked it away and crammed a large spoonful of cereal into his mouth.

"I know you feel it too, Nick. Between us, I mean. It's not working anymore."

"If you say so."

"It's been tense for such a long time, Nick, and I don't want the girls to grow up in a house where the parents hate each other."

Nick stopped chewing. "I don't hate you though," he said, without a touch of warmth.

"And I don't hate you, Nick. But we'll get there if we keep going like this, you know we will."

"Sure, okay," said Nick with the tiniest of shrugs.

"Yeah?"

"When are you leaving?"

Pain.

"I thought... maybe... right away. To keep it clean and make it easier on everyone."

"And you'll take the girls, I assume."

"I thought that would make the most sense, given your job demands. You can see them of course, as much as you want. We can work out a schedule for holidays and summers. You're a great dad and they need you."

The weather was up next: light rain, chance of fog. Nick listened impassively.

"What's his name?" he said finally.

"I'm sorry?"

"The new guy. What's his name?"

"Nick," stammered Nancy. "I don't think…"

"Well, I hope he makes you happier than I did. I trust he'll pay out your half of the remaining mortgage?"

"I… We can work all of that out, Nick. We can sell the house, or I can give you my half of the value or whatever it is you prefer."

"And of course you'll want alimony."

"I mean, we can talk about child support or whatever, depending on how much time the girls spend with each of us, but I'm not expecting…" Desperate, she grabbed the remote and clicked off the television. "Nick, look at me."

"Why bother?" said Nick, tilting his head towards her with a violent expression. "You've made up your mind. My opinion and needs are, as usual, totally irrelevant."

Nancy felt a small tingle of fear in her abdomen.

"Nick," she pleaded. "It's for the best, I promise."

"I have to go to work," stated Nick, leaving his breakfast half-eaten and walking stonily out of the room. As he disappeared upstairs, she heard him punch something – the wall, by the sounds of it – and curse. Nancy put her head in arms and started to cry.

Four months later, the papers were signed and it was all over.

2022

Nick followed Vanessa into the kitchen and watched her throw the first course dishes into the sink with such force that he was surprised any survived the impact.

"Can I help?" he offered, nudging her away with his hip and starting to put them into the dishwasher.

She slammed two pots of water onto the stove to boil and, catching him looking, explained that one was for the gluten-free pasta. "Because it's disgusting and the rest of us shouldn't be forced to eat it, but Becca's apparently got a leaky gut now."

Vanessa set about sautéing shallots, pushing them around the skillet as though they were being disciplined for bad behaviour. Nick watched her for a few moments.

"I'm going to be fine," he said.

"I'm not worried about you," replied Vanessa, carelessly dumping in cream and lemon zest and stirring viciously. "I'm just so sick of her."

"Who?" asked Nick, genuinely confused. "Becca?"

"Yeah," said Vanessa. "This dinner is supposed to be about Conrad and like usual she's making it all about her."

"I think she's concerned…"

"She's concerned about herself, is what she's concerned about."

Nick stood awkwardly by the now-empty kitchen sink. "I mean, she can't help it if she's gluten intolerant I guess?"

"This isn't about the goddamned pasta, Nick," scowled Becca. "Pretending she's all worried about you, getting all involved with your business as if she has any right to say anything about anything. Making sure everyone at the table is looking at her, listening to her, paying attention to her. And that… Max."

171

"What has Max done?"

"Nothing! Just being there!" said Vanessa, scattering dry gluten-free pasta shapes across the counter and stove top as she carelessly dumped the contents of the box into the boiling water. The regular pasta received only marginally gentler treatment. "Becca's always been like this and we always put up with it. Oh I'm an actor! Oh I'm a lawyer! Oh I'm a vegan! Oh now I'm a lesbian! How very on trend of her!"

"That's not really fair, V," asserted Nick, inefficiently collecting dried pasta from the floor around Vanessa's feet. "They've been together for years now."

"So she's committed to the bit," said Vanessa, "it's still a phase. Organic vegan lesbian anti-vaxxers who spend their lives in the gym and the salon – she's an Instagram cliché and I don't buy it."

Nick stood up and stared at Vanessa through squinted eyes. "Fine for you to judge," he replied, "with your fancy job and your fancy house."

Vanessa stared at him, eyes huge, sauté paddle dripping great globs of white sauce down her hand and onto the floor. "Excuse me?"

"Who's the problem, Vanessa? You sit here in in your four bedroom –"

"Three!"

"Five, three-bedroom house, just you and Robert, all this space and SO MUCH STUFF."

Behind her, the fiddleheads started to boil over. Neither noticed.

Vanessa's voice dropped low and throaty, almost a growl: "You know why we have all the bedrooms."

"Boo hoo," said Nick, "get a dog then."

Nick could see and feel the words buzzing in the space between them.

"Get out," hissed Vanessa.

"And ruin your perfect dinner? Whatever would the others think?"

He could see Vanessa's wheels turning, the options being weighed: ruin the dinner party or spend the rest of the evening playing nice. Her face read alarm and incandescent rage.

"Get out of my kitchen," she decided. "Tonight's about Conrad."

"Of course it is," he agreed with a smirk. As he left the kitchen, he could hear her taking out her emotions on the smoked salmon.

"Everyone," he said calmly on re-entering the dining room, "the main course will be a few minutes yet."

Robert looked concerned. "Does she need any help?" he asked reluctantly.

"She's fine," said Nick. "All under control."

Robert sunk back in his chair and resumed drinking, visibly relieved. "Conrad was just starting to tell us about the time he joined a cattle drive in Wyoming. *Very* interesting stuff."

Nick took his seat.

"Couldn't even ride a horse when I started," laughed Conrad, "but I sure could by the end of the week, let me tell you! Those long days in the saddle, crossing the land, eating over a campfire, sleeping in our long johns because of how cold it got at night. Really life-changing, paradigm-shifting stuff. So, one morning before the sun had even come up, I'm woken up by Darren – that was one of the ranchers – shouting for help. I grab my boots and head out to see what the commotion was all about, thinking maybe it's a wolf or something, but it turned out one of the cows was in labour but in really serious difficulty. Darren asked me if I had any experience with cows and I said no –"

"Only goats," quipped Becca with a snarl.

"I said no, but told him I was ready to help as I could. And oh my god you guys, I won't give you the details as we're about to eat but let me tell you, I will never forget watching the sunrise, covered in that cow's sacred life liquids, cradling her new-born calf in my arms. In a way, we were both born that day."

"Wait, why was there a pregnant cow on a cattle drive?" said Max. "Seems high risk."

Conrad blanched. "I mean, we were on a ranch…"

"So it wasn't a drive, then."

"I mean, not like a long one, but we did drive them," he admitted, looking cross. "Have you ever done anything like that?"

"No," replied Max, "I've mostly focused on building a life and career."

"Burn," said Robert while refilling his wine glass, his cheeks pink.

"And I've mostly focused on ensuring my life has some meaning beyond materialistic trappings," said Conrad.

Robert slapped the table with his hand happily and took a swig of wine.

"Max isn't materialistic," said Becca. Max gripped her hand and kissed it.

"Oh yeah?" said Conrad. "What are you driving now, Maxine?"

"None of your business and it's Max," replied Max.

"Gotta' have the right car, Max," said Conrad, "otherwise how else will you know you've made it in life?"

"I drive a Toyota," offered Robert, wanting to be a part of the game.

Vanessa appeared in the doorway with the rigid mouth of a manager about to give critical feedback on a team member. "Are we ready for the next course?" she said with steel-boned sunniness.

The pappardelle was brought out in grand style and laid lavishly in front of her guests.

"This looks delicious!" said Robert with enthusiasm absent in the rest of the guests.

"Pappardelle – or gluten-free shapes – in lemon cream sauce with fiddleheads, and, for the less picky among us, smoked salmon," said Vanessa, her hand on Conrad's shoulder. "Black pepper in the grinder if you want it, and salt is in the little pots with the spoons."

"We're not picky," sniffed Becca, "we simply love animals too much to torture them for our consumption."

"It's just fish, Becca," said Vanessa.

"You'll find 'just' fish have complex social structures and emotions actually," said Max.

"Is this cream-cream?" asked Becca, sniffing her plate suspiciously. "Only that's very hard on the arteries."

"Do a hundred extra squats tomorrow at the gym then," chirped Conrad.

"Vanessa, stop," said Nick.

Vanessa smiled wanly and sat down. "Bon appétit," she said.

"This *is* delicious," said Robert, coiling an impressive spool of pasta onto his fork and attempting to force the lot into his open mouth.

Vanessa turned back to Conrad. "So Conrad, your epiphany…"

"I don't want to talk about it anymore," said Nick.

"Well," said Vanessa diplomatically, "technically we're talking about Conrad, Nick."

"But we're not," said Nick. "You'll all pretend you're talking about Conrad, but everything he says you're all gonna' be thinking, 'I can't believe stupid old Nick has fallen for this.'"

"You're being selfish," said Vanessa.

"She" – he waggled a thumb in Becca's general direction – "is one step away from calling in Social Services, she's so convinced I've lost it completely."

"It's an opportunity!" bleated Conrad. "A life opportunity!"

"An opportunity to lose money," said Becca. "Max researched it."

"97% of people in pyramid schemes lose money," said Max.

Conrad's knuckles were white around his utensils, pasta dangling impotently from his fork. "It's not a pyramid scheme!" he repeated at some volume.

"It absolutely is," said Becca. "You just don't want to admit it now that you've roped your friend into it too."

"I mean," said Vanessa, the spite rising, "you have to admit that it does seem like a pyramid scheme, Conrad. You're making money when you get other people to sign up as your downline. That's literally the definition of a pyramid scheme."

Everyone around the table nodded, Nick included.

"And I knew what I was getting into," said Nick. "I'm tired of living according to everyone else's rules: I've tried that and look where it got me.

Look at my life! My kids hate me, my job is meaningless, my life sucks, so I coughed up some money to have an experience, maybe learn something. How much worse could it get?"

A chorus of coos, except for Conrad who sat gape-mouthed and incredulous. "You think this is a joke too?"

"Better a joke than a materialistic cliché," muttered Vanessa angrily.

"Was that supposed to be about me?" snapped Becca.

"At least I'm trying," flung Conrad. "Isn't that what you've all wanted from me this whole time? For me to settle down and commit to something? Well I'm doing that now, no thanks to any of you who never support me, ever."

"And just how are we supposed to support you, Conrad?" sputtered Vanessa, "when all you've ever done is seek adrenaline hits like a crackhead?"

"Which is so different from you and your ever-changing career path, is it?" hurled Becca. "You're so busy changing jobs to distract the world from realising that you're even more of a slacker than Conrad is!"

"Hey!" slurred Robert with some merriment, "my wife is not a slacker! She works very hard and she worked very hard on this dinner and I think we should all calm down and enjoy it."

"Sorry," said Nick.

"Yeah," said Becca.

"Thank you, honey," said Vanessa with an acidic scowl at Becca.

A truce, without a white flag. Silver tines clinked against bone china, wine burbled as it was poured into glasses, noodles caused inadvertently hilarious slurping noises that went some way to taking the edge off the negative energy in the room.

Conrad polished off his plate, wiping the last of the cream sauce out with a crust of bread, and wiped his mouth with his napkin. "That was actually really delicious, Vanessa," he offered as a proverbial olive branch.

"Thank you, Conrad," replied Vanessa, peripherally in his general direction.

"Really," he said, rubbing her forearm, "thank you for doing all this for me."

She placed her hand over his and held it there. "Thank you for taking the time to acknowledge that. It means so very much to me."

They clasped hands and gazed tenderly at each other, on the verge of an apology.

They could have stopped there, and it would likely have been a perfectly nice rest of the evening.

So close.

"It's really interesting," observed Max, "You two sure touch each other a lot. Way more than you touch Robert. Anyone who didn't know you might think you two were the couple."

Robert and Conrad both froze as the headlights of conversation came bearing down upon them. Vanessa, pure panic ripping across her face, stared at her husband.

"Uh oh," said Nick with a hint of a smirk.

"They dated," whispered Becca to Max.

"But you knew that, Robert!" said Vanessa with dread.

"And it was a long time ago!" added Conrad.

"A very long time ago!" said Vanessa, reaching out towards her husband.

Robert slowly rose to his feet.

"Honey?" asked Vanessa with concern.

"Robert?" echoed Conrad.

Robert stood, unmoving, swaying slightly from all the wine he had consumed, as if caught in a breeze.

"Super interesting dynamics," finished Max. "It doesn't feel entirely over, does it? That must be weird for Robert."

Robert calmly and coolly picked up his dinner plate and the remnants of his pasta and threw it across the room. It shattered against the wall, a few noodles sticking to the wallpaper and one ending up draped elegantly over a lampshade.

Vanessa exploded. "THAT WAS OUR WEDDING CHINA, ROBERT!" she hollered. "DO YOU KNOW HOW EXPENSIVE THAT WAS?"

Robert looked evenly at Vanessa and threw his bread plate as well, the half-eaten bit of bread clipping Max as it flew across the room.

"Fuck the china," he said.

"ROBERT!" screamed Vanessa. "STOP!"

Robert reached for his wine glass but Vanessa lunged to wrestle it from his grasp. There was a physical altercation, Vanessa shouting mostly unintelligible things as she tried to climb Robert's arm – he was too tall for her to reach for it – to save her crystal wine glass.

"God damn it, Robert, don't you fucking dare!" she yelled.

Another plate shattered against the wall, from elsewhere in the room.

"NICK!" screamed Vanessa. Nick's face was bold and challenging. His fingers itched to throw another.

Max went to stand up with her plate but was stopped by Becca, who was otherwise clearly enjoying herself.

"Have you gone insane?!" shrieked Vanessa, prying the wine glass from Robert's hand and stepping further than arm's reach away from him. "How could you –"

"Enough," thundered Robert directly to Vanessa.

The room fell silent.

"Enough," he said to everyone.

All eyes were on Robert.

"You –" he said to Conrad, "grow up and get a real job."

"You –" he said to Nick, "take some responsibility for your life choices and stop expecting the world to hand things to you."

"You –" he said to Becca and Max, "stop thinking you're better than everyone else because you're so 'woke'; you're just arrogant and pretentious."

"And you –" he said, turning to Vanessa, "my wife and my best friend, my heart and my soul, if you're going to fuck Conrad, please just fucking do it already."

The room exploded in chaos and noise. Becca shouted at Nick, who was shouting at Conrad, who was shouting at Robert, who was shouting at Vanessa. Max was pulling at Becca, holding her back by a fistful of hair. Someone was being a total bitch; someone else needed to go fuck themselves. Food flew: Robert's cheek was streaked with lemon cream sauce, smoked salmon oozed off the edge of the table and onto the floor, bread rolls became buttery projectiles. Somehow the centrepiece ended up ripped into three parts, scattering tiny Canadian flags and daisy petals everywhere. If more plates met their doom, it would have been impossible to hear over the cacophony.

And then the doorbell rang.

"I'll get it," said Robert with oddly marked composure as he exited the room.

The five guests remained where they stood, the fight on pause: trembling with adrenaline, fingers high in judgement interrupted, straining futilely to hear who might be at the door.

Robert returned. "That was the police," he said, with the stoic timbre of an overstretched schoolteacher. "The neighbours called in a noise complaint. We are to keep it down."

The entire room exhaled.

"I'm going to go work on my book," said Robert, walking soundlessly out of the room and upstairs. Everyone watched him go without moving.

Vanessa straightened her back. "It will have been the Richardsons across the street," she surmised.

"They've always had it out for you," said Becca, meekly collecting the shattered remains of the dishes from the floor.

"Always," said Vanessa, going to get a cloth from the kitchen to wipe sauce from the wall.

"I remember them from the mail fiasco," reflected Nick, peeling pasta from the lampshade.

"They're probably just jealous," decided Max, neatly stacking the surviving dishware and cutlery. "You have such a beautiful house."

"Oh totally," agreed Becca, trying to make as little noise as possible as she dropped shards of dishes onto an empty plate. "Just jealous."

"I guess dessert is off, hey?" asked Conrad, still sitting in his chair, dazed.

2016

When she was 40, Becca met the love of her life.

While a raging success in so very many aspects of her life, when it came to romance Becca's friends worried about her: her entanglements were few and far between, and in the in-betweens Becca didn't seem particularly bothered to fill the role.

There had been Bradley, the painter from Nunavut, who breezed into Vancouver one summer to see if he could handle the big city. Becca showed him the sights like a tour guide and the perks like a real estate agent, but within a month Bradley was mournfully painting scenes of arctic solitude and complaining that he was feeling compressed. Conrad felt the loss more than Becca when Bradley eventually gave in and returned north, having found in him a brother of sorts.

Keith the accountant had stuck around longer – over a year – but Becca's friends despised him. He was brilliant but patronising, used long and complicated words when simpler ones would have sufficed, and got a kick out of provoking them for the pleasure of watching them rise to it. He was rakishly handsome and knew it, and it was this quality, and only this quality, that Becca saw in him. That relationship fizzled out when the three friends grew bored of his drama and stopped responding; Keith moved on with little fanfare.

George the actor was a particular favourite of Vanessa's, and by far Becca's longest relationship. He held his alcohol better than the rest of them combined and was a shameless entertainer, frequently ending evenings with impromptu late-night sidewalk concerts of Frank Sinatra classics. He and Becca had a jovial if competitive relationship: Becca confessed to Nick over cocktails one night that she struggled to hear him talk about his career

179

despite being quite at peace with her decision to leave the industry generally. Her parents, on the other hand, absolutely loved him and were despondent when he decided to move to the United States to pursue his dreams of true stardom. "Are you sure you don't want to follow?" they asked her, knowing the answer already. George and Becca attempted long distance but, after 10 months in the gentle decline of life minutiae no longer shared and 28 months dating in total, they called it quits.

In between those were the odd snippet: a date here and there, a romantic tryst, a fling on a beach while on holiday. It annoyed her friends immensely that this seemed to be enough for Becca.

"Don't you want what me and Robert have, though?" asked Vanessa one evening over dinner at the couple's house. Robert beamed like a child getting his school picture taken.

"I do," Becca admitted, "but it doesn't happen for everyone and I'm okay with that."

"What do you think the problem is?" asked Conrad, while the two waited in the queue for popcorn before the latest *Lord of the Rings* movie.

"There's no problem," replied Becca, "it's just not the most important thing in my life."

"What if you end up old and alone?" asked Nick, watching the server place down their Denny's breakfast skillets gingerly and warning them not to touch the very hot plates. "Aren't you afraid of that?"

"Not the greatest reason to be in a relationship though, is it?" replied Becca, smothering her potatoes in hot sauce. "And who's to say it would last that long anyway? Anything could happen: divorce, a heart attack, the sudden appearance of a twenty-something Brazilian supermodel with a penchant for middle-aged Canadians."

"Be careful," warned her mother lovingly while folding laundry during a visit, "a woman's beauty only lasts so long. That's why your father left."

"Your problem, peanut," said her father over the phone, "is that men still fundamentally want to marry down, and there aren't very many men above you."

"You guys are all lovely," she would say, "but I'm okay, really. I have a full life the way it is. I don't need a relationship to be complete."

In actuality, Becca yearned for it, ached for it, on a handful of occasions even took to her knees before bed and prayed to a god she didn't believe in just in case it might help make it happen. She witnessed her encroaching spinsterhood with a growing dread that, despite all her successes, she had failed in this most important and simple of all things – to be loved by another person -- and that this failure was down to her own blatant, inherent unlovability. Unwilling to risk repeating 2002's Great Unravelling by addressing that, however, she simply pushed the act of dating out of the

Top Ten of her life priorities and got on with the rest of her life. "Men have pornography," she would repeat to herself as a mantra whenever the pangs started up, "and women have Hollywood."

The acquisition of Maxine ("Max, please") to her life was therefore a complete shock, as much because Max was a woman as that she was there in the first place.

There was no bolt of lightning, no shuddering of the earth, no illumination of the Empire State Building, literal or proverbial, when Max hired Shacklady & Hatcher LLC to review the contract paperwork for a potential partnership with a major hotel chain to sell her organic, soy-based, eco-friendly scented candles. Nor in truth was there anything seismic for Max either, beyond noting that the assigned associate and the articling student were both very attractive women. In fact, until their final meeting, there had been nary an unprofessional thought on anyone's part.

"I've been in touch with the hotel." Max jiggled in her leather chair in the firm's stoically opulent meeting room.

"And...?"

"They've accepted the terms in principle."

"Oh gosh," cried Becca, "that's fantastic!"

"They said they didn't have a single thing they were concerned about or wanted to push back on."

"And they were okay with shaving down the non-competition clause?" asked Becca, checking her notes.

"Entirely!"

"And the maintenance of minimum inventory SLA in the exit clause?" confirmed Becca, ticking off something and crossing out something else.

"Totally happy," gushed an ebullient Max. "Thank you so much for your suggestions and wording. You're very good at this."

"Aww," said Becca, clapping her hands together, "isn't that tremendous news! I'm delighted to hear it." She instructed the mousy-haired articling student who sat typing furiously on her laptop on the other side of the table to go print out the most recent draft of the contract for final review.

"Of course," said the student, pushing her glasses up her nose with her index finger.

Becca turned back to Max. "I'll run this past senior counsel to see if they have any final comments, of course, but I think we're pretty much ready for signing." She raised her water glass: "Congratulations, Max. You did it."

Something about the way Becca was looking at her caused Max to suddenly come over shy. "I couldn't have done this without you," she said.

"I'm just the nerd making sure all the paperwork is in order. You're the artisan."

There was a sudden and heavy weight in the air. Their eyes met and lingered, until Becca dropped her head and vigorously began a final once-over of her notes. She made a point of rustling papers for several minutes until the student returned with the printed contract.

"Great," said Becca with relief, "thanks Joan."

"Fantastic," purred Max. She touched her lips unconsciously, then realised she had and, with embarrassment, sat on her hands.

"I'll have the finalised version over to you by close of business Friday, and then we can get this baby signed!" said Becca, protectively patting the stack of paper.

The two women stood up and collected their papers, making the usual small talk: Nice weather out there. Is that your bag? Where shall I leave my coffee cup? I might steal a couple cookies for the road. Of course, of course.

Becca conspicuously tucked a blonde curl behind her ear.

"It's been a real pleasure working with you, Max," she said as they headed towards the front door of the firm and extended her hand, "and congratulations again on this incredible opportunity for your business. I am sure this is only the start for you."

Max took Becca's hand in hers. It was warm and soft. "I hope it is too," she said with a squeeze.

Just as she was about to leave, she paused and turned back. "This might not be entirely appropriate but I'm attending an event for artisanal SMEs in a couple weeks that might be of interest to your firm. Might be a good opportunity to network with potential clients, if you have any interest in expanding your business negotiation side of things."

"Sounds interesting," said Becca, noticing the glimmer in Max's eyes with a tickle in her stomach. "Email me the details?"

"Will do," said Max. "I hope to see you there."

Becca glanced over at the firm's two receptionists, who both pretended to be busily inspecting something terribly important and complicated on their respective computer screens.

Oh my god, said Conrad via Facebook Messenger the next day, *That is so totally a date.*

It's a networking event, that's all.

It's a date.

It had better not be. She's my client.

Do you want it to be a date?

She is my client.

Are you attracted to her?

SHE IS MY CLIENT.

And are you attracted to your client?

When he sent her a gif of a child in a tutu pelvic thrusting, Becca stopped replying.

Of course it wasn't a date, Becca reassured herself, as that would be unethical. She would probably have to report herself to the Law Society of British Columbia if she dated a client. She would definitely never make partner if she started dating clients. It could be the end of her entire law career, only four years in, which would be the end of absolutely everything she had worked for and she would have to go back to cheesy jukebox musicals and tv residuals.

So, no, this wasn't a date, it was just a networking event suggested by a client.

And, besides, Max was a woman.

Becca spent the remainder of the work week with a stomach ache that she attributed to excessive consumption of Diet Coke and coffee. She attributed the effort to polish herself up to her dazzling best on the night of the networking event to her commitment to bringing in more clients to the firm. She attributed her nerves to her relative inexperience networking as a practising lawyer.

The event was being held at the Fairmont Hotel Vancouver. Max met Becca in the lobby, wearing a smart fitted black suit, unbuttoned, with a white bandeau top underneath that showed off her taut stomach. Her short dark hair was gelled and combed strenuously back, and her eyes heavily outlined in kohl. She smelled of musk.

"I'm a lesbian cliché," she said, holding out her arms.

"You look very chic," Becca told Max, kissing the other woman on the cheek politely. This is a professional relationship, she reminded herself.

Max waved her hand at the chaos in the ballroom behind her. "They're just getting set up in there. Do you want to grab a drink in the hotel bar or something?"

Flutter. "I mean, don't let me interrupt you if you have work to do," hastened Becca.

"My assistant has it covered," replied Max with an alluring smile. "Let's get that drink."

Over beer (Max) and vodka and Diet Coke (Becca), Max confessed that the entire invitation had been an obvious ploy. "You're my lawyer," she said, "so I'm not sure if it's allowed. Figured I'd make up some cover story in case your boss got wind of it."

"It?" asked Becca, knowing exactly what Max meant.

"You know, asking you out. But I couldn't leave the firm thinking that might be the last time I saw you."

"Oh," said Becca.

"Is it okay?"

"What?"

"This," said Max. "Us," said Max.

"The thing is…" said Becca in a rush. "I'm not actually… I'm not…"

"Gay?"

"Exactly."

Max let out a high giggle that was more Disney princess than androgynous artiste. "And yet you're here."

"And yet I'm here."

"I'm glad."

"Me too," said Becca, meaning it.

Becca collected a grand total of two business cards from the event. As soon as Max's Uber pulled away from the curb, Becca received a text: *Let's do that again xox*

"Becca's a lesbian?" said Nick, after hearing about Max from Vanessa. "I knew it!"

"I had wondered…," said Vanessa. "God, I hope she wasn't pretending to be straight for us!"

Becca was not. In fact, until that first drink with Max, and in the absence of any evidence that she wasn't attracted to men, she would have said unequivocally that she was straight. And yet nothing had changed in her that she was aware.

"Penises are super gross, right?" giggled Vanessa.

Becca shrugged: not really? I mean, they're okay.

"Can I watch sometime?" asked Nick.

Ugh, Nick.

Only Conrad seemed to understand.

> *I told you it was a date.*
>
> > *You were right.*
> > *So what does this mean?*
>
> *Mean? Mean how?*

Am I gay now?
Shouldn't I know? If I'm gay, I mean
Isn't it something you just know?

Why get wrapped up with labels, Becs? You're
a woman who has fallen in love with another
woman. It doesn't have to be more than that.

And boy had she. Becca loved everything about Max: the way she stretched and yawned in bed in the morning like a cat, the facial expressions she made during the emotional journey of reading the newspaper, the knack she had with potatoes and eggs. Becca loved the softness of Max's belly and the scent of her skin, and how they were able to communicate without the haunted socialisation of 'rules.' More than anything, Becca loved how entirely calm and centered she felt around Max. Max's confidence seeped through Becca's skin until she started to truly believe in the person Max saw in her; Becca's vulnerabilities and self-awareness polished Max's sometimes-aggressive bravado to a warm sheen.

Eight months after their first date, curled up together on the sofa to watch *Justice League*, Becca turned to Max.

"I really love you."

"It's mutual, babe."

"Let's get married."

"Okay."

"Yes?" asked Becca.

"Yes!" said Max with a grin. She rummaged around in the satchel she used for work and brought out a small box. "I've been ready for a while."

"My parents still think you're my housemate, Max."

"I bet they don't," said Max, wrapping Becca in her arms and planting a big kiss on the top of her head.

Becca's parents did not.

2022

The speed in which the five remaining adults cleared up from dinner was impressive, aided by the total lack of effort made towards socialisation to distract anyone. Each moved in a zombie-like trance, lost in their own thoughts and silenced by shock.

Conrad and Max passed silently between the living room and the kitchen, piling whole and shattered dinnerware on the counter. The decorations and assorted non-dish accoutrements were placed carefully on the kitchen table, organised by Max into neat, rigid rows as if preparing them for labelling and archiving.

Vanessa, up to her elbows in pink rubber gloves decorated with whimsical corgis in tutus, stared dully out the window while running each dish through the hot and soapy water in the right sink and placing it in the empty left sink. Becca was on her third tea towel already – the first two damp and piled on the side for laundering – rinsing and drying the dishes and putting them away. Those items for which she didn't know the homes she diligently stacked in a small pile in the corner.

Over in the living room, Nick was on his knees scrubbing creamy pasta sauce off the walls and furniture with a sponge that smelled faintly of mildew.

Conrad finished first. At a loss, he stood in the doorway to the kitchen with his hands in his pockets and his face distorted with emotional need. He watched the others complete their chores in slow motion, as though the very act of movement was painful. He wanted to grab his coat and run but everything he owned was scattered all over the guest room upstairs and he didn't have anywhere else to go. He wanted to make them understand that they were wrong about everything, but he didn't want to face the likely outcome. He wanted to make it all go away but had no idea what to try.

"Shall I start laying out the dessert?" he said.

Vanessa, in the act of rinsing the soap bubbles out of the sink, let go of the lever to stop the stream of water but did not answer. Her shoulders were tight, her neck straight and stiff. Her mouth was filled with the bitter taste of embarrassment and bile, so she placed both hands flat on the edge of the counter and fixed her eyes on the bird feeder hanging from the fence. She made a mental note to buy more fat balls for it the next time she was at the big grocery store.

Becca watched her carefully while wiping off a cleaned pot lid. "The plates are in the cupboard on the right, Conrad," she said directly to Vanessa.

Conrad watched Vanessa for a signal that did not come.

Nick appeared in the doorway behind Conrad. He held the sponge and the bowl of dirty water up like a poor offering, and said brightly, "Where should I put these?"

Becca placed her hand over Vanessa's and let it rest there, damp and soft from drying dishes. When she felt Vanessa resist and start to scrunch her hand into a fist, she interlocked their fingers and squeezed.

"Pah," said Nick, pushing past Conrad and dropping the bowl with an unselfconscious thud on the counter beside Vanessa. "There might be a stain on the lampshade," he said. "I did my best to scrub it out but I won't know if it worked until it dries."

"Thanks," whispered Vanessa.

Glowering expressions in every corner, guilt and shame and anger and hurt. Max watching Becca's hand on Vanessa's, poised for war. Conrad clutching onto the doorframe as though he could no longer stand without assistance. Vanessa visibly quivering.

Nick looked around and frowned. "Really?" he said incredulously.

Still staring at the bird feeder, Vanessa's bottom lip began to quiver. "I really needed tonight to go well," she admitted, "and it hasn't."

"Oh honey," shushed Becca, leading a droopy Vanessa by the hand over to the kitchen table and pressing her into one of the chairs, "but that wasn't your fault." She sat down in another chair and gathered up Vanessa's hand, leaning in like a parent consoling their child. "You did so well. The food was amazing."

Vanessa gave a hollow chuckle. "Even your salad?"

Becca glanced over at Max for help, who jumped in with, "Okay, the salad maybe wasn't the fanciest, but the pasta was absolutely delicious!" and took a third chair.

"And the table looked amazing," said Becca, beckoning to Conrad with the slightest cock of her head. "Don't you think, Conrad?"

"Sure," said Conrad immediately, still unhappy. "The table looked great. I loved the flowers. The little goat. Ha. Funny."

"I'm sorry I didn't do something vegetarian for you, Becs, Max..." sniffed Vanessa miserably

"Pssh," said Max, watching Becca carefully and following her direction, "we're used to it."

"I should have tried harder."

"Why should you have to change everything for two people?" added Becca. "Really, you did so well. I'm really proud of you – not just tonight but always. You do so much for us. I'm grateful you're in my life."

"You're such a good friend to everyone," said Max.

Vanessa peeked up with a snotty nose and a warped smile. "I'm glad you're here, Becs. You're important to me. You too, Max. You're like my sisters."

The women bowed their heads and held each other's hands and said "aww" and "babe" and "I love you" over and over and over.

"Great," said Nick, tipping the dirty water from the bowl into the sink, "are we done now? I'd like dessert."

Becca looked aghast, drifting to her feet with her hands held out towards him in supplication. "Nick... back there... what I said..."

"Don't worry about it," replied Nick, putting the bowl into the dishwasher and the sponge in the garbage.

Just as she had with Vanessa, Becca collected Nick and led him over to the kitchen table. "I'm fine, really I am," he kept protesting.

"I didn't mean to imply you were stupid or anything like that," explained Becca with chagrin. "With everything you've been through, I don't want anyone to take advantage of your sweet, trusting nature."

Nick picked at the seam of the table with his fingernail. "I think it just felt nice to be making a decision for once," he admitted. "I sometimes feel like the world has made all the big decisions for me."

"So unfair," said Max, "so unfair."

Vanessa touched his shoulder protectively. "You do what you need to do, Nick. This is your life and we should support you better."

Nick grinned sheepishly. This made Vanessa grin, which made Becca grin.

"Forks or spoons for dessert?" asked Max, leaping into action.

"Knives, actually, and some teaspoons," said Vanessa, standing up to unwrap the piled cheeses in front of her. "Becca, could you pass me a couple large platters? Nick, the chutney is in the fridge - it's already in its serving bowls."

The friends busied about laying out the cheeses and chutney, clucking and fussing and drawing whimsical geometric shapes on the platters with crackers. Every so often one would pause to touch or caress another, make meaningful eye contact and share a moment of affection. "I'm grateful for you," one would gush; "And I am grateful for you," the other would reply. Even Nick got into the spirit, at one point coming up on Vanessa from behind and giving her a firm yet authentic hug which she sank into, hands on his folded arms and eyes closed, humming softly.

"Shall we eat in the sitting room?" asked Max, lofting one of the platters.

"Good idea," said Vanessa, wary of the recent ghosts in the dining room, then, "Wait, where's Conrad?"

Nick and Becca looked around with surprise, having both assumed Conrad had been among them all along. He wasn't in the sitting room either when they went to lay down the platters and dessert wine, nor was he in the dining room, Max confirmed after checking.

"You guys start," said Vanessa. "I should go check on Robert anyway."

She filled two glasses with sweet wine and tiptoed up the stairs. The guest room door was open and she could just make out Conrad sitting in the wing chair in the nook, his curls silhouetted by the streetlights through the window. The air was so still she could hear her own breathing: fast from trepidation mixed with climbing the stairs. He made no sign of having heard her. She had one hand up to rap on the door frame when he spoke.

"You were right," he said, quietly. "I know you said it might happen, but I thought they might understand."

"Sorry?" she said in a whisper.

"Anyway, I'm leaving tonight. I'm not putting myself through this, not when it's so important. I won't make a big deal out of it. I'll tell Vanessa and Robert that something urgent has come up and you need me down there or something."

Vanessa could make out the faint glow of the mobile phone now. His back was to her.

"Thanks Andrew, I knew you'd get it."

His suitcase was open on the bed, already with a small pile of folded clothes inside. Several pairs of shoes were soles down on her duvet cover.

"Yeah, I'm sorry too. Yeah, I'm still sure. I'll call you tomorrow."

Vanessa set the glass of dessert wine down on the carpet, positioned in the precise middle of the open doorframe, and stepped silently away. She felt sick, panicked, wracked with guilt, yet also somehow relieved.

Where she would have expected whirling thoughts, she could only think of one thing: Robert.

She knocked on the master bedroom door and waited to be called in. "I thought you might want some dessert wine," she said shyly, holding up the glass. "Conrad's packing to leave as we speak."

"You okay?"

Vanessa took a large sip of his wine. "I'm great," she said. "I knew I would throw one hell of a dinner party."

Robert rolled from the bed, scattering papers everywhere, and pulled her into an embrace, one hand on her back and the other in her hair, their heads pressed against each other's, both smiling.

2017

Just after Vanessa turned 41, she did not get pregnant for the third time.

Prior to meeting Robert, having children had not been a priority for her. She had enjoyed watching Nick's stepdaughter Hayley grow from a shrieking toddler to a self-composed miniature adult from a distance and, admittedly, the arrival of tiny Anna in 2006 did cause the odd twinge of maternal longing, but mostly she was focused on what she was going to do next week, next month, next year.

"Besides," she mused to Becca over lunch one afternoon, "women are having children later and later nowadays. It's totally normal."

Even meeting Robert didn't change things, not right away at least. Sweet, gentle Robert, whom she met one cool September evening when she stepped off the curb while reading a text from Conrad on her phone.

"Look out!" he shouted, pulling hard on the brakes on his bike and skidding to a stop only inches away.

Jangling with adrenaline from the near miss, she fumbled with her phone and sent it tumbling near his feet. "Oh, shit! Sorry! Sorry!" she exclaimed, as they both scrambled to recover it from the dust.

He picked it up and cleaned it off with the bottom of his T-shirt. "I think it's okay," he said.

"Thanks."

"Are you okay?"

"God, I'm so sorry! That was completely my fault!"

"Oh no, it was mine."

"No, no, I wasn't looking…"

"I was looking in the other direction…"

"I was reading a text and…"

"Okay, fine, it was your fault."

He grinned at her, and she felt herself go pink.

"Was it your husband?"

"Sorry?"

"The text you were reading. Was it from your husband?

"No, just a friend," she said, then met his eyes. "I'm... oh!... I'm not married." She smiled through her lashes at him.

"Perhaps you should sit down for a few minutes, you know, to make sure you're okay," he said, getting off his bike and leading them both towards a nearby bench.

It was the slickest Robert had ever been in his life.

The two dated for exactly one year before he dropped to his knee in an elaborate choreographed event involving several of their friends, a dance routine and 365 heart shaped balloons; it took them another two to finally get married. It wasn't for lack of wanting to be married on either part: Robert was content to let Vanessa set the pace, and Vanessa for her part was distracted by frustration over her work as a part time Latin American Studies and Spanish teacher for a middling community college. The big universities, as it turned out, weren't particularly interested in the newly minted white Canadian professor of Latin American Studies regardless of her fervent passion for the subject.

"I mean, I guess I sort of understand *why*," she sobbed into Robert's chest on a semi-regular basis. "But it still seems unfair! People should be given opportunities based on how good they are, not the colour of their skin! Isn't it simply racism in reverse though? I would be an amazing professor if they'd only give me a chance."

The thoughts of having kids didn't really kick in until the wedding itself, when Robert's Great Aunt Jessie pressed Vanessa's sweaty hand in hers and wished them both happiness and many healthy children.

"Robert?" asked Vanessa a few days after the wedding, not long after they had fallen apart in tangled sheets. "If we're going to have a baby, we should probably not wait very long."

"How old are you now?" teased Robert, "like, 23?"

"Ha ha."

"Janet Jackson's pregnant and she's, like, 50."

"Mmmm," said Vanessa, kissing the tip of his nose. "Be that as it may..."

They started trying immediately.

Vanessa had always assumed it would be relatively easy: her mom had fallen pregnant with her within weeks of her deciding it was time, and her family tree was positively littered with unplanned and unwanted pregnancies. Vanessa herself in her 20s had dashed to the doctor twice for a Plan B tablet when precautions went modestly awry, presuming that she was so fertile that anything above standing downwind from a man would be sufficient for conception.

She wasn't terribly bothered by the lack of progress for the first four months of effort and chalked it up to the stress of moving into their new home. For her 38th that September, Robert gave her a card that read, "Happy Birthday Mama!" with "To Be!" inked in, and they spent an hour arguing genially over the design concept for the nursery. On their first anniversary, Vanessa and Robert clinked glasses of champagne over a wish for an addition to the family soon. The card for her 39th birthday was of three sets of footprints on a beach.

Okay, fine, it was taking longer than expected, but her mother had also been 27 when she got pregnant with Vanessa in weeks, and Vanessa accepted that she was technically a "geriatric mother" – such an insulting term for a few extra years – and it might be marginally more challenging.

The little voice in her head that Vanessa had been silencing with a strict prenatal vitamin regimen and regular pelvic floor training with her yoga teacher woke up on her 40th, when Vanessa awakened to flowers and a card from Robert that simply read, "Happiest of birthdays to my beloved wife."

She stared up at him, appalled. "What is this?" she asked incredulously.

Robert was confused. "…Happy birthday?"

"You know what I mean."

In truth, that little voice that was starting to howl inside her had been in full voice in his head for over a year by that point, so it didn't immediately occur to him that that was what she was upset about at that moment. He assumed, wrongly, that she didn't like the card itself.

"So you've given up then?"

"V, what are you talking about?"

She waved the card in his face. "'Happiest of birthdays to my beloved wife.' That's it? Just us two?"

"Ah," he said.

"You've given up."

"No, Vanessa, I've not," he tried to explain, "I'm simply letting a birthday be a birthday. You've been putting so much pressure on yourself."

Vanessa walked purposefully over to the garbage can and dropped the card directly into it. "If you have decided you don't want a baby anymore, it would have been nice if you had actually bothered to tell me."

"I'm saying it's your birthday, and let's celebrate you today."

Vanessa cocked her head at her husband. "It's because I'm 40."

"Vanessa…"

"You think I'm too old."

"I don't think you're too old."

"You think I waited too long."

"V, we've been trying since we got married."

"You think that I waited too long and now I'm too old and it's too late and I'm never going to get pregnant."

Vanessa started pacing around the bedroom, needlessly slamming drawers and clanking clothes hangers.

"You think I've been selfish," she said to no one in particular. "You think I put myself first."

Her face was a contorted mask of primal, visceral distress. "Did I wait too long?" she whimpered.

Robert waited.

"I didn't put myself first, I didn't. I was living…"

Robert waited.

"I made choices, and they were the right choices," she insisted. "I had things I needed to do first, to figure myself out. I couldn't have raised a child before this. I wasn't ready."

Robert waited.

She sat down on top of the pile of clothes strewn over the armchair with a dejected thump. "Robert, did I wait too long?"

Robert reached over and took her hand. It was cool and limp, unresponsive.

"It's not too late, Vanessa," he said, pulling from his work satchel a short stack of printed paper. "I've been researching, and IVF is covered up to age 43 in this province. We have loads of time."

Vanessa peered up at him quizzically.

"I mean, assuming everything is working as it should with both of us, we'd definitely be eligible."

"Working as it should…" Vanessa repeated, putting her head in her arms. Robert put the printouts on the arm of the chair and slid them over until they brushed her forearm.

The first round was conducted in complete secrecy. Even after the fertility specialist completed all the exams and tests and returned with a fat file saying there was no obvious reason the procedure wouldn't work, Vanessa held back from telling any of her friends. Despite Robert's constant, relentless reassurance, she couldn't rid herself of the sense of shame that she had somehow let them all down by needing professional help for something as primal as motherhood. To soothe herself, she concocted an elaborate fantasy of the moment she would instead reveal the good news to her unsuspecting friends: Conrad would cheer and declare himself the child's uncle; Nick would offer some advice from lessons hard learned; Becca would pretend to be happy but would be inwardly seething with envy that Vanessa had reached the exalted state of blessed maternity and thereby achieved the complete set of life milestones.

Vanessa profoundly enjoyed the process, including the daily injections and intrusive tests, bearing the suffering as her sacrifice for the greater miracle. With every needle in her stomach she sent out a thought to her future child. "Welcome, little one," she would murmur into the spirit world, "You are already loved beyond measure."

They did a double transfer due to her advancing years, and in the gruelling two weeks following Vanessa searched her body for signs that at least one of the embryos had taken. On Day 5 she experienced a swell of nausea that brought her to her knees in front of the toilet but conceded that that may have been anxiety when it didn't happen again. On Day 8 she developed a headache and a strange taste in her mouth, which she noted with more interest. On Day 10 she thought her breasts might be a bit on the sore side and she had a ravenous craving for kosher dill pickles. On Day 13 her teeth started to hurt as well, and she thought her abdomen was possibly a tad firmer than normal.

"Oh my god, Robert," she whispered to her husband the day of the pregnancy test. "I think this is it! I don't know how but I feel pregnant!"

Robert sat on the edge of the tub with his elbows on his knees and his chin resting on the backs of his fingers. "I hope it's a girl," he said softly.

"I hope it's a boy," Vanessa replied, holding the stick in her hand like a conductor's baton. "A boy just like you."

"But who looks like you," he said dreamily.

"We could name him Dustin," said Vanessa, "after your father."

"Dustin Alexander, after yours too then," said Robert.

"My dad would love that," said Vanessa, tearing up at how sweet her husband was and how perfect her life was.

"I love you," cooed Robert.

"I love you," replied Vanessa.

A single line appeared.

"I don't understand," said Vanessa. "There must be a mistake."

Robert studied the single line. "These things aren't perfect. I bought two, just in case."

A single line appeared.

"No," she whimpered. "How is that possible?" She could feel a lacey edge of pain beneath her sternum.

"We'll try again," hushed Robert, taking her into his arms as she dissolved into tears. "We'll try again."

Vanessa struggled to rally to the same degree for the second round. The fertility specialist gave them a 75% chance of the procedure resulting in a live birth and Vanessa was unsurprised when the egg retrieval resulted in only six eggs, which dwindled down to two blastocyst embryos.

"It's enough!" said Robert, rubbing her hand vigorously to warm it up. "We only need one!"

Vanessa looked up at him with dark eyes. "I guess," she said. "I don't want to get my hopes up."

She went through the motions, the injections, the exams, listlessly and without any of the anticipatory joy of the first round. As she pinched her stomach for the daily needle, she wondered why she was bothering. "Are you even out there?" she would send into the universe. "Am I wasting my time?"

"How do you remain hopeful?" she asked Robert in bed one evening.

"I just am," he said, burrowing his face into her hair.

When the single line appeared again, Vanessa went in an instant from numb to rubble.

"We'll try again," said Robert, rocking her in his arms on the floor of their ensuite.

"I've failed you," mouthed Vanessa into his tear-stained shirt.

"No you haven't."

"I can't do this. My body can't do this."

"You can," replied Robert sternly, clutching her cheeks and wiping away the tears. "And you'll be a great mother. We'll try again."

"But the cost..."

"It's just money. It's just money. This is more important."

"I want to do this for you," she murmured, the fire blazing behind her bruised eyes.

For the final round of IVF, Vanessa went all in: the very model of the perfect patient and mother-to-be. She swapped out their casual grazing with a rigid Mediterranean diet of lean meats, legumes, and avocados, and stripped their house of all household items made with endocrine-disrupting chemicals, formaldehyde, parabens, triclosan, benzophenone, BPA, brominated flame retardants, perfluorinated compounds, dioxins, and phthalates. She choked down the maximum recommended dose of folic acid, fish oil, and Vitamin D, and spent hours practising health mama/healthy baby yoga positions. She drank coconut water for the bloating and Pepto-Bismol for the nausea, focused on staying hydrated and keeping her body temperature low, did deep breathing exercises as she walked and swam. She got acupuncture and bought herself flowers. Every time she pinched her stomach for the injection, she would say her mantra: "This will work."

And the single line still appeared.

She didn't have to say it out loud, Robert was thinking it too: no more, it's over.

"You did good," he whispered into her hair.

That night Robert bought them plane tickets to an all-inclusive adults-only resort in the Dominican Republic for an extended beach holiday to give them both space from a world that might accidentally ask if they had children.

"That's so romantic," sighed a clueless Conrad when he swung by to pick up the keys for house sitting. "A surprise second honeymoon."

It was nearly a month before Vanessa started to feel glimmers of the self that existed before the fertility treatments. She allowed herself one final week of seclusion and then re-emerged into daylight having reconciled with the pressure to be the woman who had it all. When she arrived downstairs that afternoon, she discovered a flyer for the master's in business administration programme on the kitchen table and Robert with the face of an excited child.

"I thought, since things are going to be... not exactly as we'd planned... maybe it was time for you to pursue that MBA you'd been considering?" he said.

"Yeah," said Vanessa, cricking her neck, "that's not a bad idea."

2023

The wedding was predictably gorgeous: a small but impossibly stylish outdoor Buddhist-Anglican-secular ceremony that worked exhaustively to ensure that everyone's possible needs were met.

Becca wore an expertly tailored ethical cotton and humane synthetic silk traditional, off-white, A-line dress and flowers from an organic garden centre in her hair: "That's a butt that does a lot of squats," observed one wedding guest as she floated past. Max went for an unbleached linen sheath hand painted with subtle silver thistles in tribute to her Scottish heritage and white Converse All Stars so that she could dance all night. They read each other florid vows they had written themselves and kissed too long to the strains of "Rainbow Connection" while 60 of their closest friends and family applauded and cheered.

Over at her assigned seat in the far table by the hedge for dinner, Vanessa twisted the napkin in her lap into the beginnings of a noose as Max's geriatric Uncle Sidney to her right attempted to make a connection.

"Cake's not bad, eh?" he said, severing a mighty chunk and stuffing it in his mouth. "Awful dry, though. Don't you think it's dry?"

"It's vegan."

"It's what?" said Uncle Sid through his half-chewed mouthful.

"It's vegan," repeated Vanessa. "It doesn't have any animal products in it."

"Why would a cake have meat in it?"

"No, like, no milk and eggs and butter or anything like that. Nothing that comes from animals. Not just meat. That's vegetarian."

"That's stupid. Whoever heard of a wedding dinner without meat?"

"Ha," agreed Vanessa unconvincingly. She had in fact very much enjoyed her vegan portobello mushroom wellington and planned on making it for Robert one day.

"So are you one?" Uncle Sid asked. He daubed at a smear of icing stuck in his overgrown moustache, missing it entirely.

"Sorry?" asked Vanessa. Over on the other side of the garden she saw Becca stand and survey the crowd. Vanessa gave a little wave to try to attract her attention.

"A lezzer," said Uncle Sid loudly, spraying himself, the table and Vanessa with crumbs. The remainder of their table – an assortment of miscellaneous relatives – and a handful of people on the next turned to watch. "A dy-"

"Ah!" interrupted Vanessa hastily, disguising her blush by fussing ostentatiously with her braid. "No," she said quickly, "I'm married. To a man. I'm married to a man."

Becca saw Vanessa and lit up. She held up one finger and leaned over to Max for a departing kiss.

"That's good," approved Uncle Sid. The look in his rheumy brown eyes was aggressively penetrating.

"Right," she said. "Yeah. Absolutely."

Becca arrived at the table, radiating happiness.

"It's not natural, two women," said Uncle Sid to Becca decisively.

"Well hello there, Uncle Sid," said Becca warmly. "Are you enjoying yourself?"

Uncle Sid wheezed and ruffled and was about to answer when Becca skilfully interjected: "V, I'm glad you could make it! It's been ages!"

A tinkly peal of laughter, her fingers placed just so against her naked throat, her curls quivering delicately.

Vanessa released her twisted napkin and placed it on her empty plate. "I wouldn't have missed it for the world, Becs. You look beautiful."

"Awww," said Becca, posing and resplendent. "Come, let's grab a fresh drink and have a quick catch up while everyone finishes eating. I'm going to steal her for a few minutes, Uncle Sid!"

Vanessa clutched her friend's hand as they headed over to the bar.

"Uncle Sid's a bit of a trip," admitted Becca. "That's why we put him at the corner table."

Vanessa couldn't bring herself to ask.

Becca ordered two glasses of champagne from the bartender, handed one to Vanessa and then threw hers back like it shot. "Sorry," she said, wiping her mouth with the back of her hand, "I starved myself for two weeks to fit into this dress, and I am making the most of tonight!" She ordered another glass and leaned back against the corner of the gilt bar. "Where's Robert?"

Vanessa smoothed down the front of her dress. She had tried several times to convince her husband to come to the wedding but Robert just laughed long and hard. "He's at home tonight finishing his book."

Becca wrinkled her nose like a parent humouring a child's uninspiring drawing. "Always beavering away at that book, your Robert," she cooed. "So industrious."

"He's actually received an offer from a publisher," said Vanessa, "who has given him a really harsh deadline, hence his having to miss out on tonight. He sends his regards and congratulations. I had hoped he'd come with me tonight, but he said…" She nervously ran her finger along the rim of her champagne glass. "He just really needed to concentrate."

"Good for him!" said Becca, oblivious, holding up her glass. "To Robert and his book!" and then that glass too was emptied. The bartender, watching the bride carefully, had the third glass ready and waiting.

Becca studied her friend wetly. "You know I love you, right, V?"

The sudden sentimentality caught Vanessa off guard. "I know, Becs."

Something like regret flickered across Becca's expression, her brow furrowed. "I should have called you after the dinner party. I meant to, often, but what with work and planning the wedding and…"

Vanessa nodded, understandingly. She had intended to call a thousand times herself but had found the concept daunting, as though everything they had ever been and would be hung on that one call. Instead, she had made excuses.

"I don't think I've always been very nice to you," said Becca.

"Oh but you have, you have… Maybe in your own way sometimes but I've never doubted…"

"In my own way, yes."

Her head back in laughter, her lips swollen from kissing, her cheeks flushed with joy and champagne. Had Becca always been quite this beautiful, Vanessa wondered, or was bridal radiance really so potent? Vanessa felt quite smitten.

"You've always really inspired me, the way you live your life without a map," said Becca. "You're like a jellyfish – a beautiful, kind, wonderful jellyfish – bobbing along, going with the current, seeing where you end up. And now you're about to get your MBA and go be a… whatever business administration professional… and it's just really great and I'm really proud of you. I hope you know that. You're my best friend, V."

Becca gazed at her as though she were about to accept an Oscar from an esteemed colleague. Vanessa looked at her friend's face, gaunt and flushed and perfectly contoured, and wanted desperately to fall platonically into her arms and drink bad red wine and put the world to rights like they used to do.

The substantial diamond on Becca's ring finger glinted in the halogen lights. "It's ethical," said Becca when she caught Vanessa eyeballing it. "Canadian, from up north. Max and I were adamant about that. Did you know 65% of the global diamond trade comes from Africa and the Kimberley Process Scheme only addresses if it directly funds a rebel war? Someone could have been enslaved or murdered to mine a diamond and it can still be called 'conflict free' – can you believe it?"

"I can't," said Vanessa with wry affection.

An older woman in a powder blue sheath dress and garish rhinestone brooch appeared in a puff of rose perfume. "Rebecca, you look wonderful!" she gushed, pressing a fat envelope into Becca's hands.

"Thank you, Aunt Lillian, so do you. And thank you so much for coming!" beamed Becca. As the woman moved on, Becca rolled her eyes at Vanessa. "My Albertan side," she sniffed. "There will be a hundred bucks in here, tops. They take out cash in fives and tens to make it appear more impressive. But at least they try, right? Oh! Speaking of trying, any word from Nick. I did make sure to invite him."

"He got Covid finally. Not particularly sick though, is the good news." Vanessa raised her eyebrow. "Thank god for vaccines, eh?"

"Not tonight, you troublemaker!" replied Becca with a merry laugh.

A younger couple approached, ducking their heads apologetically for interrupting. "We have to run, Rebecca," said the hollow-cheeked man, lightly touching Becca's elbow.

"Babysitter," added the large-eyed woman.

"But thank you for inviting us –"

"– you look beautiful –"

"– and congratulations to you and Maxine," he finished.

Becca pressed them into hugs from left to right. "Thank you both for coming," she said, accepting their envelope. "Cousins," she noted to Vanessa as they left. She pinched the envelope discretely before putting it and the other envelope into a hidden pocket in her dress.

Over at the main table, Max gave Becca a beckoning wave. Becca threw back the remainder of her glass of champagne, let out a perfectly charming belch, and giggled. "Gah!" she cried, "Sorry, V, it's really great to see you again but I should probably get back to my wife." She touched her face with wonder. "My wife! Who'd have thought?"

"I'm happy for you," said Vanessa sincerely.

"I know you are," replied Becca. She gave Vanessa a drunken slobbery kiss on the cheek. "Restart Pilates when I get back from Bali?"

Alone again, Vanessa opted to go for a walk outside the wedding space rather than return to her table and Uncle Sid.

The wedding was beautiful, she texted Robert as she walked. *Wish you were here.*

His reply came back quickly: *Have made great progress. Glad you're having a good time. See you when you get home. xx*

Vanessa sat down on a small stone bench beside a koi pond and heard the music start up behind her.

The wedding's beautiful, as is Becca of course. How are you feeling? Beer when you're better? she texted Nick.

A few minutes for the reply: *Yeah, sounds good.*

Becca tossed a blade of grass into the pond and watched a large spotted orange and black fish nibble curiously at it.

You didn't come to Becca's wedding? she texted Conrad, her stomach churning.

Somewhere off the coast of Spain, on a tall ship named the Sea Cow peopled with volunteer crew/tourists, Conrad's phone chirped.

"What is it, baby?" asked Jess, the blonde British girl eighteen years his junior with whom he had struck up a close friendship shortly after boarding.

"Spam," said Conrad, switching off his phone.

Jess crawled into the tight confines of his bunk and nuzzled into his shoulder. "Hey," she said, "do you have any more of that rose quartz? It's been really helping with the sea sickness I think."

"Sure thing, babes," he said, rummaging around in his bag with one hand. "Borrow mine and we can put in an order for you the next time we dock."

"I'm excited about this business partnership," she said, cozying into him.

"It's a real opportunity," he replied.

1977

Just after 6pm on a warm Friday night in summer, Vanessa opened her mouth, took a deep breath in, and screamed for the first time in her life.

"What lungs she has!" said the nurse, approvingly. "You've got yourself a future opera singer there."

"And beautiful," said the doctor. "She's going to be a real heartbreaker."

"She can be whatever she wants to be," murmured her mother as the squalling infant was placed on her chest.

A popstar.

A writer.

A nurse discovering the cure for pneumonia.

A lion tamer.

An astronaut.

A princess.

A special snowflake.

"Anything she wants to be," agrees the new dad, holding his wife and their new-born daughter in his arms, bright eyes to a shining future of possibilities.

ACKNOWLEDGMENTS

This book would not exist without the support, input, and flagrantly stolen life plot points of many people, but especially:

Miranda Thomas, Jenny Rust, Carly Smallman, Angela Pagano, Emily Langley, Charlotte Crewe, Cheryl Plambeck, Tim Sorrell, Andy Louder, Mwice Kavindele, Heidi Mavir, Constance Peach, Elizabeth Moffatt, Paul Savage, Arkane Sin, Bryan Shacklady, Horace Gooden, Lizzie Ludnow, Joanne Ojerinola, Hamish Khanna, Marcus Latuske-Hearl, Kate Wall, Maria Smolar, Anna Baumbach, Monique Méthot, Amy Cadman, Kerry Norman, Velveteen Hussey, and Ken Norrie.

Special thanks to Hannah Tottenham for her tireless cheerleading, for this book and for so much of my life.

And to Lorna Higdon-Norrie for telling me when I was a teenager that I could win the Pulitzer someday.

AUTHOR BIO

Erika Norrie is a dual Canadian and British citizen living in London UK with her geriatric Mexican cats. She is currently a senior project manager for a boutique Mayfair law firm, via stints as an actor, theatre administrator, ESL teacher, international trade consultant, English/Spanish editor, corporate trainer, IT business analyst, cabaret producer, and seller of furniture to Hollywood stars. *Generation Karen* is her first novel.

Milton Keynes UK
Ingram Content Group UK Ltd.
UKHW041355070823
426453UK00004B/359